The Preacher Bird

RC Wallace

Inspired by a true story

Robert Clifton Wallace

Books By Robert Clifton Wallace:

Ka-Batin-Guy

Mons Graupius

The Preacher Bird

Copyright © 1995 by Robert Clifton Wallace

All rights reserve. No part of this book may be copied, utilized or reproduced in any form without the written consent of the author.

The Preacher Bird is a work of fiction based on actual events and the lives depicted herein. However, the names have been changed and any similarity to other persons living or dead is purely coincidental.

Printed in the United States of America

ISBN: 0-963-4992-2-X   First edition

Published by: PRETANI
               268 Sayre Street
               Lakeport, CA 95453

Cover design by Robert Clifton Wallace
Cover-art by Carol Dellinger

The Preacher Bird is a story I felt begged to be told. And so this book is for Mary, Bob, and Claire, and all the others who lived to tell about the experience of that time, or like so many others it might have perished forever in the mist of forgotten memories...

One

Atlanta, 1977

This is not the first time I find myself standing in line at an airport waiting for a payphone; scratching my head and agonizing about making a call I know I'll make anyway. After landing I hurried to check the terminal monitor and found my departure time for Mobile was still scheduled at 4:10pm. A glance at my watch showed the time; 2:22pm. That still left one hour, forty eight minutes to burn.

    I found myself mentally recounting the times I had done this in the past. Scrambling for a payphone between connecting flights. It seemed almost an involuntary act, nurtured by some hidden urge to learn about my roots. There is never any rationality about it—just something I do instinctively when there is time to spare. The name I searched the endless columns for was always there, but it had not been the right Marshall. Atlanta is a big place. With my finger I traced down the column of names; there... an R. Marshall, a Richard and finally a Robert; and two more Roberts. Could this be the right one? And there it was staring at me as if in bold letters, and then came the apprehension all over again. At times I had felt so close; this time there was a difference, as if demanding attention. Robert S Marshall... 1723 Ponce de Leon Ave. I had never been sure of the middle name; the S could be for Steven or Stanley, or. . . maybe Sydney. I hesitated, not knowing what the voice might say if a person on the other end answered.

Might such an unexpected call be an intrusion; opening old wounds? Even if he was my father maybe he wouldn't want to hear from me.

I hesitated, as I had so many times before, weighing the consequences. Oh what the hell, this wasn't the first time I had found a Robert S, and wasn't Atlanta the last area he was known to be in, or at least Warm Springs, Georgia. But that was 1932 and 1933. How could I not try. Weary travelers in the other booths were busy with their own brand of menial chatter. I wondered it they too had ever agonized over such decisions as I now faced.

After dropping in coins came the hesitant ringing. . . then it stopped. Someone picked up the receiver at the other end.

A man's voice greeted me. "Hello." It was a pleasant enough greeting, and why shouldn't it be, after all hadn't he been a singer and lecturer, naturally he would have a pleasant voice.

"Hello," I countered, then pausing. . . "Is this Robert S Marshall?"

"This is he," the voice replied.

"Would this be the same Robert S Marshall who went to Ohio Wesleyan University and who came from Waterbury, Vermont?"

"It sure is," the voice replied. "Who am I speaking with?"

I paused—what next? "Is this the Robert Marshall who married and had a son in 1931?" A flurry of thoughts and questions flooded through my head, all scrambled up. . .

"Why do you ask?" Came the voice.

"I don't think you know me. . . by name that is, but—" to myself I wondered; can this be true? Is he really the right one? After all the other times I've tried.

"Hello, hello," came the voice again.

"Ah yes, ah, my name is Robert Milton."

After a brief silence. . . we both tried to speak at the same time, then came the simultaneous hesitation all over again.

The voice at the other end seemed to reclaim some measure of composure while I struggled. "Are you trying to say that you're my son— that I'm your father?"

"Yes. . . I think so."

Then came a long sigh, followed by more hesitation.
"I'm so glad you called, you don't know how often I've hoped that some day... Let's see, this is 1977 and it has been forty six years—since, since 1931. I can hardly believe it's you, but... here you are... Where are you?"

My brain flooded over with past memories and the many times I had tried, and how close I was at this very moment. I must have known that someday it would come to this...

"We have a lot to talk about. Where are you?" asked the voice.

"I'm here, in Atlanta, at the airport. I'm on my way to meet with a brother at Mobile and I have a two hour layover." Checking my watch, I realized there was less than an hour and a half left.

"Oh!" The voice said, disappointedly. "But we have so much to talk about... and a lot of catching up. Maybe I can come to the airport. Which terminal are you at? Can you wait?"

All of a sudden a mélange of thoughts flashed through my mind. Why hadn't I thought this far ahead, nor had I ever in my wildest dreams expected it to come to this. I just went through the motions born of compulsion. But here we are, and he is willing to come to meet with me. I should have known he couldn't do that in his condition? How could he park and get around? Why hadn't I thought this out? How stupid of me.

"Listen, this is more important than anything else," I managed to say. "I'll catch a cab... and come to your house. How far are you from the airport?"

"About thirty five minutes. But..."

"That wouldn't give us any time and I probably couldn't get back here in time for my connection. Still, after all this time, this is more important. Tell you what, I'll check for later flights, then catch a taxicab. Let's see, your address is..." reaching for the telephone book I read it aloud; "1723 Ponce de Leon Ave. I have it. I'll be there as soon as I can."

"Good, good... I've been hoping for this for so long." The voice replied, and yet there was apprehension there too, or was it simply nervous expectation?

"Me too. I can hardly believe it." I said, sensing the elation. Suddenly the air filled with excitement—I wanted to shout and almost did. Those souls next to me should know—then mixed feelings of anticipation and doubt flooded over me, confusing my senses. What a fool I was to think he might not want to see or hear from me.

We exchanged simultaneous goodbyes, but this time goodbye meant I'll see you later, like the French say, *"au revoir,"* or better yet: *"a la prochain."* Till we see again, or till something. Never goodbye; goodbye sounds too final. This felt like a beginning.

"I'll be there soon."

"I'll be here waiting."

As I hurried to the ticket counter, I was struck hard with the sudden impact of what I had done; what do I call him? Just now on the phone, he was a voice, Mr. Robert S Marshall. And I forgot to ask him what the S stands for.

Outside the terminal I found myself hailing a cab and the next conscious moment leaving the airport. I gave the address to the driver; "1723 Ponce de Leon Ave."

In the back seat I tried to sit back and relax as I retraced the events in my mind. . . to standing in line at the ticket counter. The agent had given me the limited availabilities. Two more flights this evening. One at 6:40pm and the last one at 9:36pm. Both had a few seats left. I had taken a reservation on the 9:36pm and had my ticket changed, then placed a call to my brother on Dolphin Island.

I paid little or no attention as the cabby took a right here and a left there and somehow I hadn't heard his questions. Something about first time in Atlanta; where you from?

As thoughts flashed at me like bees in a frenzy, I realized I knew very little about Robert S Marshall. Mom had called him Bobby once and said he didn't care for the nickname, something kids had tried to pin on him. Then it had been Bob or Robert.

The big question continued to haunt me; what should I call him? I had a father, or rather a stepfather. I had been called Tay, or Taylor. When Mom remarried, they had changed my name from Marshall to Milton. I didn't know that my name had been Marshall until I was about fourteen or fifteen. That's when she told me about Robert and that he had been a theology student at Ohio Wesleyan in Delaware Ohio—that he had been very athletic, especially in basketball, he liked hiking, and they had gone bird watching a lot. She had explained that they had met at church during choir practice and her mother invited him home for dinner one Sunday, and later he lived there and delivered donuts and baked goods, and that he had a beautiful bass voice and loved to sing. That he had lectured; usually about the Bible and Bible history—also nature. She thought he had tried boxing and he had left college one year to join a traveling circus. . . she had given me two photo's of him, one a small portrait taken about college time; the other in a wheelchair with a blanket over his legs. A curious contrast. She said it was taken while he was at Warm Springs, Georgia. He was of Scottish and English ancestry, she had said, and his family had a farm in Vermont. That's where he had grown up and had gone to school . . .

The taxi-driver interrupted and explained about some construction work. "What kind of work you do?" he asked. An identity card on the visor read: Arthur Brown, with Art in parentheses. That was the first I noticed he had an identity.

"Construction." I answered, still lost in distant thought. I guess that's not much. Still I wondered what to expect, what would he look like, and what to call him. I think, yes, that's it, Robert. He would expect that. Certainly not Mr. Marshall. That would make both of us feel stuffy and like erecting a sort of formal barrier.

Two

At 1723 Ponce de Leon, Robert Marshall sat for long moments after replacing the receiver in its cradle, thinking about the phone call he had just received. Then he maneuvered his wheelchair over to a desk. Nearby stood a bookcase filled with books, and on the desk lay a Bible with visible place markers. Opening the drawer he removed a packet of letters and separated one which had never been addressed, then two small snapshots. He held them in his hands. One was of a pretty, young woman and the other of a young child, a baby. He studied them at length as his mind drifted... back... back to Delaware, Ohio and another time long ago. In his head he sounded her name, and the thought gave him a surge of pleasure and unwittingly he shifted his carriage to square his shoulders, as if the act all by itself helped him reclaim some measure of youthful strength and persuasion over his condition.

The month of May had been closing in on the summer break of 1930. One Saturday evening Robert stopped by a boarding house after school. It had been a day like so many others, with little else to do, except to visit friends from church where he sang in the choir. He found Edith and her daughter Mary busy in the kitchen preparing the evening meal. Edith asked if he would like to stay for dinner.

"If you stay," said Mary, "we can practice some songs afterwards."

"Sure, that sounds like fun. The only practice we get is at church for the choir. What time?" he asked.

"Be ready in just a little bit," said Edith.

"Can I help with anything?" he asked, watching Mary while she skittered about, all the time preparing the table; place-mat first, knife and spoon on the right and fork on the left over folded napkin, then plate and soup-bowl, all precisely at each place in a proper setting. He studied the lightness in her movements, delicate and filled with subtle harmony, and then the coquettish twinkle in her eyes, like she was flirting; so young and girlish, he thought, and always filled with girlish things. In another year she won't be able to hold the boys off.

"How are your piano lessons coming?"

"I'm always learning new pieces. Want me to play something for you?"

"Why yes, I'd like that."

Just then Joe, Mary's younger brother came charging in, "When's dinner?" he demanded. Joe had a thing for the back screen door, like crashing into a line in a football game, dishing out punishment, demanding respect, or simply because he was filled with that energetic urgency in all things except washing his face and hands and combing his hair.

"Just a little while Joe. Go wash up and sit down in the parlor," insisted Edith.

"Ah Mom, do I have to. I'm not dirty, really."

"Joseph! Wash your face and hands, and comb your hair also." She heaved a great sigh and gave him that trademark stare of despair.

Mary fluttered a napkin and made a funky face as he stutter-stepped by, crouched ready to charge, the ball tucked away and stiff arm in her face.

"Mary, why don't you and Robert go into the parlor and play something."

"Come on," she said, taking him by the hand. " I'll play *Fur Elise*; see if you like it."

As he started to sit down in a nearby chair, Mary said, "not there silly, here by me."

The two boarders came in and watched for a minute. "Hi, Mary," they chorused on their way to the dinning room; "looks like Mary's got a beau," they chuckled.

"Dinner's ready." Edith called from the dinning room.

At the table Robert was invited to say grace and gladly accepted and small conversation circulated around the table. Someone asked Joe about school.

"What will you do this summer, Robert?" asked Mary.

"Back to Waterbury and the farm. There is always lots of work at the farm and I miss the family. I'll get a chance to see some old friends."

"A girlfriend too I bet." said Mary, flashing a coy grin.

"I may have a chance to do lectures and maybe some ministerial work also," Robert said, without changing pace.

"Do you plan to return to Wesleyan this fall?" asked Edith.

"I hope so. My brother, Bill and I both expect to continue this coming semester... But with four brothers and two sisters, we take turns at the farm and going to college. George wants to return to Michigan University next fall. I guess a lot depends on how much we can earn this summer."

Sitting across the table the two boarders waited, like setting a trap for a new victim. Junior had the look of a donkey with the bit clenched between his teeth, and he he-hawed like one too. His brother Jack slouched so his belly stuck out like a mare about to foal. His he-haw had a scratchy bite to it, like a crackling fire. "Well, jobs is sure hard to come by," he said; "you know, what with so many people out of work. Things sure is hard, and ain't no money for regular folks like us. But that new president Hoover, now he's got plenty, so's he ain't gonna fret none about the rest of us. Why, ever since that stock market thing crashed. . ." Jack Owen would have continued, but was interrupted by Edith in a delicate voice; "now Jack, you know rules of the house, we don't talk on politics at the dinner table—" but he and his brother worked for the railroad and dressed the part. They worked hard, and it showed in the striped bib coveralls they wore. They liked to joke around too—mostly with Joe; but there was a college guy there now which meant new meat—if only he would take the bait. . ."

Jack took the hint like an actor in a stage play.

Edith came back from the kitchen carrying plates with hot apple pie.

That got Joe's undivided attention.

Junior, his eyes wide, hesitated momentarily, as if his mind was set on an earth shaking idea and his tongue was already in motion. "You know, all of them guys over at the Washington capital are fat and they none of em care much about us little folks, but this here New York Governor Roosevelt, now there's a man to look up to, got a head on his shoulder and an eye for the little fellow too. Even though he's a Harvard man and comes from a rich family; he's a man gets things done, Back in nineteen and twenty when he was nominated vice-president people knew then he was a man for the working folks. If him and Cox would'a gotten elected instead of Harding and Coolidge things might'a been different for the whole country today—"

When Junior paused to catch his breath, Jack Owen grasped a chance to get in his own two cents worth. "Then he got hit with polio, but even that didn't slow him down none—even if he is in a wheelchair. He's governor of New York now and he'll be president; you can make bet on it—"

"Call themselves the polios—" Jack he-hawed.

"Here's your pie. Mary will you hand me the dishes please?" said Edith, nudging the Owen brothers again. They got the message this time. "How do you travel back to the farm in Waterbury?" directing her question to Robert.

"Hitch-hike mostly, any way we can. Bill and I go together.

Someday we plan to buy a motorcar," answered Bob, happy to help change the subject. "Joe, what are your plans for the future? What about college? Do you have a major in mind yet?" Robert asked.

"I haven't decided yet. Guess I'll just play football and basketball, see what comes along."

"I want to study music," Mary said, "I don't know where yet, but I still have another year to decide."

He nodded approval and considered her momentarily. "Your voice is coming along... and you certainly have a gift with the piano."

"Do you really think so?"

"Yes definitely, you can do anything, if you're willing to work at it, and it shows that you have, and if you keep working at it, no telling how far you could go."

"Humph." Joe stuck out his tongue.

Mary stared back with daggers.

"There is a piece of piano music, for competition mostly, called *Juba Dance*, do you know of it?" Robert said, at the same time pasting a generous portion of butter on a slice of fresh-baked bread.

"No, I haven't heard of that one," she replied.

"I'll get it for you. It involves a lot of hand over hand work—shows the judges your level of development. That's what they look for in competition. Just your style." He made it sound like a promise, as his eyes held her there with the sensitivity of a scholar.

She looked back longingly—the look of an artist filled with expectation—vulnerable, and smoldering with a lingering desire. Then, as Edith came back from the kitchen she looked down to hide the girlish blush.

"More apple pie anyone?" Edith offered.

"I'll take another piece, Mom," piped Joe quickly.

"Me too," Jack and Junior chorused. Then Jack said, "maybe you could go out to see if there's any work with that Blanchard circus outfit while they are in town, out to the Cavendish field east of town."

"I saw the posters around town, thought I might hitch a ride out there to see if I could get something," Bob said. "No more pie for me, thanks. That sure was some delicious meal and I'm full up," he added, patting his stomach.

When Mary started removing the dishes he came to his feet and said, "here, let me help."

"That's okay; anyway its not men's work and Joe can help," Mary said, as she shot her brother a piercing stare. It seemed she spoke as much with her eyes as with words.

Joe blinked at his mother. "Maybe Bob and me can go over to the park, shoot some baskets, and play some man-to-man."

"Another time, okay but tonight you have studies young man; and there are some chores," Edith said.

"That would suit me better too. I really must go. I too have studies too. Thanks again for the fine meal and for such an enjoyable evening, Mary; Mrs. Swaren."

"You don't need to rush off so soon," Mary said.

"I'm afraid I really must go. Studies you know, and with exams soon. . . but thanks again."

"You're welcome Robert. . . goodnight." answered Edith.

As he walked, he thought how nice it would be to rent one of their rooms next fall, if he could afford it. Six dollars a week she had said, includes room and board. And boy what meals! That would sure beat living at the crowded dorm, and he could make deliveries and still peddle donuts to the other students in the mornings. Sure would be easier living there. He had heard that sometimes she took in students as boarders, and he knew she liked to help, especially the ones studying theology. I'll talk to her about it tomorrow, he decided. . .

Alone in the kitchen with Edith, Mary said, "Mom, how come Robert didn't say anything about his father? Doesn't his father live and work at the farm?"

"His father died in the 1918 flu epidemic."

"Oh Mother how awful. I was only six years old then. Did a lot of people get it, the flu I mean?"

"Oh yes, child, So many people were affected. Robert told me about it one morning when he came to pick up donuts. His father, James, was down with the flu and he got up to work in the barn or do some chores, I think Robert said, and then he came down with pneumonia and died from that."

"Couldn't the doctors or anyone do anything for him. . . to help?"

"The whole family was down with the flu, all except their

mother, and she was the only one able to go out and do the farm chores."

"All of them sick at the same time, how awful."

"Robert was only fourteen at the time, the oldest of the boys and I should guess he tried to shoulder most of his father's responsibilities after that."

"How many brothers and sisters does he have?"

"One older sister, then Robert—seven in all, the mother and seven children have managed ever since."

"How dreadful. . . Mom, how did she manage, with seven children, and a farm. . . no man, all by herself, how could she?"

"A body just does the best we can, child. Well, the Lord set a mighty task for her, that's for certain. . . and we just keep doing the best we can, praying for the Lord's help."

"Mom, why don't you and Pops live together? What happened?"

"Land sakes alive, Mary, so many questions; you shouldn't worry yourself with such things. Besides, it's a long story, and not one for you to be concerned with," Edith said, with finality. "We're near done now. You can go to your studies, and practice your music some more."

Three

At 1723 Ponce de Leon Ave, Robert Marshall sat poised in his wheelchair, still holding the letter and photo, and he wondered just how different his life might have been if he had taken that other fork in the road, or had considered all options and alternatives, and if he had not gone to see about work at the circus that fateful Saturday.

It had been an early spring day in Delaware, like so many others in the past when he had fallen into a pattern of self-doubt and indecision, and his third year at Wesleyan University. The first semester had gone pretty well, but the second had brought troubles. He had been unable to find any part-time work, and when he had played basketball everything had gone great at first, but disagreements with his coach had brought more difficulties.

Each year had been like a dilemma repeating itself; at first things went great, but as the term's end drew near the motivation just wasn't there. This year he had been determined to make it work. Then his grades went into decline and things were just not going well at all. He had begun to agonize over his situation. There was just not enough time or money to play sports and work. In the course of time he became more disenchanted until his downward spiral seemed headed for new depths.

He had seen posters around town and on campus of a traveling circus that would be a few miles east of town the coming week. Perhaps he might find work. After all, it did look exciting and he just might get to see the circus.

Arriving early on a Saturday morning, he had managed to get on with the yard-gang doing odd clean-up jobs. Later on Sunday, the second day, when it came near show-time, the foreman who had hired him came to get him. As he followed the big man's long strides he thought of the obvious; Burt was his name, and his years as a seasoned foreman of tough men was all to apparent in the lines of his leathery face, his hardened body and callused hands. He was a husky man with a gruff voice and bushy eyebrows. Bob had wondered what he might have looked like as a youth—and when he might have joined the circus.

At the rear entrance to the big tent, he had noticed some of the performers gathered around. Burt told him to stand guard right there at the entrance. "You're a big enough guy," he had said, "and don't let no one in here, and don't let nobody bother the performers. No autographs, no nuttin. You unnerstan!" Sure, I understand, he had answered in his distinct college voice. After all this sure beat raking straw, shoveling manure and picking up trash, he thought, and even get to watch the show.

And he did watch with affected enchantment, gaping wide-eyed as the performers lined up preparing for their grand entrance; the clowns, the jugglers, and a man and woman in colorful costumes with their group of little dogs with bright frilly ribbons tied around their necks. He watched, enchanted as they darted and leaped through rings and over each other, then playfully in and out of boxes.

Briefly, the animal smell reminded him of his home at the farm. Then came the other smell, of popcorn and taffy and caramel apples, and again the animals.

The small band was playing *The Daring Young Man on the Flying Trapeze,* and automatically his eyes and attention became fixed on the athletic figures poised high in the tent-top as they began to mesmerize the audience with their death defying leaps and acrobatics.

Then, as another fragrance touched his nostrils he suddenly became aware of a figure standing beside him. As the alluring fragrance of her perfume and body drew his attention, he turned to see that she was watching him with affected interest. Pictures of women like this he had seen before. . . yet not this close, nor in person. . . She just stood there, almost touching so that he could feel her, even taste the sense of her presence.

"I have not see you before," she intoned, with the fixed gaze of doeful eyes. "You like, monsieur?"

"Ah. . . yes I like very much," he stuttered, surprised that she spoke to him.

The eyes held him there, with the intensity of a woman who knows how to affect men with her will. Momentarily he broke the spell to study her raveny black hair tied back in a ponytail and loose pin-curls dangled by her ears and forehead beneath a golden gem-studded tiara.

"I am called Josette," she said soft and whimsically. "Josette Lebeaux. I ride ze horse." With a subtle nod and hinting glance she indicated the ring in front where a costumed man with a whip directed a trio of magnificent animals trotting in a circle.

"You have. . . *travailler,* how you say; work, with ze circus, *mais non*—? I have not see you here before."

"Yes, but just part-time. I started today. I'm a student at Wesleyan," he said, still studying her, trying desperately to fathom her sudden intimacy. He had not seen a woman up close with make-up like this before. Had she materialized there from some innate fantasy; glamorous and beautiful beyond his dreams. He supposed her age to be at least thirty, yet she looked much younger. "It sure looks exciting," he added. "I mean with all the glamour, and flying through the air, up there," he pointed, "I sure would like to try it."

"You can do these?" she said, blinking her eyes in that same subtle gesture again, but this time there was a hint of surprise written in her expression.

"I think so. I'd sure like to try."

"Mae-be I can talk *avec*, with Monsieur Blanchard for you, *mais non*—?" Pointing to one of the trapeze artists, she continued, "Helmut is leaving after the last show, *ici*, here, to go weeth a big-gar circus. They will desire. . . umm, how you say, want someone for heem," she hesitated, and shrugged slightly with her shoulders and hands as if dismissing the thought for the moment. "Yes, mae-be you can try."

"I'd like that—and you could arrange it?" he asked, as he mentally recounted his troubles at school.

"And now . . . ladies and gentlemen. . . for your pleasure may we present: *the beautiful and talented.* . . JOSETTE." The words erupted from a powerful voice at the bandstand. The music had stopped while he made the announcement, but were preceded by a drum-roll as the figure beside him turned to bounce lightly on the balls of her feet toward the arena. With a twinkle of her eye she turned and danced away.

Leaping upon the horse's back with the graceful agility of a well trained athlete, she rose to her feet, ponytail streaming behind, as her horse trotted in a circle. She offered herself with hands outstretched to the crowd as they jumped to their feet and applauded.

Later, when most of the visitors had vanished and the entertainers had returned to their wagons and tents, Burt approached him and told him to report to Jack Murphy; "over there." He pointed to a short man in a checkered shirt and derby hat. "He's the labor foreman, he'll tell ya what to do."

He was helping the laborers with clean-up when his attention was drawn to Josette at a distance. She was talking with a tall man dressed in black trousers, shinny black riding boots and a bright red coat with tails down to the backs of his knees. The man was listening intently as she turned to point. He guessed she must have said something more about him because the man turned to glance in his direction also.

This must have been the man she spoke of, Mr Blanchard. . . the same name on the posters, *The Blanchard Circus*. He wondered if she was serious. Was she really asking Blanchard to give him a try?

He had continued working when they parted and disappeared. It seemed like only a few minutes had passed when Burt approached him again. He realized no one had asked his name yet, not even Josette.

"What's your name, lad?" asked Burt.

"Robert Marshall."

"Robert, it is then. Okay Robert, you can report to Mr. Blanchard's office."

He looked around bewildered... office? "Where?"

"It's the big wagon with the word CIRCUS painted on the sides, out back with the other wagons," Burt said.

Filled with misgivings he went in search of the office wagon. What did Blanchard really want, and if he was to be given a chance, what would he tell his mother and the rest of the family. And what about school? He couldn't leave, just like that—or could he? After all school wasn't working out for him anyway. And there was Josette. Ah yes, Josette. What was there to loose, and this just might be his big opportunity.

He knocked twice on the door and heard a deep voice tell him to come in.

"I'm Blanchard. Some call me mister, but most just call me Blanchard," he said, offering his long-fingered hand. Robert realized that the other man was a towering figure, and height seemed to have burdened him with a slouching posture suggesting his shoulders carried a heavy weight of responsibility. He had changed into a gray smoking jacket and some leisure clothing. His hair was medium brown with a balding spot in the center and graying sideburns. His eyes were small, deep set beneath heavy brows, slightly close, yet they were bright and immensely alert. He wore a mustache beneath a beak of a nose and a perfectly trimmed goatee at his chin. A man of respectable distinction.

"What's your name, young man?" he asked. "How old are you?"

"Robert Marshall, Robert I'm called. I'm twenty four," he answered, taking notice how the other man shifted and squared his carriage—as if to correct the tiresome slouch.

"Well Robert Marshall; Marshall is a good name in the circus business. I hear you would like to work with the trapeze. Any relation to the Marshall family of Hagenbach and Marshall; the circus people down south of here?" he said, as he moved to settle into a comfortable looking chair behind his desk. At the same time he indicated to Robert to take the one opposite him. He paused again, obviously a man who selected his words and thoughts carefully, all the while watching for the younger man's reaction. Then he resumed, "Have you ever worked with the circus before?"

In response to the first question he said: "I understand there is some family connection if you go back far enough." It was not a total lie—he had heard of them, but in the rush of things had forgotten it. Then he added: "They are legend in my family. No sir, I haven't worked with a circus before, but I'd like to try, I know I can learn, and I'm no stranger to hard work." Inside him there had welled up a powerful uncertainty born and nurtured by being out of ones element, and so he tried to pledge his words with confidence and sincerity.

"Good spirit," Blanchard said. "I like that in a man. And confidence, I like that as well." He paused again with eyes still fixed intently on the younger man, then continued. "We'll be moving south, near Cincinnati for our next show in a couple days. You can report to Burt; he'll tell you where to bunk and introduce you to Fritz for tryout and training. Simple basics at first, you understand. Then we'll see how you do. You're a well built young man, athletically built, should look good—important how a man presents himself as well as he performs. . . We'll see."

Robert wanted to ask about collecting his belongings at college, but decided to wait and ask Burt.

"What about pay?" How much does the work pay?" he asked, almost biting off his words.

"We'll see what you can do first, and then we'll talk about money. Report to Burt and he'll show you the rest." He spoke in a tone of finality as he settled back in his chair and touched a lighted match to a pipe he had been filling.

Robert sensed that Blanchard had something else to say, but changed his mind. Perhaps he would find out what it was later.

It was getting late when he found Burt talking with some of the other men. Most of the work was done. When he had explained his situation, Burt told him to gather his belongings and report the next morning for instructions, and explained that meals were prepared by their own people and he could join them if he wished. He had further explained that he would introduce him to Jolly the clown for his bunking arrangements.

It was a windy overcast morning when Robert arrived early and eager to start on what he perceived to be his new adventure.

He had explained to his brother Bill, and though Bill had disapproved, he finally agreed not to tell the family, and further, he agreed to forward Bob's letters to their mother as though he were still in college, at least for the time being, until he got this wild notion out of his system and came back to his senses.

Robert had not seen Josette again that night and had said nothing of her to Bill.

Excitement ran high when he joined the other performers for the morning meal. Their own, however was a casual and almost complacent nature. He felt an inward flush flood over him from inside to out. And wondered if it showed.

Burt had told him to get a bite to eat and later that morning he would introduce him to Fritz and Helga.

Fritz was a dour-faced man with short blond hair and sharp features. He had trained Helmut and they had worked together for many years, but now Helmut was leaving for a better position with one of the big circuses. That meant he would have to train another man all over again, a task he in no way held great relish for. He had gone through some twenty different men before finding Helmut and didn't look forward to the same ordeal again. Most circus performers came from the ranks of family members who grew up in the atmosphere. Smaller circuses had to settle, for the most part, with leftovers. The trapeze ilk was one of those where top talent was always in shortage, and where a willing individual with limited ability had a small chance to get his or her foot in the door, and could in the long-haul be trained to function in a limited capacity. All too often, young men had shown up hoping to get on with the circus. But few ever made it. Those established individuals on the inside resented how they always had an eye set on the fun and glamour, and expected it would launch them into a career of fame and possible riches.

Fritz eyed his new prospect with the same skepticism, but finally agreed to test him, but only after considerable persuasion by Josette and Blanchard.

Having studied them as they had flown through the air, the last evening, flipping and somersaulting like birds enjoying themselves at play, Fritz was their recognized leader, and though shorter than himself he was muscular and powerfully built. He had that lean iron toughness about him; not only in his physique but in his face and in his look. Obviously his expertise was a result of many years of hard work and dedication, most likely a skill born of talent from his own parents.

Fritz considered him again. "First; those clothes, they will not do, and shoes, you will require special athletic shoes for such big feet. If you must wear sneakers, wear them other places, but your bare feet will have to do for now. Well," he said abruptly, "lets see what you can do." He pointed up—to a small platform where a ladder rose to the very top of the big tent.

The net was in place, as it always was during practice and Bob could see Helmut swinging up high from a bar like a child at play—casual and filled with mischief. A female figure leaped from another to meet him in mid-air.

Climbing the ladder, he recalled Blanchard's words of last evening. "You'll start with the basic moves first, then we'll see," he had said.

Flashing back his mind remembered the thrills of climbing Mount Mansfield and Camel's Hump and how he used to stand at the edge of a giant rocky outcrop at the very top and marvel at the world below. And always he had wondered what it would be like to soar like the eagles he often saw there.

When he reached the top the woman greeted him warmly, "I am Helga and this is Helmut."

Helmut was an adonis of a man with pearly-white teeth and blue eyes bright with amusement which he displayed often. It was the mouth turned upward at the corners in a perpetual smile. The dimples helped too, especially during performances.

Helga was shapely and trim, probably thirty five or forty, yet she appeared in excellent condition and in possession of a full head of blond hair which she kept neatly braided and cinched to the back for performances. Helga seemed to float like a mist, even when she was standing still. When she moved it was like fantasy and a sylph, and thrills all rolled into one. Flashing that performer smile, she said, "watch me closely." She raised from her heels to her toes and swung smoothly and easily to the platform on the other side.

He studied her movement just as he had studied all three intently the night before. He had been entranced by their graceful monkey—like feats as they had leaped through the air, and then as if to fall they would catch one another or another swing. The crowd, with eyes transfixed had watched breathless and then came the inevitable oohs and aahs, then the gasps as they appeared almost to miss or fall. Sometimes they would tumble in the air, and then into the net, only to swing gracefully to the floor, bow, raise their hands and again climb the ladder to resume their daring feats.

Glancing down, he realized how high up in the air he was. A few people had gathered below to watch, and others went about their business of practicing their art. Everything from his viewpoint seemed like toy miniatures; he gulped to swallow the lump in his throat.

Helmut caught the swing as it returned from Helga, who stood waiting on the opposite platform. "One thing you must remember, *always*, you must concentrate. Do not look down. Ignore their calls and claps, and sometimes their boos, yes, the boos. This one thing, you must concentrate on—what you will do next, and how. Only that alone," He said, seriously as though to stress his point, then the teeth sparkled again. Helmut might not give the same warning twice.

Bob took the swing bar and placed his hands as he was instructed. He stood for a minute and felt a hand on his back, raised onto his toes, took a deep breath and released it as he flew through the air. Quickly, it was over. One instant you are here, and the next; there. And yet the sensation lingered, like the scent of Josette. Like the thrill of yesterday and tomorrow. . . Just like that he was on the opposite platform and Helga was helping with his balance. For fleeting seconds he had experienced the sensational, he had flown. Now he understood fully—why they are called aerialists, and flyers. He could feel the adrenalin surging throughout his body as he turned to look back for Helmut's approval. I did it, I flew, he almost shouted aloud. Then he returned to Helmut as he was instructed, and performed the same feat several more times, each time with more delight than the time before.

"You're doing well my friend." Helmut patted him on the shoulder; "but you must breathe to your toes, then exhale. Now is time for your next move, but first you must know this, when you descend to the net, or if you should fall, you must roll." He made a rolling motion with his hand. "Roll in the air and land on your back, like floating down—and do not hold your air."

He makes it sound so easy.

Helmut continued, "now when you release from here, do not land on the other side as before. I want you to kick your feet in the air and return to this platform. Like this." He demonstrated what he had just explained.

Bob repeated the maneuver several times and then returned to the opposite platform where Helga awaited, smiling approval. Again, he repeated the maneuvers and increased his momentum in the air before returning to the platform. His confidence was growing and it was at one of those high swinging times that he lost his grip, slipped and fell out of control, tumbling awkwardly into the net below. Struggling to the side he rolled over to the floor below as he had seen the others do many times, so easily. He staggered as a seaman does after being at sea for a long time while others watched for his next move, and headed for the ladder and up he went again. Now he knew, he would have to learn to fall more gracefully.

Climbing the ladder, he started to realize how talented and skillful the others really were. How Helmut made it look so easy when he caught Fritz or Helga in mid air. Such precision in timing, he realized it would take years of practice and dedication to attain even a fraction of Helmut's ability. And Fritz, truly Fritz was the master.

He had practiced the same moves over again and again and still he had fallen to the net. One time as he had swung to the floor, he had seen Fritz and Blanchard standing nearby with Josette. He overheard them as Fritz was saying, "yes, he does have a certain talent, though crude."

"Ah yes, and, he does have determination," added Blanchard. "But we shall see." When he climbed the ladder again he realized he had passed the first stage.

When lunch-break came round, he stopped only after Helmut had insisted. Soon he was back, with Helga and Helmut showing him some maneuvers to practice. He realized it would be some time before his wrists would be strong enough to attempt a catch. They explained other exercises he could do on the ground such as stretching and strengthening. Helmut explained how Fritz had learned from his father in the old country, and he in turn had learned from his father, and that Fritz and Helga longed to visit their homeland and to perform there someday. Helmut said he too yearned to perform in his homeland and when he joined the bigger circus he would get his chance. He went on to explain that they would have to change their routine until he, the new man could be worked into the routine. It had been seven years since he had started training with Fritz, and he felt he owed him everything. But they understood he must move on even though they envied him the opportunity and would have liked to have gone as a team, but they could not all go, as they owed much to Blanchard.

That same evening when he dropped to the net and spun over the edge to the floor on his way for a shower and dinner, Bob found he could barely walk. He had become sore and stiff in the process of using muscles in a way he hadn't used them before. Struggling to the meal tent, he forced himself to walk. Later when he visited the big tent, he stood looking up, to where he had spent most of the day. Studying the curious apparatus for long moments, in the recesses of his mind he was leaping about fully synchronized as in the playful flight of performing birds.

Then a familiar voice reached his ears. "You have do well these day, *Monsieur* Ro-bare."

He loved the way she pronounced his name, Robare, instead of Robert, from her lips it took on a sensuous quality bordering on eroticism.

"You like?" she intoned, with eyes bright and wise, ". . .up there?"

"Oh yes, very much, its very exciting. . .and challenging. *Mais oui*, I like." he said, mockingly, in her french accent.

"You speak French? *Oui*, yes."

"Oh no—well maybe a few words. I studied it one year in school," he said, humbly. "It's a very musical and expressive language. . . and I'm fascinated with your accent. But no, I didn't learn very well, I'm afraid."

She considered him there, with dark searching eyes that missed nothing. "Mae-be I can elp you to learn bet-tar, *Oui?*"

"Why yes, I think I'd like that very much" he said, hesitating at first. "When can we start?" he asked, his words intuitively falling into a whisper.

"Now, tonight... ah *oui, ce soir*," she nodded. "Yes we can start tonight."

He had watched her full lips as her mouth had formed the words. "Where?" he asked, glancing around.

"*Chez moi,*" she laughed, "see, you have already to begin. Come to my place."

"Where—?"

"*Lá,*" she pointed out back to where he had seen the circus wagons. "My wagon with the lavender and white... and my name; JOSETTE on the side." She made a little dip with her head. "One hour, *bien?*" she said, holding up one finger.

That's what did it, that one finger so close. He wanted to take it and touch it to his lips right there, but the urge gave way to some inner discipline; his first lesson in French might not be about the language... unless, it would be body language.

A circus in full business swing can resemble a beehive of industry whether in operation during performances or in preparation for a move to the next location. To the average outsider it is a thing of beauty to witness in either case; a thing born of energy and mystery—still a thing of beauty to see. But to suddenly become a part of such an elaborate and thriving operation is beyond the realm of comprehension for most. By comparison it resembles something more akin to a beehive in full sway—every being and every element down to the smallest nut and screw has its own place and function. There is a sort of hidden buoyancy that floods over all those serving that ultimate purpose—a duty and a place, from the boisterous roustabouts to the main performer, like that of the hive where the function flows in surging rapture from queen through drones and each worker. All have a specific function and specific purpose that is fed by infectious chemistry that courses through every fiber and gland. With bees the figure-eight dance is the highlight of excitement when a food source is located and reported by scouts; then they all gather to watch and follow the dancers pulsating rhythm, all the while growing more rapid and finally culminating into a frenzy the closer they get... When a circus gets ready to move it greatly resembles the swarming of bees by the thousands in a perfectly coordinated effort, then comes the dance of arranging and raising the big tent with all the ornaments and trimmings, where that glorious finale erupts when the queen appears along with her drones, workers, and soldiers to perform the magic—the magic of the show that pours forth the golden honey.

To have an active part in such wizardry was beyond the wildest dream, and yet, that is exactly where Robert Marshall found himself, among the diverse personalities, considering each creature and wondering about their place in the overall scheme of things. What would his place be? They all seemed extremely tolerant of each other's eccentricities and yet he sensed there existed a critical limit; unwritten laws that could be broken by an unfortunate outsider. Ethics that were etched in stone and even blood, and yet nowhere put down in pen and ink as written guidelines. To cross that obscure line could arouse a wrath of intolerance; could mean expulsion and condemnation, as it had in pagan times when the lawbreaker was sent away in disgrace.

And yet he had been invited in to the strange uncharted future, and very possibly by none other than the queen bee...

Among the roustabouts he found they were no less affected, and none at all were concerned with his wondering presence. They were all too busy in preparation for the move that would take place in a couple days. Burt had explained that he would be expected to fill in at other odd jobs. Perhaps with the elephants or horses, and probably in the big parade as a clown. He had told Burt he would be happy to help any way possible. He was aware that his eagerness showed and he was anxious to be a part of the big show.

In a few days the equipment would be set up again near Cincinnati. There he would experience performing for the first time in front of a live audience, and he understood this was what *it* was all about. Even if his role, for the present was to be a minor one, he would be introduced to the excitement and cheers of spectators.

Again, he was reminded of Helmut words: "Concentrate on what you must do."

At the workday's end he found himself wandering about casually until he located Josette's wagon, and now he stood poised to knock at her door.

Again, the pain and stiffness struck as a reminder of his day's exertions on the high trapeze.

The door opened.

"*Entrez cherie,*" she said, as she studied him closely.

Inside the lights were low like smoldering shadows, and he stood poised, stunned by her beauty as she waited before him, with shinny black hair that had been loosened to flow freely about her shoulders, clad only in a silk lavender gown clinging loosely to her body and casually open at the front. Only a tie around her slim waist prevented its opening completely. The points of her breasts and her full thighs shows clearly as the soft light from behind suggested the remaining curves and hollows of her body. . . What was her game, he had wondered? approval—adoration? She already had that. No; she was a creature above simple prevarication—a woman who knew and controlled her emotions, and to a greater extent managed those she allowed within her inner circle. . . Why then, had she chosen me, he wondered? A toy, perhaps? At that time it had mattered little in the overall scheme of things—he had fallen completely under her spell.

For a moment he glanced about the wagon interior as though taking inventory. He was amazed at its spaciousness and how the habiliments attested to her exquisite taste.

He saw some books in a small wall case and recognized one, *Lady Chatterly's Lover*, and another of poems. He wondered if they were in French.

His eyes returned to her form as she beckoned with a finger for him to sit beside her on the couch. As she shifted persuasively her gown opened further, revealing the inner smoothness of her thighs—she made no effort to cover them as he sat down beside her, but leaned towards him allowing the silky upper portion to loosen.

He must have winced unwittingly as he moved.

"Have you pain, *cherie?*" she sighed, concerned as her expression changed to sympathy, and her eyes searched for the problem area.

"Oh just a little stiffness. . . and maybe some sore muscles. You know, but it'll go away, I'm sure."

"*Ici,* here?" she touched his thigh and pressed a little with a practiced expertise. "Here?" touching the other, her eyes testing all the while his for reaction.

"Josette weel help you to feel bet-tar," she promised, reaching for one of two glasses and a bottle of wine setting on a small table nearby.

    She poured, and handed him the first glass, then continued, "*la*, there. It is *vin rouge* from Bordeaux—my family is at Montreal and have, how you say—connections." She allowed a wry grin to cross her face, a grin that said it all. "The best wine in the whole world ees made in Bordeaux. Eet tis my home." She was looking at him as she motioned for him to drink and sipped conservatively from her own glass.

    He noticed that her mere act of sipping wine was by itself casting another spell.

    "Finish you wine," she said, replacing her own glass on the table nearby. "Josette weel fix zee pain for you, *cherie*."

    She moved gracefully with her silken gown flowing behind, he thought it must be silk. And for just a moment he seemed to drift away, weightless carried in a cocoon of fuzzy tethers with teasing sensations; pain became another time; another world; forgotten. He marveled how she could move with so much grace, and gentle as a lamb in one instant, and yet in another she could leap upon a horses back with ease and balance of a trooper.

    "*Venez, ici*, come here," she beckoned, to the bed partially visible at the other end of the room.

    She folded the bed cover and put it aside as he focused on a bottle of lotion nearby.

    Standing close, he felt he could almost taste her smooth flesh as she unbuttoned his shirt slowly. She said nothing, but removed his shirt and slowly traced patterns with her fingertips in the hairs of his chest, touching ever so lightly with her fingernails. He stood motionless, unprepared yet willing to enjoy whatever she would do, realizing the wine, or was it a potion or something was already having a magical affect, and the tethers took hold once more. Unbuckling his belt and lowering his trousers she eased him down onto the bed. Then removing a shoe and sock, then the other. As she leaned over him, he caught a glimpse of her breast when her silken garment opened a little more. While she was removing his trousers he was treated to a partial glimpse of her black lace panties, the only other piece of clothing she was wearing. He was then guided further upon the bed and turned face down into the lush scent of her bedding.

As she knelt beside him he felt the smooth cool silk brush his body soothingly.

Time melted into another dimension, and he settled into the lethe of pleasure he sensed her movements, barely aware of the soft music, probably from a phonograph he had noticed, sometime between his ephemeral drift she had mounted him, straddling him and caressing him in a special way.

She had started by stroking his back after spreading the exotic scented lotion. Beginning at the base of the spine and sliding her hands firmly up to the neck, then sweeping outward across the shoulders, then returning down the sides. She repeated this several times and then, slowly worked upward by pressing and holding for a few seconds at the side of each joint of the spine with her thumbs. Thumbs he thought, though he was only certain of that greater sensation; the caress of her inner thighs on his buttocks and legs.

After a time a certain conscious awareness returned—filled with sensations that aroused and beguiled. His shorts had been removed, yet he did not know when. He guessed she must be naked also, because he had felt the subtle touches of her nipples and mouth on different parts of his body. Now, she was exerting pressure under the muscles of his shoulder blade, at the neck, and while never loosing contact, her hands moved ever so skillfully, downward to work their magic on his feet.

With practiced ease she urged him over onto his back, again kneading his shoulders and arms, then to his stomach and groin muscles. Oblivion seemed as though threatening to take over his very being. He was aware then of a hushed darkness and was certain now that she had removed all that she had on and was as naked as was he.

At times other parts of her body had brushed his, and her hair had teasingly crossed his face as she had remained close for long indeterminable periods so he could smell her sweet erotic fragrance.

While she stood at his feet and bent over to massage his inner thighs, he thought he could feel her pubic hair brush his toes and feet like a feather's touch; or was it mere fantasy born of a rampant imagination. Sometimes from this position she crouched above him and stretched to reach his shoulders while at the same time lightly tracing her fingernails across his chest on their way down to his feet, then she would pause, nipples barely touching his stomach and hips, and then, her hair and face traveled slowly over his abdomen and genitals.

As he returned to life, suddenly he felt as arousing energy, an impassioned energy. . . and now she lay fully on top of him, guiding their flesh together in that gifted way she had.

When the filtered light of morning came, his eyes did not pop open with their usual alertness, rather they eased casually to accept the moment of memories past—then POP! Slowly, then he strained to focus as he scanned the interior. Spotting a clock that read, 8:31. "Eight thirty one!" he blurted aloud. Turning to sit up, he searched the mound of covers but there was no Josette.

Neatly folded over a nearby chair he found his clothes. While he dressed hurriedly, he realized how starved he was, and in his mind he envisioned the events of the last evening, and night. He smelled her perfume as it had mingled with their body smells and he felt a part of her still remained on his person as a uncertain claim over his body and soul.

Outside, the sunlight was blinding, and squinting his eyes he noticed the bustling activity all around. As he staggered in what he perceived to be the general direction of the shower tent to wash and clean up a bit he could see some others laughing as they nodded and expressed greeting to him. What a night I must have had, he mused, and hoped he was not too late for something to eat.

With the passing of three months since his audition and acceptance with the Blanchard Circus, Bob recalled a certain day when he stood watching the high wire performers in one of their practice sessions. His respect for Fritz and Helga had been born of sound sincerity and it had brought big dividends, they had in turn accepted him and taught him well. Helga at first had responded with immediate and open affection, and in time Fritz had come to welcome him into the daily fold—eventually showing willingness, and at times eager to fulfill his role as teacher and mentor. He had come a long way in just three months. He could fly while hanging upside down and do a single somersault effectively, plus effect a smooth transfer with either Fritz or Helga. No longer did he feel awkward and clumsy as before. At last, he was one of the team.

Still he had miles to go. Soon he might do a catch, probably with Helga as she was lighter, and their timing was excellent. Perhaps a double somersault soon. Helmut was long gone, yet they often remembered him. Bob had come to enjoy the thrill of performing in front of a live audience and rejoice at their applause, but always he remembered Helmut's words. "You must concentrate on what you will do next," he had said. "Nothing else."

On occasion, after the last show he had been sent ahead with the roustabouts to assist in the set-up at the next location. During these periods there had been no chance to see Josette for two or three days, but he did get to start his practices sooner, and they were always eager to meet when she found him. Sometimes she would just stare, watching him from a distance with that look she had. At night he would go to her wagon.

He recalled how he had watched her from a distance on several occasions. She had become engaged in an argument with Pierre LaFranc the animal trainer, and she had turned to stalk away in anger.

He had come to compare Pierre with himself for some uncertain reason. Both were about the same height and build, with Pierre slightly shorter but of a more muscular physique, with light brown hair, shallow and bony facial features and deep set, steel blue eyes. He always wore shinny black boots and tight pants. Most of the time he wore only a sequined vest. Bob thought Pierre liked to display the two scars on the side of his stomach and another on the right side of his face like medallions of honor. He guessed they were reminders of his past encounters with the big cats and he observed that Pierre had responded as though he was glaring back with intimidation and resentment.

Once, after having observed an encounter between Josette and Pierre, he realized she was angry, and he had asked her, "what was that all about?"

"*Rien qui vaille*, it means nothing," she said, angrily. "I am Josette, and no man weel own Josette," she answered, her face still set hard with anguish. "He is ver-ry dangerous, you must stay away from heem. He like to drink and that make him very mean." Bob remembered how he had held her hands together in his own, and pressed them to his lips. A gentle impassioned expression replaced her anger and he sensed she wanted to melt next to him.

"*Je te amour,*" she whispered, "*je te'aime, cherie.*" They stood close that way for all to see, and he spotted Pierre scowling in the distance before skulking away, and as they parted, she whispered:"*Ces't soir Cherie, Ces't soir,*" and her lips formed a kiss from over her shoulder.

As he turned to walk away, he wondered if he too was becoming possessive, guessing that the trouble was Pierre's jealousy and possessiveness and Josette's fierce independence. In the past, they must have been involved, he concluded.

Then he was reminded of an incident just a few days ago while he was standing at the entrance aisle with some of the other performers, and talking with Jolly. Jolly was one of the clowns he had become close friends with, having bunked with them on occasions. It had been Jolly who taught him to use make-up, and how to dress and act the clown when they had marched in the big parade and the gala event. Jolly was always cheerful and even when not performing he often acted the part of a clown. Suddenly, Bob had felt someone hit him hard from behind, jolting him aside. It had been Pierre hurrying on his way to the cage of the big cats, whip clenched in hand.

Jolly had been serious this one time, and had warned him. "This man is very dangerous, and vengeful. You must be very careful of him," he had said, and then hesitatingly he continued: "years ago, there had been another man. . . and Pierre had cornered him with his whip, like an animal; he treated this man like a wild animal, and with his whip, he severed one of the man's ears. There was another time, a year later, or maybe more and this time it was another man. In the same way he was blinded, in one eye. Be very careful my good friend, to be always a clown is better perhaps."

Bob had tried to put it from his mind, still it had haunted him, even as he practiced.

He had almost forgotten the incident this day, as he strolled toward Josette's wagon after a practice session. Suddenly, he saw Josette and Pierre arguing again at her wagon. She turned to walk away again as she had before, but Pierre grabbed her and spun her against the wagon, pinning her there and slapping her repeatedly.

Impulsively Bob rushed to them, and grabbing Pierre; jerked him around and pinned him against the wagon-side. Pierre reacted in a violent rage as he raised his fist to strike. . .

Instinctively Bob's body coiled into a boxers stance, at first in defense, then the opening was there—reflexes became automatic; he shot one quick, hard left jab, then another to Pierre's face as his nose swelled to a bulbous red and he staggered backward, eyes glossy and shaken as blood trickled down his mouth and chin from the swollen and throbbing nose. The basics of boxing once set in a man's body mechanisms become automatic and instinctive. The right cross was cocked and ready for delivery, that same right cross that had put a few men down in the past, and yet there were other imbued instincts at play too, and so he held back. Perhaps there had been an underlying pity he felt for the man, like himself who loved and desired Josette—and to this point in time had been the looser in her game of unwritten rules.

Sobered now, Pierre was shouting threats and obscenities as some men dragged him away.

As others who had gathered dispersed, he turned to see Josette standing there glaring at him in a manner he had not witnessed before; hands on hips, poised in a provocative stance.

"You do not fight for Josette!" she declared, her eyes staring wildly at him. "Josette weel care for Josette." She waved a finger in his face. "I, *moi*, weel care for *moi*," stabbing the same finger at her chest, she said it bluntly. Sometimes when excited, she confused her French and English, and the tenses and genders even. "Josette does *not*, how you say, will, wish, want you to fight for heem," and in a posture of finality, she turned to stalk away.

Confused and puzzled, Bob found himself standing alone, wondering what to do. As he started to walk, someplace. . . anyplace, he noticed Burt's approach.

"Robert, just a minute," he called out. "Mr. Blanchard wants to see you in his office."

"Now! Right now?"

"Yes."

Standing at the door of the wagon with words Blanchard Circus painted in big letters on it, he knocked, twice.

"Come in," the voice returned.

"Burt said you want to see me," Bob said, stepping inside.

"Ah yes, Robert—have a chair, sit, sit down man," he said nervously, leaning back in his big chair, his expression in the manner of a man beset with many problems and compromises.

He held an envelope like a man on tenterhooks, as if weighing its contents and then leaned forward to push it across the desk.

"I must let you go Robert. In the envelope, you will find a letter of recommendation, and your pay. You have learned fast, and you have been a good trapeze man," he said, pausing momentarily to let out a great gush of a sigh—like releasing a heavy burden, then he went on as if straining for words. "The recommendation, it is the best I can give, and you will be missed. I will miss you. And we all wish you the best. You may do well in the circus," he paused, then continued grimly. "But this with Pierre is a sour business; as the big cats are the main part of my show. Pierre has been with me for many years. . . and he can be a vengeful man. I cannot have dissension among the troupe—it would be very bad." He hesitated again, then continued, "Josette has been with many men, but always she has returned to Pierre." With this obviously his final words, he rose heavily to his feet and offered his hand.

Even more confused, Bob had found himself standing outside again. So much had transpired in so little time, like a flash of light, bright then vague and misty. A short distance away he observed Josette talking with another man; one he had not seen before, and at first she ignored him. But as he started to walk away her head turned so their eyes met and held for one last time. He had learned much about French. And lately their affair had become more of a sexual marathon anyway.

As he departed he thought he discerned a certain regret and wetness in her eyes.

"*Au revoir*," he said softly, "*Au revoir ma cherie*, Josette." This he whispered into the wind.

He had gathered his belonging and after saying his goodbyes to Jolly and Helga and Fritz he was on the road. This is a good time to see the family and the farm, he thought.

At home he would decide what to do next.

Four

Staring out through the taxi window I saw the bewildered look on Mom's face that many years ago, when I said: "I knew Milton was not my real father—" She just stood there staring at me with her mouth agape, teetering like a wounded tree ready to topple over. I realize now that it must have taken a big effort for her to muster the courage for this declaration, all for the benefit of my heritage. I had no reason why I knew or felt this uncomfortable detachment towards the man who raised me as his son, and I hesitated to call *father*. Now that I think of it, I just didn't call him anything—I don't think I ever called him father, and later on it was Milton. Perhaps that was the reason for the rift that developed between us. And a simple thing like calling him dad could have meant so much and given him the simple satisfaction he needed in his troubled life. But the record had been set straight; he was step-father, a term I never dared relate to him because of some obscure courtesy.

I was a tender but hardened 14 years old when Mom first told me my real name was Marshall instead of Milton, and that Francis Milton was not my real father—she didn't tell me much more that day—I guess she thought I was too young to understand, and the shock I had handed her hadn't helped.

What should I call this man I was about to meet for the first time? Bob, Dad, Mr. Marshall, Reverend Marshall, had he ever become an ordained preacher? I had a stepfather but, I now consider *him* Dad. What does he look like? Will he embrace me and do we look alike—will I recognize any thing about his features or manner? Are there any common redeeming qualities I should look for? Just now I don't feel very redeeming.

"They be working on this same spot of road for over a year now—think they be done by now—so many guys just standin round—puttin in time—causin a goddamned traffic jam—we on I 85 now headin north into downtown Atlanta. Two miles up the road here to the interchange where 85 and 75 join we hit another jam—they be workin on that one over ten years—times it just sits there—a mess of concrete and iron like some dead skeleton or ghost in a goddamned war-zone—"

"Yeah, I know what you mean," I said. "I didn't think such things bothered taxi drivers, with the meter running anyway."

"Well it does, we pay taxes too. And I hate to see those guys standing round doing nothing."

"I know what you mean. There is a strip of highway north of San Francisco and the Golden Gate Bridge that's been torn up for 20 years that I know of. There's places with only single lane traffic, one hellish traffic congestion there every day."

"Yeah? Guess it's like that at big cities all over the country—you from California huh?"

"Northern California. I lived in Los Angeles for a few years."

"No shit. You a vet?"

"Korean war—but I got lucky and spent my time in France. Air Force. How about you?"

"Yeah—Army. I was a sergeant. Not so lucky though. Oh maybe lucky compared to some guys—I got this bum leg from a land mine—cramps up when I got to just sit still too long. But I did my time."

Art was quiet then for a spell, his concentration on the road workers, like he was working on a solution for a dilemma they cared little about.

"What kinda work you do in California?" he got out at last.

"Construction." I started to say building contractor. At one time building contractors were considered high on the ladder of prestige along with teachers, doctors, and librarians. But not any more. Too many con-artists have plunged our integrity to a new low in the public eye. Now we're lucky to be on a level with politicians and others of questionable and nefarious character. I think we rank somewhere down there with lawyers and insurance people.

"Yeah?" Ain't that funny—when I got out the Army I wanted to go to California and be a carpenter there..."
" Why didn't you?"
"This damn leg. I don't think I could climb around so good—drivin cab's not so bad—on a good day, I get good tips—airport is a good run—uh-oh here we go again—"

Mom didn't tell me much about my real father then, I guess because I had not formulated any questions. Somehow my statement—once blurted out had been as much a surprise to me as to her, and later it didn't come as a surprise though. I think I suspected all along my name shouldn't have been Milton and that Francis Milton was my stepfather, there seemed that undefinable barrier between the two of us. He knew so much that I didn't, and could never know, like he could hold it over me whenever he chose—in time I learned he wasn't like that. He never let on or spoke of anything before he and Mom came together. At least not to me.

Perhaps she only told me then because I was going north to Delaware, Ohio by train with my sister to visit with Grandma and Grandpa—Mom's parents, the Swaren's. They knew it all; the whole sorted tale and the tragedy of their time.

And maybe she decided it was time I was told—or maybe it was a load she had carried for a long time and wanted it out. At any rate it didn't register much with me at the time. My identity was Taylor Milton, or Tay as I was sometimes called. Just leave it to other kids to peg a nick-name on you. It must be a game we are all born to in our youth. A kid called me Tay-bear once and I punched him.

Later when the questions mounted, Mom explained how she and Bob Marshall had met and that he was a third year theology student at Ohio Wesleyan. She said he wanted to be a preacher then, and he had performed with a circus at one time. It had been a brief stint in his life which passed like a whim, and he only mentioned it once.

Five

*O*delia Bright stepped into the room on Ponce de Leon Ave where Robert Marshall sat in his wheelchair. She was a large-boned woman with a handsome figure and an understanding face. When she paused there in the doorway to get his attention she filled the space so that the mere act made her presence felt. In his hands he still held the photo and letter as he had lapsed away into his dreamy state.

"Robert, what you doing just sitting there in your wheelchair like that?" she said. "It's a sunny day outside—you should be getting lots of vitamin D out there—"

"My son's coming to see me. . ."

"You got a son. You never told me you had a son—or even you was married, I've known you almost 30 years—even since you was lay-minister and taught Sunday School at our church."

"He calls himself Taylor Milton. . . "

"That him there in that picture?"

"He was a baby then, and the last time I saw him."

"That girl his mother?"

He nodded.

"Cutie ain't she, such nice thighs—all the time we been friends, and me your house maid and all—cook and all that time, you never once mentioned a wife and a kid—even you was married?"

"Oh yes. . . for a very short time."

"You want to tell me about it?"

"Another time maybe—"

"What happened?"

"I don't know really. It's so far back in another time I had forgotten, and now it starts to come back like bits and pieces of a puzzle—and just a drop in the bucket of a life-time—sometimes, it seems like it was never real—you know what I mean—forty-some years in this confounded wheelchair. . ."

"Robert, all the years I know you I never hear you complain bout your chair before, even bout your crutches."

"Oh, there was a time I despised every thing living and healthy, including this chair and myself. That was like the dark ages of life—splitting two life periods asunder, and after that, well the time before no longer existed. It became necessary that way, in order to come to terms with the limitations—"

"Challenges, don't you mean, Robert? The Lord set you a mighty task, and you rose above it to find yourself."

"It didn't seem that way at first. . ."

"And now your boy brings it all back. What you gonna do when he comes—and when he be here?"

"He was at the airport. He's taking a cab, probably on his way by now."

"Lord in heaven, Robert, I better fix some food then. What does he like?"

"I have no idea—lemonade maybe—yes lemonade—ice cold lemonade. . ." He muttered on in a babbled state of mind as Odelia Bright paddled away to the kitchen; his eyes focused once again on the photo and he drifted back—back to the time after he had left the circus—to his home on the farm in Vermont. . . to summer and his hike up the road—Blossom Hill Road—with his brother Bill tramping along beside him.

Arrival at home was always a happy occasion, early summer with the birds singing and the smell of grasses and flowers in the air. Maybe tomorrow he would get to see Claire. They had often exchanged letters while he was away at college. Now he longed to see her again.

The house loomed into full view through the rows of trees on either side of the rough graded roadway, rising upward and away on rich grassy slopes to their left where tall pine and maple trees greeted them from the distant horizon. This then was their legacy; their own forest where often they had sugared for the prized maple syrup. In the fields cows grazed, and they marveled at how the fruit trees planted by their father and his father had grown fruitful.

On up the roadway stood towering rows of cherry woods on both sides. Two, three hundred yards of them, tall they were now, with branches that stretched to touch those reaching from the opposite side, and formed a sort of tunneled archway beyond the summit.

To their right, the green hills sloped downward gently where on alternating days the cows would graze—milkers required lots of fuel, and then a small stand of trees about a granite outcropping, where they had often played as youngsters, and in winter skied to the bottom where a lazy, tree-lined creek meandered its way through miles of green mountains only to spill somewhere beyond into Lake Champlain.

"We're all grown up now. Leslie, the oldest, a teacher, and Aileen the youngest, even she's all grown up too," Bill said, reminiscently.

Bob nodded his agreement.

Bill continued, "this is truly one of God's marvelous creations. It must be the most beautiful place on earth, Vermont, Green Mountain, the French named it that for its beauty."

They had been recognized, and shouts from Aileen and Leslie brought the others, at least those within earshot. They hurried to gather at the roadway entrance and together walked up to the house where Mother Marshall appeared in the doorway and eagerly rushed to embrace them.

"Come inside, sit down, you must be tired and hungry from the long trip," she cried.

"Did you see Uncle Henry and Aunt Kate? When did you get there? How long did the trip take?" Aileen inquired anxiously.

As they went into the kitchen Bob put his arm around his little sister and squeezed affectionately. "How many more questions do you have, you been saving them up?" he mused, as they all found a chair. "What about George? Have you heard, and when is he due?" asked Bob, telling how he and George had hitchhiked to Ann Arbor together, so he could help his younger brother register and get settled in his first year at University of Michigan.

"We had a letter from him just a few days ago and he should be here in a day or two," said Aileen. Soon brothers John and Allen came in from the fields and again they taunted each other in teasing chatter. Milking time was upon them again. Usually John and Allen could handle it easily, but with two more pairs of hands the milking would go much faster and they could visit each other as they used to. Once, a long time ago a squabble had broken out and evolved into a milk-squirting free-for-all; evolving in whole buckets being splattered about. You would think the wrath of had God struck when Mother Marshall made her will felt for such wasteful nonsense.

Later with chores temporarily done, they returned to the house and visited some more, then a few more bites to eat and some fresh milk before bedtime. For the inevitable was very clear. Early morning would bring about more milking and many never ending projects.

The upstairs loft-room never changed. Still the same large space with two small windows on each side, set low to the floor. The ceiling, flat in the center and sloping at the sides, nearly touching the tops of the small windows and hinting at the outside roof slope. The room was big enough for five beds and five lads. In their growing years, much of their time had been spent here. The only empty bed was for George and soon it too would be filled again.

Occasionally they could hear some light chatter from the adjoining room at the front of the house where Leslie and Aileen slept. After some friendly chiding through the walls came the snores and soon all were asleep. . . all except Bob.

He could reminisce, and then plan for the days ahead. He glanced around a bit, taking in the room. Allen's bed in one corner, John's at the other with enough room in between for books, many books on shelves made long ago by his grandfather. Many long hours and days he had spent with those books and many others against another wall, how many he wondered, a hundred, two hundred perhaps. He wondered why he had never counted. Maybe someday he would though some were so old and delicate he doubted if they would bear handling.

On another wall, more old books and then a door into the hall and the girls room, and two more front rooms. A big house he thought, two story and traditional Vermont style with white clapboard siding and green shutters for window-trim.

Just a faint ray of moonbeam bounced into the room to illuminate and form strange shadowy shapes. And now he could feel a slight breeze, let in by the open windows, and smell the soft, sweet scents of the countryside, the flowers and trees. . . and cows, yes of course the cows, and that reminded him briefly of the circus and Josette.

He was thinking; a couple of days to work around the farm. For an instant he recalled something his father had said in a fit of despair; "maybe we should just forget about milking and go into the manure business—damn cows is the only one of God's creatures I know that shit more'n they eat—more'n the milk they give too. . ." He had said the same thing about chickens a time or two. But he had liked to cut and split firewood; "a man's workout," he'd say. The chicken house was in bad need of repair and the fences. Springtime and summer always brought the need of numerous repairs and he was good at fixing things and enjoyed it, and the others relied on him and looked to him for leadership, he was the elder and since his father had passed away the responsibility had fallen to him.

Maybe, after two days, he could hike across the valley to see Claire Mayfield, and to the grist mill to visit Harry Ellwood his best friend, but now it felt great just to sleep in his own bed.

Summer in Vermont, especially near the mountains has always been more like spring than summer, with the promise of afternoon drizzle—endless spring, and then autumn. After the milking, the cleaning and the ever mounting manure pile had to be moved by pitching it into a wagon and then hauled up to be spread across the grassy slopes. Though Allen and John kidded that they had saved it just for them, all were well aware that it could not be moved completely and spread onto the fields until it had fully thawed. That could be anytime now.

It didn't seem like work; it was good to be home and to be doing. Rising early, before sunrise was never a problem. Had there been a sluggard the others had seized the opportunity to prove a point by some rather rough treatment like bouncing him, mattress and all on the floor and rolling him down the stairs. George had tested their fickle determination just once.

After breakfast everyone was soon busy again. The women finished with the kitchen and headed for the garden. Soon there would be fresh vegetables and Mother Marshall had always considered the flowers a very high priority.

Bob and Allen tackled the chicken house while Bill and John applied their efforts to badly needed fence repairs.

With evening came the time to herd the cows in from the pasture across the road. As they all joined in, it was Leslie who called for attention and pointed to a lonely figure hiking up the road. Allen turned to look. Bob and Bill were farther down the hillside and John a little closer.

The girls called out, "George, it's George."

Cows can be stubborn critters at times, and possess the size and bulk to prove it and were spread about, mooing their defiance against the over zealous border collie named Josh, but whom the family often referred to as just plain *dog*. Josh delighted in the pleasures of commanding the larger and more stubborn animals and took his authority with serious relish. George found his way through their maze while Josh paid him no mind. Josh had more serious things to do.

"George, what took you so long?" chided John; "miss your train?"

He laughed, "I see they got a better connection," indicating Bob and Bill as he spotted them bringing up the rear.

"We saved it for you." John never missed a chance to poke a little fun, and anyone could be his target..

"What?"

"Your favorite, the manure pile," teased Allen.

"Oh you guys are horrible," scolded Leslie, seizing one arm and Aileen the other. "Let's go see Mom and we'll fix you something to drink and eat—we hid some lemonade from those gluttons."

At the steps George paused briefly then rushed to embrace his mother desperately and at times like this she treated them all as youngsters, though he was the middle born, and a grown man of almost twenty two, then she stepped back to look at him and to take inventory.

"Yes, you are taller, and thinner, definitely taller, a little weary and hungry. Come in and sit, rest while we fix something for you to eat," she said, with a happy glow. At last her whole brood had returned to the fold.

"Tell us about the trip,—did you hitch-hike all the way?" asked Aileen.

"Did you stop at Uncle Henry's?" pleaded Leslie.

"Girls, girls, so many questions, give him a little time to get his breath. He needs a rest and some food. Soon the others will be in from milking. It won't take long with four of them. . . and then we can all enjoy a good visit together."

"I'm really not that hungry, Mom," he said, but showed no resistance to a plate of steaming roast beef and mashed potatoes, beans, biscuits and some fresh milk Aileen had fetched.

Time at college had been good to him. After registration, he explained, and they had located a room to rent, he had also found work. It was Bob's diplomacy that helped set him up, he continued, and also Bob who got them lost in the city so that they had to ride the streetcar back across town before finding their way.

When Bob had departed for Ohio Wesleyan, George had finally settled down to his studies in Zoology and Ornithology.

Allen came in from the back room. "Looks like you made it just in time for haying. We were waiting for you, you know; college boy needs to build up those muscles."

"I got muscles. I could do with a vacation though; think I'll just take it easy and lay around for a couple weeks. . . maybe months, maybe the whole summer. . ."

"Honestly. . . you guys. . . never know when to quit. Still acting like children." Leslie shook a finger at both of them. Allen snapped his teeth as if to bite it.

Each had their traditional places at the age-darkened oak table of seven feet long and almost three feet across. This old kitchen with its great cast iron, wood burning stove was a constant reminder of the old days, and of this eighty year old place called home. They laughed as they told how their mother had sat between Bill and Bob to prevent their bickering which on occasion advanced to some serious fighting—but that was all past now—a time for laughing at old memories.

It was Aileen who reminded them of the birds and how Bob had initiated a contest to see who could document the most bird sightings. The family had always been enthusiastic about animals and birds in particular, but George had become obsessed with his precise and comprehensive documentation. Always it seemed, he found excuses to go searching for new species, often slipping away from work details to pursue a whistle or a chirping sound.

Opening the subject was an invitation for George to tell in detail of his most recent sightings in Ann Arbor. One of his favorite haunts had become the cemetery as there were always birds there in abundance. He also told of how easy it was to ride the streetcars all over the city for just pennies. Discussions continued late into the evening and well past their usual bedtime.

It was Mother Marshall's insistence which finally sent them off to bed.

But it was Bob, the elder who argued, "just one song before we go. Let's do Mom's favorite," he said.

"Okay that sounds great, but let's do *Dry Bones* first," Aileen declared, flashing a coquettish grin.

"Sounds good to me," Bob agreed.

"Bob likes *Dry Bones* just so he can show off his deep bass voice and four octave range," added John, emphasizing deeeeep.

Aileen sat at the piano with her mother beside her after they moved into the parlor, and after a few notes Bob signaled for the chorus.

"Ezekial dried dem, dry bones,
Ezekial dried dem, dry bones"

Twice more Bob signaled by lowering his hands, and then. . . they stopped as he continued,

"Now here's tha words of tha Lord,
Ezekial connected dem, dry bones,"

and he signaled the chorus. They continued until they all finished.

One tune led to another. "Only one more." This time she insisted. The last one, they agreed it must be her favorite, *Rock of Ages*.

After everybody was asleep, Bob lay thinking again; tomorrow he would work on the barn door after milking. And in the afternoon he would hike across the valley to see Claire.

Hiking down the back side of Blossom Hill Road he turned and waved to his sisters working in the garden. . . and recalled how just two days before, he and Bill had walked up this same road from the opposite direction. Another beautiful day he thought, a day filled with kindness and cheery prospects for the future, as his mind traced the events of the morning. After milking and repairing the barn door they had gathered for a big meal prepared by the girls. Then, they had moved into the parlor where John and Allen took turns reciting poems. These had become favorites wherever John went, though Allen had teased that they were *smokehouse* poetry and then had countered with two of his own, *Our Cousin Jack* and *The King is Sick*. He had found them in an old book when he was a youngster. Then he and John had recited alternate lines of *Our Cousin Jack*. Together they cranked out some hymns and folk song favorites until time to resume their chores and he had decided the time had come to visit Claire and his old friend Harry.

He would follow the old dirt road over the hill, and down to a creek that fed into a lake a few miles farther on. Recalling, again how they often went there for picnics and church gatherings in the past. His mother had told him of a church picnic and softball game scheduled for this coming Sunday.

Crossing an old covered bridge that seemed ancient yet so friendly and familiar he paused to inspect a post where he had once carved Claire's name. So she would never be forgotten. It was still there, however crude and weathered. He followed pathways to avoid the main road so he could listen to mockingbirds and larks and the any other songbird which caught his attention along the way. Other times he would sing out loud.

Stopping briefly two other times he exchanged greetings with the Charboneau's, and later with the Lester's.

Across the valley, he started up the foothills, paused to pass time with Mr. and Mrs. Mahan while recounting the past when he had attended high school with their son and daughter.

Later, he stopped for a rest and refreshing drink of cool water from a spring, then continued on his way.

How uncanny Claire was he thought; she had always sensed his coming, and had freshly baked pastries ready and how the aroma had reached him even as he hurried along the pathway to her front porch.

The house came into view as his ears caught the sound of piano music; yes that would be Claire. The tune; a rousing rendition of one of her favorites by Edward Grieg; *The Hall of The Mountain King*. She had made it one of his favorites also.

Climbing the front porch steps of the white, two story house, he marveled at her intuitiveness. His senses signaled rich smell of pastries, some of his favorite no doubt. But how could she know he was coming. They had played together for many years, and had hiked the woods alone, often hand in hand.

For some unknown reason when he tapped on the door, he recalled Mary Swaren, and how she and Claire were so much alike, about the same age and size, although Claire was slighter in build and more petite. Both possessed the same qualities; vivacious and boundless energy—both were happy and quick of wit, and both had that flirty eye.

Claire would probably be wearing a soft flowery dress with lace around the neck, loose sleeves and long curly blond hair, she would smell sweet and clean and he could see her in his mind's eye now, like springtime and laughter all year round.

As the piano playing continued, he watched through the glass panes till someone came to answer his knock.

"Good afternoon, Mrs. Mayfield," he said, in a low greeting.

"Well Robert Marshall, come in, how good to see you. It's been such a long time. Do come in. Claire is in the parlor playing, as I'm sure you can hear. She'll be so glad to see you."

"Thank you, Mrs. Mayfield," he said, as if on cue he tip-toed softly toward Claire and the music.

Momentarily he waited there behind her; "guess who!"

"Bob," she gasped and turned in surprise, then jumped up, she threw her arms around his neck and hugged and kissed the side of his face near the corner of his mouth. It was more intimate than he had been prepared for at the moment. "Where did you come from, how long have you been watching me?" she demanded, then the usual coy grin flushed across her face, "you sly fox."

"I wanted to watch you, for just a moment," he said, stepping back a little. "Let me look at you, yes you've grown, and prettier than ever. You're a woman now, I remembered you as a girl."

"Well sure," she flushed, coquettishly, "I was a woman then, but you just didn't notice."

They stood there, gazing into each others eyes until she spoke. "Where have you been? How long have you been home? Come and sit down, tell me about the family, Bill and George, I mean. I see the others from time to time in church, but you three have been gone so long."

Bob looked up to see Mrs. Mayfield enter the room carrying a tray. "I bet you would like a bite to eat, some pastries Claire has just baked, and a glass of cold milk," she said.

"Oh, yes thank you, ma'am," he said, thinking to himself, cold milk, a special treat. There was no icebox at his home and only occasionally did they have cookies. His mother preferred to bake bread mostly, and pies. But how did Claire seem to know when he would be coming? How did she always manage to have some treat ready? Maybe it was because she was always making something. He had asked many times before, but always she had given him that same sheepish grin.

"This is a real treat. Thank you, thanks, both of you," he said. He remembered that Claire never ate her own goodies. She just found pleasure in preparing them for others.

"How did you get here? walk I suppose, the six miles as you usually do most of the time," said Claire, inching the cookie tray in his direction.

"It doesn't seem so far; a few hops and skips," he said, after finishing a cookie and holding another in his hand, gulping down a couple swallows of cold milk. "Bill and I arrived two days ago and George came in yesterday."

"And all of you hitch-hiked, I suppose," she said, "but I want to know what's been happening with you?"

"Uh-oh, I just realized something; I meant to bring you a surprise!"

"You don't have to bring me anything—oh a wildflower maybe," she grinned. "At least you noticed I am a woman."

"A whole field of wildflowers then—next time." He felt boyishly guilty as he bit into a cherry cake square and finished the last of his milk.

"Have you heard about the picnic this Sunday?" she asked, "I'm sure you men will have a softball game, as usual."

"I plan to stop at the grist mill to see your father and Harry. John said he's still working there."

"That Harry Ellwood," she said. "I catch him looking at me sometimes," she added, holding him there with a demure smile that spelled suspicious curiosity.

"I'll have to talk to Harry about that."

"Don't you dare, you just leave Harry be."

"Harry's been my best friend for years, even before high school. If I'm to talk to anyone about you, it should be Harry."

"Don't you dare Robert Sidney Marshall, that's all, just don't you even dare," she said, stabbing her finger at his chest.

He smiled at her; a teasing smile. Coming to his feet he reached for her hand. "Let's go outside for a walk or a sit on the swing," he said.

"Okay" she cooed, "Do you remember that time two years ago when you took me for a hike, and we were supposed to catch up with the others, my brother and your brothers and sisters?"

"Oh yes, and I left you alone in the woods while I climbed some rocks to hunt for the others."

"You left me alone, and you got *lost*. That's what happened."

"I wasn't lost, I was just looking for the others."

"Then my father came along; said Mrs. Jones had told him—she acted suspicious and she saw me go into the woods with a man."

"And when he found you, you said, 'I'm with Bob, Daddy.'"

"Yes, he found me, and he left me standing there in the woods, all alone." She snickered, a little thing, crinkling her nose and squinting her eyes. "'As long as you're with Bob, then you must be safe', he said."

"Your Dad thought it was very funny." They sat down in the front yard swing—both were silent for while.

"Soon, maybe tomorrow, I'll have to look for work, there is plenty to do at the farm, but I have to earn some money to continue at college," said Bob, his voice becoming serious.

"You worked at the radio station last summer, maybe you can do that again, you know singing, you and Aileen. And you gave some talks. You're really good at it, and you have a natural voice for that kind of thing," she said.

"I'd like that, it sure is close to the farm and I could live at home and still help out there. But it doesn't pay anything, oh maybe a little, but not enough. I have to look for something else."

"I heard Daddy say there's not much work anywhere," she said, hesitatingly. "You know, something might turn up Sunday. A lot of people will be at the picnic."

"I sure hope so, perhaps Harry or your dad will know of something. Bill and George are both looking too. It's getting late, I'd better head for the mill soon."

"Don't go yet, lets sing some songs," she pleaded, jumping up to take his hand, "Come, I'll play and you sing. . . *Deep River* and *Amazing Grace* and. . . and we'll get Granny, you know how much she loves to hear you sing in that deep voice of yours, she just sits there in her rocking chair, and rocks, and smiles, and then when we finish, she always says 'that was nice Robert, that was nice'. Come on."

He thought, how clever she is, so cheerful and resourceful, and always when he needed it most.

With his spirits raised, Bob hurried down the road toward the grist mill; a mere fifteen minutes by way of a brisk walk. In the past even her letters had cheered him up and had helped to set him a positive direction. He was thinking how fortunate he was to have someone like Claire.

As he passed a two story white house with green trim and a white picket fence, he shouted greetings and waved to Mrs. Conrad, who was tending her flower garden; so many clean white houses with green or red trim, all similar, yet different and individual, and how their uniqueness added to the beauty of the countryside and traditions of each quaint little town. They reminded him of a storybook setting.

Approaching the mill, he could see Mr. Mayfield standing just inside the door.

"Good afternoon Mr. Mayfield," he said.

"Well hello there, Bob. How are you? It's been a long time, let's see, last May wasn't it?"

"Yes sir, just about then, I think."

"Looks like college is treating you good these past days."

"Just stopped by the house to visit your misses, and Claire. Thought I'd stop here, hoping to find out about some work. See if maybe you might know of some leads."

"Not much around Robert. Things are kinda slow, but I'll sure check about for you," he said. "Sure wish I could use you here, but you can see, we're running a little slow too."

"Sure Mr. Mayfield. Guess I'll see you Sunday at church and the picnic. I'd like to have a word with Harry over there, if its okay with you."

"You just go right ahead, it's good to see you again. . . and give my best to your family."

"Hi buddy," said Harry raising his voice above the noise, yanking back a lever that operated the mechanism which metered grain flow.

Bob noticed that Harry was the only man, but there were

seven young women working about. "You sure are the lucky one Harry, the only guy here and all these pretty girls," he mused, saying pretty girls a little louder, so he got a few cute looks from some roving eyes.

"There's only one girl I care to be with, and that's Claire Mayfield. Sure would like to know her," Harry countered.

"Why didn't you say so sooner, that's no problem. I'll introduce you. She's my cousin."

"That a promise?"

"Promise."

"Well at least I wouldn't go off and leave her standing all alone in the woods."

"Oh you heard about that, did you? Guess I'll never hear the end of that one."

"Well, what are you doing back here among the civilized? Haven't seen you for a while," Harry said, yanking on the lever again, checking to see if it was secure. "They kick you out of college again?"

"Come to check on you, see if you're doing your job. Maybe take it away from you."

"Ha, if you could you mean."

"You know, it might be worth it, what with all these pretties around. That could do a lot for a guy's morale."

"Well, I'll tell you one thing for sure, I'll take you up on that introduction to Claire."

"Right now any work would be worth looking into. Do you know of anything, for the summer that is?"

"Not much to be had, maybe you can get a little at the fruit sheds, or cheese factory. Things are getting a little slow here and I think George, Mr. Mayfield is some concerned, but he won't show it, least so's anybody can tell."

"Are you going to the picnic after church Sunday?" Bob asked.

"Sure thing. The guys are planning another softball game. How about you and your brothers?"

"Wouldn't miss it. With my brothers and you and me, that's almost a full team right there, and we can take on anybody. Just like the old days," Bob said. "Think I'll head on home now, leave you to your work."

"You hiking?"

"Don't think so. Walked over. Think I'll trot on down to the main road and see if I can hitch a ride, part of the way at least." Turning to leave, he waved goodbye to everyone while tossing a kiss to one particular cutie with a wicked roving eye.

"Don't wear yourself out now, I wouldn't want to make you look too bad come Sunday," shouted Harry, with a quick salute and getting in the last dig.

With a chuckle, Bob went on his way. He had never thought of Claire as a cousin before, still she was, and they had talked about it a few years back.

The ride he got took him part way, and another, on a hay wagon, let him off at the foot of Blossom Hill Road. He walked the rest of the way uphill to the farm. And he remembered the time he had hiked over to Camel's Hump Mountain. That had taken four days round-trip and, he had slept out at night and had eaten wild berries along with biscuits and jerky he had carried.

They would probably start haying in about two weeks, he thought, as he reached for the door.

His mother and sisters were busy, setting the table and preparing food for the light evening snack. Almost always, they hummed a little tune while working.

"Well hello Robert Sidney. Did you have a good afternoon?" asked his mother.

"Very enjoyable." He explained about his visits. "But nothing of any work, though."

"Reverend Murray stopped by," said his mother. "He spoke with your brother Bill. He wants to see you before service Sunday. Has something to talk to you about."

As the door opened, Reverend Murray invited his young visitor into the pastor's study.

"Robert, how good to see you. You're looking well in the Lord's keep," he said, reaching to shake his hand. "A glass of cool spring water, or milk—?"

"No thank you, sir."

He always offered a warm firm grip, first with one hand and then firmly clasping the other on top with a sincere shake as a strong reminder that he was a man of God. From his grip he passed on a gift of energy. Bob considered the man before him; his wavy white hair came neatly to a point at the top of his forehead; friendly deep-set and dark eyes beneath heavy brows; his ageless features bespoke of endless energy. And though slightly shorter than himself, he stood erect and proud with shoulders squared when he moved, giving the appearance of a much taller man. Bob remembered hearing that he had studied and preached in Britain and Europe, as well as all around this country. There was no mistaking how this man's influence reached out to touch those around him.

He had chosen to live here for its natural beauty and its closeness to God he had said, he liked the people, and the small towns. And Bob wondered if he could be like the good Reverend Murray in his coming years.

"I am well, Reverend Murray."

"And your studies, they're progressing as well, I presume."

"Oh yes, quite well." There was hesitation in his voice, and the other man seemed to consider it momentarily.

"I suppose Bill explained why I wish to speak with you?"

"Yes he did, briefly," said Bob, hesitatingly, "but I think he would be much better qualified than myself, since he has just graduated and is nearly ordained."

"Have a chair," said the Reverend, settling into his own behind his desk.

"True. . . still other circumstances come into play, and it is a wonderful opportunity for either of you. However it seems Bill may have other commitments."

"Yes, he did tell me of other work he might get, and I know he wants to return to Wesleyan for another semester for some post-grad work. He feels that would further his chances for an assignment," explained Bob.

"Of course, I quite understand," agreed the man in the dark suit and clerical collar. He leaned forward and placed his clasped hands on his desk. "Let me start from the beginning," he paused, momentarily, inclining his head, raising his hands together, touching his chin and lips as if collecting his thoughts into words. Bob had studied this technique before as a means of gaining a listeners attention. Having organized his thoughts, he continued. "The opportunity has come up to appoint someone to the summer pastorate of two churches—small, mind you. I have discussed the possibility of your brother Bill or yourself to the board members. Also that I would highly recommend either of you. They have concurred with my recommendation and if you choose to accept, I have been empowered to have you start next Sunday. The fact that both of you and your father have acted as lay ministers here and at Waterbury many times was very convincing and much to your favor."

Bob leaned forward in his chair anxiously.

"There is more. The widow Simpson needs some carpentry and other repair work done and is willing to pay you and would exchange room and board for some of the work. As her house in East Calais is situated just across the road from our Lord's house; this could prove to be an added convenience." The clergyman paused, his eyes still measuring the young, eager man sitting across from himself.

"I appreciate the opportunity," Bob said. Then with certain reservation he continued: "with rain due any day and I should help with the hay gathering at the farm... and..."

"I'm sure that would be no problem. You could be spared those days you're needed, and we might even arrange for some transportation for you," he said. "Oh, incidently there is a bicycle available at the church and you can use that to get around locally. I might add that Bill thought you would be much better qualified since you're the one who likes fixing things, and he said you are pretty good at carpentry."

"I'll have to thank him," Bob said, smiling. "True, Bill doesn't care much for carpentry, though he's just as good at it as I am."

"You will be free in time for college in September." Easing his chair back, he asked; "would you like to think on it for a while, before giving your answer?"

"No need. I accept. It is better than I could have hoped for, and thanks for your confidence. I shall do my very best."

"I am convinced you would." He rose to his feet and squared his carriage still considering the younger man. As he rounded the small desk to place his arm about Bob's shoulder he said: "I shall make the announcement during service and we can discuss the details later, and when you wish to go."

"I don't know how to thank you enough, but thanks again," Bob said gratefully.

"I'm well aware that the pay isn't much, but it will help, and having known your family for many years and how they like to keep doing, especially your wonderful mother, I know you will

do your best."
"She will be pleased, I'm certain."
"Its been so nice talking with you." At the doorway, they shook hands. "And now, with service approaching, I must prepare."
Bob returned his handshake with their second hands clasped on top of each others. . . and he wondered again, could he be like this man in his later years, possessed with an endless reserve of energy which he passed on to others.
Stepping outside, he knew that shortly people would be arriving. Some, old friends he had known for many years, yet hadn't seen for quite along while.
He wanted to tell everyone the good news. Then, he remembered Reverend Murray's own words. He said he would make the announcement at the service. He couldn't precede the good Reverend, yet could he tell his mother and family, and Harry. . . and perhaps Claire. . .
Suddenly he stopped in his tracks, did this mean he would not get a chance to spend time with Claire and other friends like Harry. For Claire he would have to make time, somehow.
When he found his way to the church front people were already arriving. A few came in automobiles and many still showed up with horse and wagon as his family would. They would probably be last, what with the milking and all. A few others walked to church from homes nearby.
The first pangs of guilt caught him unaware as he thought of being absent from the farm when so much help was needed. He wondered how George and Bill would fare in their search for gainful employment.
When he glanced around, his eyes caught Claire as if waiting on him. She was standing with her mother, father and brother who were busy speaking with others he knew. He saw her in a way he had not thought of before. God, she is pretty, he thought. She was standing still, in a light flower print dress that gave hint to her femininity, her hair and smile caught the light as she winked, a little thing, with a crinkled nose. Now he understood why Harry wanted so much to meet her.
As the congregation entered the church, so went the Mayfield's locked in conversation. George Mayfield himself was bent in serious talk with other men about him. Undoubtedly they were concerned with business and the economy.

He would tell Claire of his good fortune later. Then he saw Harry's approach with his family and he hurried to greet them. Just as he reached them some others joined in and they exchanged greetings also.

"You can go ahead with the others, Harry. I'll wait for my family and see you later," he said.

Aileen and Leslie met him first, "What did Reverend Murray want to see you about?"

Then his mother said, "we must hurry. We don't want to miss the first hymn, its one of my favorites you know." As they plodded along in an effort to catch up she continued, "and Bob, do tell us of your visit with the good Reverend."

Bob had started to explain, but they were joined by another late family whom they all knew well. Again pleasantries were exchanged at the church steps, as they hushed to listen.

The congregation sat and the Worship Leader, a generous sized woman, stood poised as she invited announcements and greetings.

"But first," she said, "I would like to invite everyone to the picnic just a short piece from here. You all know the location down by the lake park and of course," she spoke smoothly and in a pleasant gentle tone, "we will be joined by the congregations from two other churches that we all know so well. One is the Wesley United from Waterbury and the other from Stowe. And, of course there will be lots of fine food and refreshments." Her words flowed out in bubbly way. "I'm told there will be some canoeing as well, and swimming. Also, I understand that some of the men are planning a softball game."

There was another announcement of a childrens and a ladies group meeting, and a reminder about summer Bible studies.

When they were finished Reverend Murray stood and declared his personal delight on a few announcements of his own. "One being," he said, "the acceptance of Robert Marshall as summer lay-minister for two small churches, one in East Calais and the other at South Woodbury." He went on to explain that he took particular delight in doing so, since he had known Robert and indeed his family for many years and even his long departed father, James who had served as lay-minister for this very house. He went on to say that he had personally recommended Robert to the board, and they had unanimously

agreed on his selection and explained that Robert would be living at the widow Simpson's and working there also. Then he added, "I know we will all want to remember him in our prayers for the Lord's work he has been chosen to do.
"And now, all please rise and bow our heads."

At the park, while so many were busy setting up tables, children dressed in their best dashed to and fro in search of mischief.
Many friends came to Bob to congratulate him as so many others had after church had let out. He realized that he still hadn't talked with Claire and had no opportunity to introduce her to Harry. And so he knew he must excuse himself and look for both of them.
He caught sight of her and headed to intercept her. "Well, congratulations," she said, and added a friendly hug. "Why didn't you tell me?"
"I didn't hear about it until after I saw you on Thursday," he said. "And then nothing positive until this morning."
"It sounds wonderful. Just what you always wanted. I know you'll do so well."
"Can we excuse you from your family? There's someone I'd like to introduce you to."
"Sure, but who?" she asked, glancing about—her eyes excited and puzzled.
"Well Robert, congratulations on your appointment. We're so happy for you. . . and your mother will be so proud," said Mrs. Mayfield, then George marched up to shake his hand.
"Thank you," he said. "I'm sure she will, and I'll do my best."
"We know you will Robert. You always do—give your very best at every thing you undertake."
"Thanks again," he said. "Would you excuse Claire and me for a little while, I promise she'll be right back."

"Well, who is it?" she pleaded, impatiently. "This person you want to introduce me to!" as her eyes sparkled with curiosity.
"You'll see," Bob said. "Someone who is very fond of you, and has wanted to meet you for a long time." They strolled towards a group of young men called out and motioned to one; "Harry, can you come here for a minute?" He wanted to separate

him from the others.

"Harry Ellwood!" she gasped.

"I have someone I want you to meet, Harry."

"Claire, this is Harry Ellwood, he's been dying to make your acquaintance."

"Harry, this is Claire Mayfield."

He reached out to take her hand, at first as a man would take another, then to hold it instead, like a butterfly's wing, less it should bruise. Harry Ellwood was a man at odds with himself now that his wildest dreams seemed fulfilled; betrayed by the burden of shyness, and the cast of reddishness in his brown hair seemed oddly ready to catch fire.

"Hello," she said, musically.

He had practiced what he would say if the time ever came. But now, this close and touching her for an instant, he felt weak-kneed and tongue-tied. His lips moved but no words issued.

It was Bob who broke the spell. "Excuse me," he said. " I'll leave you two to get acquainted for a while."

He turned and moved to intercept and steer a group of men away so Harry and Claire could be alone.

"Bob, are you ready to play ball?" one asked. "We figure you and your brothers, that's five, and Harry is six, and Jim, Curley and Frank, against us and the rest of the guys. How does that sound? We know the Marshall's always like to play together, and well, I think you probably know the rest of the fellows."

The Marshall brothers did like to play together, especially in basketball as the five of them made a team. Often they would travel to the nearby towns to challenge all comers with Bob as their team captain at center.

Bob was well aware also that given the chance, Bill would rather go swimming, recalling that he practiced all his spare time at college, hoping to compete for a position on the Olympic swim team, but finally had to give up his dream. He had to work and with studies there just was not enough time. Bob remembered how he liked to swim also and for two summers he and Bill had been lifeguards.

"What position do you want, Bob?" asked Frank. "I'll take first base, and Harry likes second and the rest is a toss-up. "

"I'll take center field, if that's okay with the others," he answered. He was thinking when he played baseball he liked to pitch or play shortstop.

Remembering Claire, he decided he should return her to the company of her parents as he had promised. She was a popular girl and by now three of the guys had forsaken the game to join her and Harry in conversation.

"Bye Claire, see you later," chorused some of the guys.

"I'll hit a home run for ya," promised Frank, waving.

"Let me walk you back to your parents," offered Bob.

"I'm a big girl. I can find my own way," she reminded him. "You just go on with the boys and play your little game."

Someone flipped a coin to determine which team took the field first and who batted first.

Spectators had started to gather on the sidelines to cheer on their favorites as a wild game developed quickly, soon long, and hard balls were flying off of the bats.

After a few innings, a "food's ready" call came to interrupt the competition and a time-out was declared with the game to resume later. Not a few were reluctant to give up or postpone the game even for food and drink. Finally, the canoes were beached and swimmers hailed in from a floating raft anchored offshore.

People from three churches had participated, so there was quite a large group, and everyone had brought something. There were tables arranged in rows with food and drinks, as well as fresh fruits, vegetables, fresh baked breads and pastries. Some tables covered with red and white checkered tablecloths.

In that park meadow beside a small lake, a white haired man stood before his flock with his head bowed to give thanks.

Bob and Harry had filled their plates with all they could carry and joined Claire and her family while most of the others scattered around at random to mix with their friends. She sat between Bob and Harry, and seemed sincerely pleased with the attention being shown to her.

This was a feast to be sure and all to many would be heavy footed with swollen bellies when the game resumed. The Reverend Murray had presided and was later evident moving among the people to shake hands and speaking to each one individually. Bob watched as he worked his way, always smiling and giving comfort. He was learning many useful things

The Preacher Bird

as he observed the man in the dark suit moving easily among the others.

Later, when Bob had left the others, he strolled pensively into the trees; not in meditation, though deep in thought. Reverend Murray joined him and they walked together, and talked.

Shouts arose from the ball field; *play ball*, and once more the action started. Young pranksters with full bellies and mussed hair roamed in search of mischief again.

After the game Bob went for a walk with Harry. He told his family he would catch a ride and see them later at home.

The game had been a wild one and had finally come to an end with everybody shouting and cheering. It had been close right up to the last out, with bystanders just as much involved as the players. Even Reverend Murray had become a little overzealous in his encouragement.

Alone now, the two old friends walked together laughing about the incidents of the past game.

"How did you and Claire get on," asked Bob, "I saw you together from time to time."

"I don't know. . . I had it all figured out, what I wanted to say. But when the time came, my tongue was, well you know, all tied up."

"It looked to me like you were both enjoying yourselves. I could tell, and she likes you, that much is obvious. If she hadn't it would have shown—she is a very genuine individual, especially about her feelings."

"Really, well buddy, you can see more than I can, that's for sure."

"She wants to see you again. She told me so,"

Harry's spirit rose visibly. "I saw you talking with Reverend Murray. What was that all about?"

"Oh, we covered a few things—this and that, mostly about East Calais, and South Woodbury. And what I'm expected to do there, duties and such, you know."

"Yeah, sounds like it'll be a good break for you. But you can do anything. You were always good at sports, especially basketball and baseball," he said, thoughtfully. "I bet you could still try out for the pro's. Heck Bob, you're only twenty three;

that's not too old, and you're in top condition. You should give it a try, I bet you'd do great in baseball, and well, church bells, you even took boxing that year at Montpelier and wrestling while in high school. You take good care of yourself—and you're—well, you dare to get around, and do things. Things most of us don't even think about. You're willing to take a chance—not like me. My aims are simple—a place of my own right here, or there," he shrugged a little shrug, his eyes still on the ground as they walked. ". . .with some security, and a cute girl like Claire, and a machine to tinker with. . . Well I don't need to tell you; you know I'd be as content as cat-fur in kitten britches. . ."

"I joined a traveling circus for a while, this past spring."

"A traveling circus! you did that? Why you sly old fox! You never did say anything about that. What was it like?"

"It was interesting. . . and very educational," Bob smiled as the thought aroused memories of the past.

"Interesting! and educational. . . hah! When was that."

"Bill was the only one who knew. I wrote letters to Mom and sent them to Bill, and he would forward them to her so she didn't find out."

"If your dad knew, why I bet he'd throw a conniption, even in his grave; your mom too. . ."

"Dad, maybe. Mom, would just have been hurt, and showed it. That's the part I couldn't deal with. The hurt look."

"Well anyway that just proves what I was saying. Because you have that certain quality—determination, and you refuse to give up or accept loosing. That's why we won that game—not just that—there was other times; lots of them. "

"I appreciate what you say Harry. but I've chosen my path, and its the Lord's game I want to play in. . . His work I must do, or whatever He has for me." This he said calmly in a matter-of-fact voice, then added. "That will be my way."

At home, and in his own bed again, Robert Marshall lay gazing about the slightly moonlit room. It has been a busy day. He recalled that when he had arrived home his family hadn't said much. Still he knew, they were proud of him, especially his mother. She had that gleam of joy and pride on her face, and yet she had not said much about his appointment, realizing the proof would be in the pudding. That's what Harry might say.

He felt dreamy, as his gaze circled the darkened room. This room is home, the books, a Tennyson book of poems and the James Fenimore Cooper stories packed with thrills and heroism; *Pathfinder* and *Deerslayer,* those days of the past packed with adventure and history stirred the urge to explore and push on—and there were other voices as well, not necessarily intruding voices, but something telling him he had to choose, make a decision on a worthy thing to do—and give it his best. At times there came a flood of uncertainty gnawing deep inside of him—to travel and explore, and do other things. If he were to classify it; the circus had truly been an adventure which had lingered like a taste for good food—women with worldly passions. Then came the guilt and pressure followed with expectations to follow the mainstream. If only they could be united in a common goal? Reverend Murray would understand. He too must have followed his dreams, and made his own decisions. Often when he was away from this place and filled with doubts and uncertainty, here is where he longed to be, perhaps because all things seemed clearer and in focus here, sort of like returning to the womb.

In his mind he returned to the talks with Reverend Murray, he would have two days to help on the farm. On Wednesday morning the good Reverend would pick him up and they would drive together. He would be introduced to his new environment.

What was it he had said? Oh yes, a Mrs. Johnson would help him in East Calais and Mrs. Waymer at South Woodbury. But, what would be his first message? his first sermon there? Reverend Murray had said their biggest challenge was attendance. The young adults in particular, who required a bit of persuasion—it was they who constituted the future of the church, and they who most need to be shown the way.

Sleepily, he wondered, what would he do? What could he do to gain their interest and support; to bring them into the church and hold their interest.

A scenic wonder of rolling hills of lush and staggering greenery unfolded before the mountainous back-drop and invited their imagination to wonder, like opening the pages of fairy book tales as they drove the country road to East Calais this bright summer morning. Reverend Murray breathed a mournful

sigh; "Easy on the eyes, isn't it Robert."
"Yes sir, it is; easy on the eyes..."

Scattered clouds drifted across the sky going nowhere, yet, on an endless journey to some other place—to let off accumulated moisture so mountains and meadows could flourish. It was a good plan, this thing God made to work, to bring on and stir all elements in the nurturing of life; a never ending cycle. Though he had traveled many roads and trails in his growing years, he had not been this far on this road before. He wondered what sort of adventure unfolded along this road?

True he had hiked to the top of Mount Mansfield, also Camel's Hump Mountain. And always he had taken time with most every step to marvel at the beauty, whether it had been with a winter snow cover or a spring of velvet... or the luxuriant fall colors of oranges, reds and golds.

"This day is certainly a splendid example of God's fine work," Reverend Murray said, easing him back to consciousness.

"Yes sir, it is," replied Bob. "It does seem to have a certain entrancing charm, doesn't it... I was just thinking of the tasks before me, and how I must go about doing God's work."

"There are many ways for one to serve the Lord God while on this earth."

"Yes sir, I agree." After pausing, thoughtfully, he continued, "but for now my first sermon for Sunday is my main concern."

"Sermons come rather naturally with meditation, and of course getting to know the people of the parish," Reverend Murray spoke evenly and convincingly, as if making a point for the practical side. "At utmost importance is bringing the people into the church and attending to their spiritual needs. But certainly there is the challenge of the young ones, the teens and young adults; these, who are more inclined to stray with other interests, of the young of body and mind with, shall we say, the fears of irresolution tugging at their heart-strings. It is our task to see that they are kept in touch with the Holy Word."

"That too is my biggest concern. Can you offer any suggestions, Reverend?"

"There's a bicycle—at the Rectory. And with a little repair work I think you could use it to visit the homes of the parishioners. Invite their comments and learn of their interests. I'm sure they can offer many fine recommendations. This is where your clues will come from."

As they entered the small township of East Calais they were greeted with the usual array of houses; white clapboard siding with red or green shutters and trim. Some had low white picket fences and others with flowers as a border in front, but all presented a colorful array of flowers. In the rear and side yards each had a well tended garden.

The main street was unpaved, yet everything was neat and presented a picturesque setting. At the approximate center of town Bob could see the church. It appeared just as he had suspected. As churches go it was a small building of traditional size and style, white with green trim and a steep roof with a tall pointed steeple; very neat. . . in fact, picture perfect, he thought.

"I think we should visit Mrs Simpson's first, so I can introduce you and she can show you to your room. Mrs. Simpson is a recently retired school teacher and her husband passed away almost two years ago. She has no children, but is very active in the church. She knows everyone and can be of immeasurable assistance to you." The Reverend paused, then resumed in an even voice; "after that, we can walk across to the church and I'll show you where everything is. It has been quite a few years since I last presided here at South Woodbury. However, I doubt that things have changed that much."

Mrs. Simpson answered the door shortly after their knock, obviously expecting them.

Bob saw that she was a kindly woman with smooth features and graying hair. He thought her hair seemed so natural, it must have been like that most of her adult life. It was hard to believe that she had no children; she possessed that elegant and matronly quality so common and domestic to New England women.

They were welcomed graciously and shown to the parlor just off the entry hall, nicely furnished. An upright piano seemed waiting by the bay window bordered with lace curtains, polished to a brilliant sheen. A couch and two high-back chairs lined one wall behind an ornate cherry-wood coffee table. He glanced around at the pictures on the walls of pastel wallpaper. Near one corner he noticed a glass enclosed bookcase filled with books and tastefully arranged porcelain figurines on lace doilies. He wondered what some of the titles could be, but decided not to look closer. There would be time later.

She excused herself, only to return momentarily carrying a tray with cookies and a pitcher of cool milk. Placing it on the table, she again invited them to sit down and enjoy while she poured each a glass.

"So, Mr. Marshall, you're to be our new parson," she said easily, yet with the preciseness of conducting an interview.

"Yes ma'am, at least for the summer," he said, as he started to take a sip of the cool milk. "You can call me Robert, or Bob."

"If you wish?" She smiled; "if you agree not to address me as 'ma'am'. I understand that you are a carpenter, and handy at other types of repair work?"

"Yes ma'am. . . ah, excuse me, I mean yes, I do," he glanced at both seeking approval.

"My late husband, bless him, was also a man who took pride in working with his hands."

"I thought it would be fitting for the two of you to meet, and perhaps you can show him where he'll be staying. Then I shall introduce him to his duties. Later he can return to work out the details," said the Reverend Murray.

"Of course," she agreed. "We'll have more time to talk later. Mrs. Johnson should be here any minute and can join you."

"That will be fine. I do want to introduce them. I'm sure she will be a tremendous aid to Robert this summer," added Reverend Murray.

"I see you have finished your milk, Robert. I'll show you to your room now and you may leave your belongings until you return later."

Bob followed her up the stairs and into a front room on the corner. There was a window on the front and side walls, a dresser and a bed with a chair in the corner placed precisely before a small but adequate study table with a lamp. It was a friendly room with white ruffled curtains. The appointments were delicate and a bit feminine, he thought. . . as if it had been intended for a female. Still a friendly and inviting room; he could be comfortable.

"The bathroom is just down the hall to the right, and there is another downstairs at the end of the hallway," she said, "I hope you will be comfortable."

"Oh, I will, thank you," he said. How could anyone not be comfortable here, he asked himself. At home he recalled, we haven't had an indoor bathroom until recent years, yet here there are two. Everything seemed perfect, almost sterile and he wondered what kind of repairs could possibly be needed.

Downstairs, Bob observed the arrival of Mrs. Johnson. Reverend Murray had met her at the door and they were engaged in conversation. She was short, and possessed a sweet round face, a little pudgy with short wavy chestnut hair. She had a cute smile and an even cuter little waddle to her walk that matched her smile. I'll bet she has several children and a well kept husband, he mused. Obviously, she possessed a quality of boundless energy and complete fulfillment—it all showed, and a smile that begged to be kissed.

Crossing the street toward the church, she pointed to her own house; this to indicate where she could be found when needed. She always played the organ and helped with the choir in addition to conducting children's Sunday school classes, she was saying.

The pastor's study with a small desk was a small chamber of a room at the rear where it remained cool even in the warmest days of summer as little light found its way through the one window shaded by a close hovering old maple tree. It was a room obviously intended for meditation and solitude. There was a chair and a bookcase with the necessary hymnals and other aids. He stopped to study a picture on the wall, of Jesus on the Cross, then two wooden chairs in front of the waiting desk.

The first floor had a low ceiling and was divided into one large and two small rooms for classes. He was very familiar with this style of church. It was a common and practical design for the long cold winters. The rectory would be upstairs, and if he were a betting man, he would wager that the church in South Woodbury would be almost identical. To himself, he recalled the word *Church*, from the Greek word meaning The *Lord's House*.

"The ladies try to keep everything as neat and clean as possible," she said, proudly, as they stood quietly and momentarily observing the alter and choir box. "Mr. Johnson does his best to keep the grounds mowed and cleaned when he can, and of course Mr. Jones and Mr. Williams help, too."

"It's immaculate, everything is perfect. All of you are doing a fine job in keeping the Lord's House. You can be very proud,"

Reverend Murray complemented, as his younger novice echoed the same sentiments.

Reverend Murray turned to Mrs. Johnson, "Its been so nice seeing you again, but I'm afraid we must be moving along now. We must visit South Woodbury yet this day and acquaint Robert there also. He will call on you when he returns. And thank you ever so much. Please convey my good blessing to Mr. Johnson and the children."

"And mine also, Mrs. Johnson," Bob added. "It's so nice to meet you and I know we'll enjoy working together."

Sitting behind the small desk of the pastor's study in East Calais he started to review the events of the day. They had driven to South Woodbury and had met with Mrs. Waymer as planned and had toured the church building. It was just as he had expected, very similar, in fact almost identical, and the study room was very much like the one he was sitting in now.

Mrs. Waymer had been a pleasant lady, almost as tall as himself, and with full thighs, as though she had spent many hours sitting. She was soft spoken lady with a charming manner and obviously well organized in the responsibilities for the church's well being.

When he returned to Mrs. Simpson, they discussed the conditions of his assignments. She had prepared, in detail, a list of the work he was expected to complete; the school teacher propensity for discipline and order an obvious quality.

Later when she observed him studying the piano, she asked if he played. "Only a little," he replied. "But I like to sing, and expect to work closely with the choir."

"That's fine," she said, "of course you must like to read?"

"Oh yes, I see you have a fine collection."

"There are many good books here, and you may help yourself to any," she allowed, then added, "perhaps after dinner we can sing a few hymns together. You may look around if you wish. Dinner will be ready shortly."

He sensed that she missed her husband still, and would enjoy having a man around once again to fix meals for.

A glimpse of rare sunlight peeked through the small window from behind the maple tree outside. He leaned forward to rest his elbows on the desk, then placing his hands together as if to pray, inclined his head slightly, touching his forefingers to his lips. He sat motionless for a time, lost in thought. The youth, what can I do for the youth? Reverend Murray had implied that would be my biggest and most important task. . . he was silent for long minutes. . . and then, just as a light bulb turns bright, suddenly so did his eyes, and his mind leaped into action. "Of course," he said aloud to the empty room. Its right here in front of me, that wise old owl must have known all along what to do. *Baseball*, or maybe softball, yes a tournament. Or perhaps a league. That should certainly interest the young people, and a picnic for the children and older adults, just like he did at Waterbury. Maybe even a league that would involve other churches as well. He could have advised this but instead he planted the seed by timing—then let me figure it out for myself—the crafty old rogue, in clerical dress.

Now what about the sermon Sunday. He would make the announcement then. And about the bicycle. He must organize his time, he thought. Tonight he would examine the bicycle and see what repairs it needed.

Tomorrow morning he would rise at five thirty, maybe five. Yes five. He would dress, cross the road, and here he would devote two hours, maybe two and a half to meditation and his sermon.

Mrs. Simpson had said breakfast would be about eight. After breakfast he would concentrate on her list. She had already shown him the tool shop and after eating, he could go right to work. In the afternoon he would visit the parishioners, and prompt them for their comments.

Bounding across the quiet street he was eager to explain his schedule to Mrs. Simpson; and to seek her advice and approval.

That night as he lay in bed trying to fall asleep, he thought of Claire and how he had expected to be with her more of the summer. Perhaps he might find time to see her yet, and how about Harry? Twice they had found time to talk, and then only briefly. He wondered if he would have time to see his best friend, or maybe Harry might find time to visit him. Wasn't Harry surprised when he had told him of the circus incident; how had it started; in his mind he drifted back to that time at Delaware when Josette had materialized beside him. . .

The following morning Bob sat at the pastor's study in East Calais. He sat with his Bible open in front of him. He had risen early as planned. It was Friday morning and he had walked in the early morning hour before first light, listening to the birds singing and had smelled the flowers and other scents that permeated the fresh morning dew. He had watched as the first rays of sunlight struggled to unfold in unusual contrasting arrays, eventually setting in motion the machinery; rising steam and misty sky in the never ending cycle.

The Parables, he thought, perhaps he would read from one of the Parables. The Sermon on the Mount was another favorite. Yes, either would be fitting for his first sermon on Sunday morning, or the Travels of Paul. Leafing through the pages he paused to read from Luke 10: 30-37, The Good Samaritan, and then he reread about the stranger who had been beaten and robbed by thieves. How fitting and appropriate it would be for his first service, he thought. This Parable that shows the virtue of neighborliness. He considered it for a time, then paused, and decided to base his sermon on a theme of *Love Thy Neighbor*.

A glance at the clock, showed it was almost eight and he realized it was nearly time for breakfast. He didn't want to keep Mrs Simpson waiting. Just a few more lines to write down and he would be finished.

It was a glorious morning, and he felt it in his fibers and bones as he bounced lightly across the street; satisfied with his efforts he had come to many decisions. With such conclusions a boundless energy wells up inside a man, giving him the confidence to run forever at full tilt—climb mountains, forge raging rivers. Robert had uncovered the source of that energy in his conclusions that forever fuels the spirit—the spirit of the soul and faith, but alas—the spirit gives way and succumbs to the rigors of the flesh. A gnawing urgency in his stomach reminded him of his need for nourishment. At the kitchen door he sniffed; bacon frying and maybe, yes, eggs and potatoes and cocoa, his favorite; also some fresh squeezed orange juice, he hoped. All that heavy thinking must have stimulated a powerful appetite.

"Good morning Mrs Simpson," he said, remembering that she had been up and about in her garden when he had left the house.

"Well good morning Robert. I'll bet you're starved. Breakfast is good for a young man, especially when he has been up early doing the Lord's work."

"Sure smells good, and hmmm hot cocoa, my favorite," he said, glancing around the table.

"Won't be long now. Soon we'll have some fresh strawberries to go with rhubarb and some blackberries too. Then it'll be time for pies and cobblers. . . you just go ahead and wash up now."

On his way to the tool-shed, Bob studied the list of repairs again. Broken sash rope in upstairs window; won't open, cellar door has loose hinge, gutter pulled loose from roof at rear door stoop, stair newel loose and another has crack; rear fence gate broken, and a second page. . .

Think I'll start with the cellar door and fence gate first, get as many of the easy ones done as I can, then the harder ones or ones requiring parts last, he concluded.

He had stopped briefly for lunch, and now checking his pocket watch, he saw that it was a little past four o'clock. A good time to work on the bicycle, and upon inspecting it he found that it needed a little oiling, chain adjustment and a tire patch for the front wheel. All minor, for a master mechanic like himself.

He then washed up a bit and after explaining to Mrs. Simpson how grateful he was for the long summer days, he went riding along the Old Hill Road.

While he worked on the bicycle Mrs. Johnson stopped by and she and Mrs. Simpson explained where to find several local families. First the Albertson's, then the Grey's, the Burton's, Grants, and Smalley's. Also he could find the Romano's at the fourth house on the right, about a mile and a half. He was told that they were Catholics and do not attend our church. He said he would stop by just the same, and introduce himself, and invite them to the picnic and ball game. The ladies had agreed it was an excellent idea.

It was Saturday morning when he again sat at the pastor's desk, thinking of the families he had met and the few who had heard of him and had stopped by this day to exchange greetings. He was pleased at their suggestions, and their acceptance of his ideas. He hoped South Woodbury would be as receptive. Tomorrow, he would find out when he arrived for the eleven o'clock service.

There was the problem of the nine o'clock service in East Calais and whether he could manage the necessary time to travel the nearly four miles to South Woodbury, and conduct his service there. It was a small thing requiring timing. Of course, he would have the rest of the day to meet and visit some more of the local people. He hoped the bicycle wouldn't break down. If it does, I'll just have to leave it, and walk fast, he mused.

Already he had formulated his sermon for the next Sunday which would deal with family, and togetherness. The importance of the family life-unit within the church. Leafing through his Bible, he started to read again, searching for the most suitable parable for this next sermon.

Many of the faces in the congregation were familiar, and as he scanned out over them he saw that there were also many more whom he had not yet visited in his evening sojourns.

After the prelude, the choir entered and stood, singing *Nearer My God To Thee* while Mrs. Johnson played joyfully at the organ, and Mrs. Simpson received them as the little church swelled to capacity.

When the choir finished Mrs. Simpson stood at the pulpit, quiet and poised, then speaking in a clear even tone, she invited greetings and announcement after expressing her satisfaction that so many chose to attend and welcome their new summer parson. She paused there for a time to let it settle in, then resumed: "I am so sure you will all be pleased that he is with us at this time. . . Although he has been here only a few days, many of you have already met him." She paused as again some of the congregation showed their agreement. Once more, after a warm smile, she continued, "I am equally certain that many of you have already heard his rich and wholesome voice as you have passed my home. On one occasion he has joined in practice with the choir at this very church. He has many other messages to share with you on this day. I'll let him tell you. . . in his own words, and now may I present, Mr. Robert Marshall."

Bob rose and dipped his head in gratitude, and when he felt settled, he thanked Mrs. Simpson for her fine introduction and the generosity and hospitality of her home.

"I also wish at this time to thank Mrs. Johnson for her many fine deeds, and also the opportunity to join with so many talented singers in the choir. Again our thanks to Mrs. Simpson, for without her guidance, who knows how we might fair in all things. I'm sure everyone is well aware of her never ending devotion to our community and to God's house as well." He paused, breathing to his toes before continuing. "I wish to add that I am not yet graduated, nor am I a fully ordained minister of the church at this time. . . But with the Lord's good grace, I shall be in another year. I want all of you to know how very pleased I am to be here with you, and that as I have only been able to visit a few of you so far, I intend to get around to everyone, *if* my bicycle holds up." That brought a few chuckles, he tried to sound serious again. "If anyone wishes, I can be reached at Mrs. Simpson's during the day. . . and available in the morning from six o'clock to eight o'clock right here at the pastor's study. . . except for a few days during haying of course, week after next. That is something I'm sure many of you here share in similar commitments." Pausing for a few seconds, he continued, "I have just one more item, and then I shall return you to the very capable care of Mrs. Simpson. . . I would like to involve everyone in some extra activities that I feel will be of interest, and bring us all closer together to our church and community. First, a picnic, and later a softball game for those with energy to spare. I have spoken with some, and they agree this would be a welcome event. Later today, I intend to speak with those interested at South Woodbury and if they too are agreeable, we can start next Sunday. I also have hopes of encouraging those, especially young people, from other nearby communities to join us in a church league." Glancing around at their faces, he felt the signs implied a good start.

Mrs. Simpson rose to her feet as he turned to extend his hand and offer her the pulpit once again.

"Will all stand and join in the introit," she said, offering a benevolent smile, "and bow our heads in prayer."

Robert Marshall moved to the pulpit ready to speak. "The message I wish to share with you this day is God's message of *Love Thy Neighbor*. But first I would like to read a passage from the Scriptures. . ."

Amazing how a trusty old bicycle can perform with a little tender loving care he thought, riding back to East Calais that late Sunday afternoon. He had been offered a ride, but had declined. Perhaps another time, he had explained. There seemed a certain fond attachment now to this same road he had traveled hurriedly just hours earlier that same morning, and for some reason he wanted to be alone.

He had been well received and his ideas welcomed and he had stayed long to greet most of the flock. Anxiously, they had agreed on next Sunday for their first picnic and ball game. They had agreed on the chosen site, a field near the schoolyard bordered by a wooded area. It was big enough and ideally located near a stream with a small rapids and a swimming hole, and near halfway between the two locations.

Bob felt beside himself with joy of his success. He had overheard a few of the older gentlemen in conversation. "This young minister fella appears to be a man to get things done," one had said. "That he does," another had added. "Yup, a might windy though, I'd say," a third declared, rather succinctly.

He patted the seat of the old bicycle. "Just a little oil and air is all it requires for good service," he said as if speaking to it with pride. So much peddling does provide a healthy appetite. Just in time for dinner with Mrs. Simpson. And now he felt he had earned a evening to relax and rest a bit with one of those books.

Once more in the pastor's study with his eyes on the Bible before him, he was lost in thought. It was Monday morning, and a whole week had passed. His sermon based on the parable about the family-life and togetherness had left him with a buoyant feeling, and the picnic and ball game had brought a large turnout as well.

In a couple days, Reverend Murray would return to take him home so he could help with the haying.

He had just returned to his Bible to renew his search for the parable he would use as the basis for the coming Sunday sermon when a knock at the door interrupted his concentration.

He went to the door and opened it.

"Well Mrs. Tyner. . . how good to see you. What brings you out this morning hour?" he asked. Remembering that he had met her and her family after service on both Sundays and several times at the picnic he had sensed there was something on her mind. Her face tensed with a concerned look about her. Her hair pulled into a bun atop her head showed early stages of graying and her eyes were serious; almost pleading.

"It's my daughter. . . Loretta, she's the one I need to talk to you about," she said, breathing heavily as she motioned for the girl to step forward.

"Yes, please do come in," he offered, observing Loretta as she lagged behind, her head tilted downward; shyly repentant.

"Come child, I won't hurt you. Come join us," he said, noticing the girl seemed determined to hold her place.

"Let me speak to you first Reverend and then maybe she'll talk with you, too," Mrs. Tyner said.

"Very well then. Please have a seat," he said, still watching for the girl through the open door.

"It's Loretta, she's only fifteen you know, but. . . and she wants to leave home with this boy. Sometimes she stays out late at night, and she won't listen to me or her father." She paused nervously.

"I would like to help any way I can. Perhaps a qualified counselor— In a day or two when Reverend Murray arrives—."

"Your sermon on Sunday—about the family—yesterday. She looks up to you. . . and I could tell, she'll listen to you," she pleaded, the desperation in her voice begging for release.

"But Mrs Tyner, I'm not a qualified. . ."

"Please, if you will just talk to her, you'll see, let me get her," she said, as she hurried after the troubled and unhappy girl.

Bob sat lamely, as his mind drifted back to another time, when he was not yet twenty, and attending Montpelier Seminary. It was the year before his first at Ohio Wesleyan:

He had skipped class to go into town where he had met two girls. One had invited him to her home for the weekend. Her parents had gone away, she had said. And they could have a party, just the three of them. He had felt this would be an excellent challenge to do some reform work, since both girls were obviously of a wayward nature.

One had asked him for some money to buy drinks and things and he had given her what he had.

Upon returning to school, he had been severely reprimanded and suspended for one week for taking the weekend without permission. The whole affair had proved to be a severe and failing test of his own resolution. And now he wondered, just who had reformed who on that *fateful* weekend.

Loretta's lack of self confidence was evident as she slumped into the chair, retreating and withdrawn.

Bob thought to himself, she could be a pretty girl if she didn't work so hard at being unhappy.

Avoiding direct eye contract, she glanced around the room and at the floor, as if looking for a way out.

"What seems to be the problem?" he asked.

"Oh you know, nothing really," she answered, as she shrugged nervously, still avoiding his eyes.

"Would you like to talk about it?" he asked evenly, trying desperately not to betray his own ineptness.

"They're always telling me what to do, or what not to do, or don't do that, or straighten up, and how come you're stayin out late at night all the time, things, you know."

"Well, you are still a young girl, and your mother and father share a concern and responsibility for you. And because they love you, naturally they feel they must do the right thing by you."

"Yeah, but I'm old enough to look out for myself. And I *can* look out for myself." She shot him a defiant look, at last trying to assert her claim to independence, then shifted back into her withdrawn posture.

"Your mother tells me you want to leave home. Is this true?" He wondered how Reverend Murray would handle this. Probably does it all the time.

"Well, yeah, kinda."

"Will you do something for me?" he asked, leaning forward while trying desperately to draw her eyes. He would have reached for her hands to stress his point, but she clenched them to herself all the tighter. "Will you do nothing for a day or two? I'll tell you why. The Reverend Murray will be here then, and I feel certain between the two of us we can work something out. Will you do that for me, a promise? As soon as he arrives, I promise we'll come to visit you." He was hoping for a commitment, but the girl gave only a nod.

Realizing that was all he was going to get at this time, he rose to his feet. "Fine, that makes me feel better. I know we can help," he said, reassuringly, as he moved around the desk to take her hand, then patted her on the back.

"Thank you so much Reverend. I'm so glad. I knew you would help," said Mrs. Tyner, gratefully.

He searched his brain for the right words—something he could say to ease her doubts. But none came. As he escorted them to the door he wondered deep within himself if he had helped at all. Some tasks are harder than others.

It was Tuesday evening when Reverend Murray arrived as expected, and agreed to visit the Tyner's and talk with Loretta. Mrs. Simpson recalled how independent the girl had been in school. Even though her parents had been patient and understanding Loretta had displayed a characteristically headstrong tendency to do as she pleased.

While driving along the same road Bob and Reverend Murray discussed his past days in East Calais and South Woodbury and as they headed for the farm Bob realized the next two or three days would be busy ones with haying, and he wondered if he would have a chance to visit Claire or Harry. At least he would have some time with his family.

Back at Mrs. Simpson, late Friday evening, Bob thought of the one day, tomorrow, he had to prepare for Sundays sermon. And once settled into the familiar bed, he planned his routine as he had done for the two weeks previously.

He recalled that when Harry had a day off, he had visited him at the farm while he was working, and they had kidded each other about old times, yet his three days had been busy ones and he hadn't a chance to visit Claire before Reverend Murray had returned to pick him up again.

The summer weeks flew by with busy and fruitful days since his return to East Calais. Mrs. Simpson's repairs had all been completed and he had found time to work on the church between choir practice and visits to the parishioners at both East Calais and South Woodbury. He was proud that he had made so many friends and that the attendance had increased with his programs.

Probably in a few days Reverend Murray would return to pick him up again. They had talked on the telephone twice and the Reverend had complimented him on his good work. He had mentioned that the board members were close to a decision on his replacement, probably a young man much like himself, though recently ordained.

He would miss the many friends he had made, yet he felt good about the progress and was painfully aware the time to move on was at hand.

What was left of summer was shooting by at a maddening pace when he arrived at the farm. After changing clothes he joined his brothers in the barn. The milking and clean-up always went fast when the brothers were there to chip in and help. Bill was especially anxious to hear of his brother's activities.

Bob started by describing his replacement and the introduction by Reverend Murray: He was a young man like himself and they had talked and visited. He was eager to continue his assignments. Bob went on to tell that the good Reverend had complimented him on his fine work of the summer and especially his capacity to increase attendance and interest in church affairs. When Bill asked just what it was he had done, he explained about the picnic and ball games, and how he tried to involve more people in Bible classes and choir recitals. To create more interest, he had introduced them to some folk songs besides hymns that were not well known, like *Dry Bones*. You know, that way everybody can get into the act.

Brother George was quick to seize the moment and chanted out a few bars and got the ball rolling:

"Ezekial dried dem drybones,"
"Now here's tha word of tha Lord,"

After a few more lines of the chorus the brothers joined in to fill the barn walls to a vibrating frenzy, that is until the cows got into the act and drowned them out.

"I wonder if we're the first to milk by rhythm?" Allen shouted above the mayhem.

As they went about their chores in a methodical fashion, it was Bill who reminded them of the time some years ago when Bob had hooked up an old organ in the barn so he could play music while the others milked. John reminded Bill how Bob had said that it calmed the cows down and made for better milking.

Bob resumed his story to tell that he realized the church activity and attendance would fall off drastically due to the oncoming winter season. Often churches in outlying areas were forced to close down for the winter months and then to get people interested they must start all over again in spring.

Bill agreed, then more on a serious note he added, "but there must be a solution."

"That's how I got this idea of volleyball."

"Volleyball," interrupted George. "I remember at Ann Arbor, its a fairly new game, isn't it? But it's just catching on?"

"Yeah, that's right," Bob continued. "I'll bet someday it will be in the Olympics. Its an excellent indoor game and almost any number can play, and its always lots of fun. Reverend Murray was fascinated also, and since he had only heard of the game, he wanted to hear more about it." Bob paused to take his bucket of milk to empty it, returned, then picked up where he had left off: "The towns-people agreed on the need for a large community room for winter activities and meetings and that the same building could be used for indoor games. Both East Calais and South Woodbury settled on the location, and when I left they were already developing plans." Bob hesitated, then added, "I only wish I could be there to help."

"You can help here, tomorrow we start haying again," chuckled Allen.

After milking and clean-up was done, Bill caught Bob by the arm and told him while he was away Doc Berry had given them his old Franklin motorcar. "You know the one. Anyway, he got a new one and gave us his old one. I figure soon as haying is done we should head back to Delaware. We'd be there a couple weeks before school starts, and that would give some extra time to look for work and get settled in. The old car Franklin is a bit temperamental though, sometimes it runs and then other times it doesn't. Maybe you can work on it, and see if you can fix it."

"That sounds like a good idea." Bob realized he should have jumped with joy. "Big thing, like a freight car. I wondered what it was doing here."

For the following days they were all busy in the fields, except for Bill who went into town to work in the mornings. Sometimes the sisters took time away from gardening and other chores to join them in the fields. The humidity was high and heavy clouds had threatened rain. Working in the barn had become even more stifling and breathing was difficult.

Bob had intended to see Claire again and visit with Harry.

One evening Harry showed up and they talked for a while. Harry explained that Claire had gone to New York to visit an aunt for a few weeks.

After Harry left, Bob found himself thinking of Delaware and Ohio Wesleyan more often. He thought of the boarding house, ah yes, donuts, for an instant he thought he smelled them, the power of suggestion. Yes, donuts and pies and sugar cookies with toasted edges, and Edith the way she looked when baking and playing the piano, when she got that glow of fulfillment, and there was Mary. He had entertained fleeting memories of Mary, so vivacious and energetic. . . and young. How could she have meant anything. . . after all she was just a girl, a young girl, a junior in high school, and not much older than Lorreta—yet packed with a certain captivating vitality. How could I begin to think of her in the sense of a woman?

Six

"We at Ponce de Leon exit, by way of Bedford Ave. It'll be shorter that way—save you a little time. They had it closed last week and had to go in by Edgewood Ave to Oakdale—but it's open now."

"I appreciate that."

"Say you from California—you don't sound California."

"I was born in Milwaukee, Wisconsin, but I grew up in New Orleans, Louisiana."

"Yeah, that's a long way from Atlanta—you got relatives in Atlanta?"

"A father—that's who I'm going to see."

"Yeah? What he do, for work?"

"I don't know—I've never seen him before today—only talked to him the first time at the airport by phone. I think he said he was a bookkeeper at a lumber yard—retired now though."

"And you going to get acquainted now—ain't that something. I had a step-dad, and he skipped out most of the time—left Mom with seven kids—then he come back for a while—slap us around and leave. He was a boxer—a real bum."

"My step-dad beat us around too—guess they figure it's all part of growing up—and learning—like it's their duty. It seemed the only thing to do for a while—because your father did it syndrome I guess—but I never hit my kids."

"Me neither—I raise my hand and they know better—that's enough—I seen enough o' that shit and I don't like it. Kids is lucky these days only they don't know it—they got too much free time and television—and no responsibility—maybe they need a strap taken to their rumps a time or two—but no fists. . ."

Arthur Brown was still talking, kicking the cab up a notch to pass some old guy—but in my head, I drifted back to recall some of the things Mom had told me; Grandma Swaren, Edith was her name and for just an instant I could picture her full matronly figure and kindly face, always dressed in gingham print dresses that flowed like a tent bottom to above her ankles, and then came the unmistakable scent of sweet spices and sugar—baking flour, pies and cinnamon, apples and cherries and berries, at first distinctive, then all blended together—and I could hear the sound of her playing jazzy stuff on the piano at night—Honky Tonk mostly—like when a coffee commercial flashes on the TV screen and suddenly you get a whiff of fresh brewing coffee that sends you to the kitchen for something to eat. Subliminal suggestion I think they call it, and they swear they don't do that kind of stuff.

Mom said she and Bob met at St. Paul's Methodist Church where she went for choir practice, and he was singing a solo—he was raising the roof with *Just a Closer Walk With Thee*. Her brother Joe had been forced to go along, Edith tugging him by the ear. Grandma Edith's sister, Aunt Violet and her two daughters came along too—they were younger—Aunt Violet played the organ and when piano was the order of the day Grandma Edith played.

Mom admitted with that look on her face that she had flirted by winking at him when she caught his eye—causing him to stutter a little on *Grant It Jesus is My Plea*. She admitted also that girls at school called her a flirt—some boys said she was a tease—she had just turned sixteen, a junior in high school.

Grandma Edith admired Bob and had invited him home for dinner. Mom said it was the cooking that really hooked him. To Edith he must have been the perfect prospect—tall, handsome, well mannered and a third year theology student at Ohio Wesleyan. Preachers were considered the ultimate catch for their young daughters in those days; even today too I guess.

They had discussed the prospects of an arrangement where Bob would make deliveries in partial return for room and board.

Then, one Sunday after church when Bob came to dinner, they had gone for a walk—and then he was gone without a word. It was mid-semester and springtime. . .

Seven

The buildings in Delaware, Ohio hadn't changed a bit and Sandusky Street was still the same north/south main artery splitting the town in two by east and west. The old Shell station at the north end of town seemed dwarfed by the successive rows of three story, square built structures of cut-brick, on both side that somehow reminded one of a Roman viaduct because of the rows of high narrow windows. A perfect study in perspective for art enthusiasts. In the center of town there was the Sears Roebuck store. In spirit and prestige Ohio Wesleyan University dominated the town at the south entrance. Sandusky was a wide street, more like a boulevard in the tradition of most mid-western towns and served as the connecting artery for the CD & M Interurban, called the electric train by the locals.

It had been raining for two days since they had left Waterbury. They had stopped in Syracuse to see Uncle Henry, and then on to Ann Arbor for George. If good fortune follows bad, he thought, then does bad inevitably follow the good—so far, as in other things the weather had favored them. There had been hard times in the past—especially when his father, James, had been struck down unexpectedly, leaving them to struggle on their own. But that was the past, and the future seemed filled with the promise of good things. It had started raining the day after they finished haying and then off and on a bit. But this day and the day before had brought a steady downpour. The hay was in; that was the best part.

The old Franklin held up pretty well, though it had given them cause for doubt on some occasions.

Clearing skies gave the buildings a freshly washed and extra clean appearance. A fresh, yet musty smell permeated the air and occasionally one could see the mist as it arose from the ground where bolts of sunlight touched it.

Bill had dozed off and squirmed upright in his seat, rubbing his eyes.

"I think we should check in at Wesleyan, see what we can find out," suggested Bob.

"Sounds okay by me," Bill said, "I think I'll stay at the dorm for a while, and check the office for any possible jobs. How about you? What's your first move?"

"I think I'll check with the office for schedules and work too. And then I'll walk over to Mrs. Swaren's boarding house. I need to stretch my legs a bit anyway."

At 16 South Liberty he paused in front of that familiar light gray, two story house with white trim and a porch across the front and both sides. The scent of flowers mixed with the lingering dampness from recent rain caught his nostrils of and he sneezed twice.

As he climbed the five steps, he saw that the front door was open. It was a handsome raised paneled door of weathered oak with decorated glass in the top half. He knocked, and recognized Edith's voice from inside.

"Who is it?" she called out, then added, "come in."

"Just me, Robert Marshall," he answered, as he stepped into the parlor.

"Well Robert. . . sakes alive," she mumbled, glancing up from her kneeling position on the floor with straight pins sticking from her pinched lips. "We didn't expect to ever see you again. What a pleasant surprise." She removed some pins from her mouth.

He looked stunned, eyes stared at the figure standing on the stool. Was this Mary, he asked himself. . . Somehow he had imagined her as a girl, but now, as if poised on pedestal, she had changed somehow, more of a woman—there were breasts of noticeable proportion where he had not noticed any before. Perhaps if he had paid attention, such as with Claire—and the obvious change now hit him in the face—she had the manner of a young woman too—especially with the subtle tilt of curving hips. The face filled up with a new boldness in her eyes and her mouth had matured as if wanting to be kissed, and yet that same coquettish look was still there, along with the hint of a young girl somewhere inside. Her dress was an ivory, satiny material, belted in a sash at the hips, with tucks and ruffles to just below the knees, a little bold for the times. It hung loose about the shoulders and bloused at the waist. He had heard the term, *flapper-bob* and wondered if that was how her light brown, casual looking hair was done. The sheen of the material revealed points and suggested curves of her hips and thighs as she moved slightly shifting her weight from one knee to the other, tilting her hips and shoulders, she lowered her head a little, widening her eyes as if amusement lurked there.

"Well Mary, I think that's it," said Edith, struggling up from her knees to stand back and study the length. "Yes, yes," she nodded approval. "This will have to do, you can run along and change now."

"That's a beautiful dress Mrs. Swaren. Do you make all of Mary's clothes?"

"Yes. . . Well most of them anyway. Some, she sews herself."

"I didn't know that. You must sew your own too," he stated that plainly as a compliment, and waited for the inevitable blush to flood over her face.

"A body can do most anything if the need is there. Then we all do what we must. But you here, now this is a pleasant surprise. We weren't sure if we might see you again; your disappearance last spring was so sudden."

"I had a chance for a job and had to take it."

"And how was your summer and your family? They're all well I pray."

"Oh yes, they're all doing just fine. We finished our work a little early, so Bill and I decided to come a little sooner in hopes of finding part-time work here for the term year. We dropped George at Ann Arbor for his second year. He found a job in a restaurant there."

"You'll stay for dinner won't you?" she said, heading for the kitchen with him trailing behind.

"I'd be pleased, and boy does it smell good. The reason I stopped, was to ask about a room. I'd like to rent a room, and stay here; still make deliveries for you."

"Yes, Robert, I think that could be arranged, Lord knows I could use the help. But about the room, that's a problem for now anyway. You see I'm full at the present, but I'm having the side porch closed into a room. As soon as it's finished of course you're welcome to it, or if one of the other boarders leaves. It should be done in about a week, two at the most," she said as she arranged some pans on the cast iron stove.

"Sounds great. I can stay at the dorm until then."

"That's *neat*," Mary said, pausing at the doorway, still tugging impatiently at the other dress to get it just right. It had taken a bit of squeezing to squirm into the thing—maybe she planned it that way. "I mean you really look *spiffy*, in knickers and your polo shirt. I like knickers, Joe won't wear his—unless he doesn't have anything else."

Surprised, Bob looked down at himself. "You really think so?" He had never thought of himself as spiffy, but why not. Knickers were popular, and he often wore knickers and a sweater or polo shirt. It was the rage in collegiate circles, and he had changed before coming here, perhaps unwittingly hoping to impress Mary.

"How about some lemonade?" she asked, opening the ice box and reaching for a pitcher. "We can swing on the front porch, and you can tell me all about your summer."

"How can I refuse an offer like that?" he said. "I'd like to hear about your summer, too."

"Oh, mine is nothing to tell about, you know the usual things—piano practice, and hanging around with my friends, and practice the Charleston and the Shimmy." She gave him a little sway, just enough to insinuate her meaning, and caught a caustic stare from Edith.

Boyfriends, how about boyfriends, that's what he wanted to ask. "Oh here's something I brought for you." Realizing he still held the envelope. "It's the music I promised, *Juba Dance*, it's a jazzy dance piece of African origin I think, the one we talked about that you wanted for competition."

She giggled with delight, and opened the envelope to examine the music sheet. "Looks busy all right. Maybe after dinner." She said, considering it tentatively.

He realized she would want to practice a bit before playing it for him.

At the front porch swing Mary listened as Bob told of his summer ministry in East Calais and South Woodbury, and of his stay with Mrs. Simpson and about the limited time he had to work on the farm, omitting the circus episode. He spoke of his trip here with his brother Bill and how they had dropped George off at Ann Arbor, also of the old Franklin that had been given to them.

"Oh that sounds great, so interesting, it makes me want to visit the farm. And you have a motorcar now. Isn't that super," she said, pausing to sip delicately from her glass, tucking one leg up under the other—not a flirty move this time—simply a girl move.

"Well it's really not all mine. . . Bill and I share it. That is when it runs," he added with a chuckle and gulped the last of his lemonade.

"Do you want some more?" she asked, with that demure smile again, indicating his glass.

"Ah—okay—if its no bother, I wouldn't mind a little more."

She returned, with a full glass. "Dinner will be soon. When you finish, you can help me set the table," she said.

At home his sisters had always done such things and he was not surprised to learn that every piece had its proper place and had to be just right to complement an elegant table setting. The large, age darkened oak table was covered with a lace table cloth and the place settings for seven people laid out, then the assorted chairs adjusted properly. Mary explained that the same two boarders he had met last spring, Jack and Junior were still with them. That in itself was unusual because boarders often changed frequently.

Even if Mary had changed in the time he was gone, the scenario at Swaren House had changed little. Robert was again invited to offer grace. Edith suggested they go ahead with the meal since the one empty chair was for Joe and he would probably be late because of playing football with his buddies.

Jack had just asked Bob about business and the type of farming in Vermont when they were all jolted by a sound from the kitchen that caused Edith to bolt in her chair.

"If Joe hits the line the way he hits that screen door, he'll go all the way for a touchdown every time." Junior made that same declaration each day at mealtime, then he-hawed..

"Yeah, he sure will, no doubt about that," echoed Jack Owen.

"JOSEPH! " Edith declared, as he flopped into his usual chair, and finally drawing his eye she said it again, "JOSEPH, must I remind you to go and wash your hands and face, and comb your hair *too*."

"Ahh Mom, do I have to?" he stalled.

"That boy," Edith gasped, shaking her head, "I declare, there's only one thing he's afraid of, and it's soap and water. Lordy be."

"He sure ain't afraid of that screen door, and that's a fact," Junior mused.

When he returned Bob said. "You sure have grown this summer, a freshmen this year, aren't you?"

"Yeah," answered Joe, "Yes sir, I mean," he corrected after a nudge from Edith.

"Bob, you can call me Bob or Robert, which ever suits you. You must be six feet or better already. At least as tall as me."

"He's gonna git a lot bigger to, I'd wager, if he keeps on attack'n them vittles," teased Junior.

"He thinks he can make quarterback his first year." Mary couldn't miss a chance to get her own dig in also.

"Quarterback, hmm, well you sure have size in your favor, do you like to pass a lot?" asked Bob.

"Yeah," gulp, "—and I like to run too," Joe said, as he continued eating, then added, "I can put it in a bucket at fifty yards, and on a run too," he boasted. "But I ain't meaning to brag. Lots of guys bigger than me though."

"What else are you taking?" asked Bob.

"Basketball and, I like baseball too," he got out between a gulp and chew.

"Basketball was my favorite, but I played a little football, and more baseball.

"Really, you did?" he said, momentarily trying to decide how a sissy kind of preacher guy could be interested in sports. "Maybe we can play a little man-to-man sometime, huh?"

Bob wondered if in his challenge Joe had hoped to learn something from him. "Academics. . . I mean, what classes are you taking?"

"Oh just the usual stuff. You know?"

"If it wasn't for sports I don't think we could get Joe out of bed in the morning, and on to school," Mary teased again.

"How about volleyball? Have you tried that?"

"Volleyball, huh that's a sissy game," Joe snapped, as he glared at his sister.

"I play basketball too," she shot back.

"It has already picked up as college competition and someday it will be an Olympic event," Bob said.

Jack and Junior paused too; as if to consider the preacher man—waiting to see if he had a point to make.

"Maybe so, but I'll still take football any day."

"Boy, I think I'm getting full up," Jack said, leaning back to pat his belly. "Gotta save some room for desert though. Don't wanta miss Edith's desert," he looked at Bob, then continued, "yesterday we had some pear cobbler, and before that there was apple pie and sometimes she makes the best German Chocolate cake, sure knows how to feed a man."

"And don't forget them sugar cookies we take for lunch, toasted just right around the edges, always got plenty of them around, and you can always smell things a bakin," added Junior, leaning back in mocking style to pat his bulge proudly.

Mary said, "Bob will be staying here when the new room is finished."

"Well you sure going to be hard pressed to keep that trim figure, I can vouch that for certain," Junior declared.

"I agree, that sure was an excellent meal. It is not often I get a chance to enjoy food like that," Bob said, grasping the chance to add his own praise, then putting his fingers and thumb to his lips he gave a little smack. "Exquisite, dee-licious."

Jack said, "anyplace you go, it don't get any better'n this."

Edith and Mary were already removing dishes and serving berries and cream on shortbread biscuits.

"After dinner I go for a walk to see Pops. You want to come along?" Mary said. "It's just a couple squares down Williams Street to the corner of Sandusky, at the terminal building there."

Bob remembered the last time they had walked and how she had taken his hand; smiled as she looked into his eyes. "You'll like Pops, you'll see. He's a lot like you."

"Like me, how's that?"

"Well you know, he's quiet and doesn't say much, but when he does. . . and he stands straight and tall like you. Just about the same size." She looked at him as if to compare the two for a moment. "He'll like you too, I just know it."

Strange, Bob thought, he had never considered himself the strong silent type. Sometimes, he even wondered if he talked too much, that's what his brothers said—a bit windy the old parishioner had said at East Calais. He had overheard it, but perhaps that too was meant for his ears.

"Pops is what Joe and I call him. His name is Ross. He's the motorman on the electric train and Uncle Jess is the conductor. Uncle Jess is married to Aunt Violet—you know; she plays the organ at church—Aunt Violet and Mom are sisters. There he is, that's him over there, see, in the motorman's uniform." She took his hand again and started to hurry. "Maybe he'll have a few minutes before they have to start off again"

Bob had started to ask about Edith and Ross when her attention shifted to her dad.

"Hi Pops," she called out, then releasing Bob's hand she throw her arms around him in a hug.

"Pops, this is Bob Marshall, he'll be staying at our house as soon as the room is finished.

"I'm pleased to meet you, sir." Bob reached to offer his hand in greeting. He was keenly aware of the older man's eyes measuring him, like he was under a magnifying glass.

"Is it okay if Bob rides with us?" Mary asked, "He'll walk back with me."

"Sure, climb aboard, we have a few minutes," Ross consented, checking his pocket watch. "I'll be along shortly."

Climbing aboard, Mary took a few seconds to introduce Bob to her Uncle Jess.

Mary sat by the window and Bob beside her as the five-o-one car rattled North on Sandusky Street. They pointed to the old two and three story buildings and some people waved while a horse and wagon waited nervously at a cross street. At Lincoln Avenue the five-o-one car turned west on its tracks and Mary explained that they would get off near Troy Road. She also told him how she sometimes rode to Columbus and back, or north to Marion just for the ride, and to visit with her father.

"How's your mother?" Ross asked, while they had stood beside him. "And Joe, up to his usual mischief I s'spect."

Bob recalled how he and Ross had studied each other and he had wondered if Ross was a card player. Yes, I bet he's a poker player he concluded, and yet he wondered what else was going on in the older man's mind, when Mary said, "Bob is a student Pops; he's going to Wesleyan, studying Theology, this is his third year."

"Gonna be a preacher, huh?"
"Yes sir, that's my plan."
At Troy Road they jumped off, and waved goodbye to Ross and Jess. They walked quietly in a wooded area, then headed toward North Liberty Street and home.
Bob let his curiosity get the best of him and decided to ask the inevitable. "Are Ross and Edith divorced, or just separated?"
"Mom and Dad are divorced," she answered, in a saddened tone.
"I'm sorry, I shouldn't have asked, it was rude of me. . . to pry about something so personal."
"Oh that's okay— I don't know what really happened, but—Mom had another baby, after Joe, about a year, a boy, and it died."
"I'm sorry, you needn't tell about it. . . "
"It was never the same for her and Pops after that," she said sadly, wiping a tear from her cheek.
At the corner they turned to walk down North Liberty Street and a passing automobile backfired to brake the silence. It was dusk now, and the sun was setting in a rare brilliance that comes after a rainy day. "Look at the rainbow," Mary gestured.
"Look Mary, a robin. . . and another there," he pointed, dropping his voice to a whisper, "You can hear their songs, it sounds like, *cheerily, cheerily, cheerily.*"
"Yes. . ." she said, her buoyant spirit returning.
"Robins are the first birds to arrive in the spring and the last to leave in the fall, some even stay the whole winter," he paused as the wheels of his head turned. "I've read, and heard that robins, when returning in the springtime eat the berries of the pyracantha bush and get so drunk they can't fly or walk, and they wobble about trying to fly, and some tip over on their backs with wings spread out, and their little tongues hang out—like this."
"You're kidding," she said, with that vibrant flush again on her face. She stepped ahead suddenly and turned to look him in the eyes. "Birds can't get drunk. . . can they?" her eyes glowed again, deep and bright with the color of livid pools, "You're teasing," she exclaimed.
Nodding, he said, "that's what I've heard, though I've never seen it myself," he flashed a wry smile then.
"You're joshing me," she said in a screechy voice reminiscent

of younger days—that girlish charm working its way to the surface again. She jumped ahead to tread backwards in front of him with her hands clasped behind her back, her gaze still fixed in wild speculation.

He continued, "John Buroughs, the American naturalist called the robin 'the most native and democratic of American birds.' He wrote: 'few birds have more dignity and beauty, or a more lovely song.'"

Her eyes seemed fixed on each word he spoke. "My favorite is the mocking bird," she countered, in a challenging tone.

"During the mating season, the males fill the air with joyful ringing notes, and when nesting the female does most of the work. She lines the nest with dry grasses, and. . . "

"Doesn't the male do anything. . . to help, I mean after he has all the fun, then she does the work while he just flies around, playing and eating bugs, tugging worms out of the ground and ruining the fruit on people's trees. It really doesn't seem fair."

"Oh yes he helps," he said, holding her eyes there, aware she was teasing and searching his own for clues of sincerity. "He gathers twigs and food and grasses. . . you know, whatever she tells him to do." He shrugged easily then, fearful he might say something that would bring on that wounded look and expose her vulnerable side again.

"Okay, that's better, what else is he good for beside showing off his bright orange-red breast?"

"Let me see, hmmm," he grinned tugging at his chin. "Well the European robins are smaller but similar, and the male's plumage is similar. According to an old English legend, this pious bird with a scarlet breast mercifully picked a thorn from the crown of Jesus on his way to Calvary, and as the bird carried the thorn in his beak a drop of blood fell from the thorn to its breast, dyeing it red," he stopped there and stared into her eyes.

"Now I know you're making it all up for sure. You're just teasing. . . aren't you? You're making it all up, just to fool me. I still like the song of the mockingbird better."

It was getting late when they approached the two story gray house that night and Bob realized he must find Bill and arrange for temporary lodging.

*T*wo weeks passed since he and Bill had arrived in Delaware. He was folding and sorting his clothes and preparing his belongings for the move. Just yesterday when he had talked with Edith she told him the room was ready.

He had asked about Mary and was told she had gone to visit her father. On two other occasion when he stopped by, he learned she was visiting her girl friends, Ardith and Dorothy. Bob realized he had not seen her since the first day when he had arrived. A glance at the piano showed him the music sheet of Juba Dance was open and in place, as if it were being studied.

When Edith asked what he was doing with his time, he explained that he had stayed at the dorm temporally with Bill, and that Bill had found a part time job at the school office, he had learned of an opportunity to sing on a radio station in Columbus, two or maybe three afternoons a week. Bob continued to explain how he had done some time on the radio station at his town in Waterbury summer before last. The studio and transmitter was situated on a hilltop not too far from the farm and he had walked it easy in ten minutes. The experience sure came in handy. After the audition in Columbus he had been accepted immediately.

"There's this girl, a student who accompanied me on piano," he added. "Her name is Angela and I'm not sure she can continue, because the afternoon trips might interfere with her classes, then it doesn't pay much yet, but might lead to something better in the future."

Edith listened quietly, puttering about the kitchen.

"Then there's the old Franklin," he continued, "twice when we were in Columbus, it wouldn't start, and I had to get a push, and then one time, up here it wouldn't start at all. Luckily there was this friend who has a motorcar and he drove us down. I'm working on it and expect to have it running in time to move my belongings."

That's when Edith told him the room was ready.

"Classes are due to start on Monday, so that works out just right. If it's okay I'll bring some things by tomorrow." At the door he thanked her again for the pie and milk.

In front of the two story gray house, Bob filled his arms with some of his belongings and a bag with clothes and closed the car door with his foot. He paused momentarily to hear the sounds of some small children playing on the grass of the neighbors home. Starting up the walk, he saw that the front door and windows were open and his ears picked up the rhythmic beat from the piano inside. It was the familiar African melody of the *Juba Dance,* from the sound he could tell she had been practicing long and hard to perfect the timing—it was a difficult piece with a lot of hand over hand work that would require a lot of patience.

He paused at the door, setting his things down gently so as not to disturb her, then entered quietly and turned to where he knew she would be sitting at the piano. For long moments he watched and listened. Once she paused to find the right key, then continued.

After the last note she stopped, as if studying the keys for an instant, suddenly aware of his presence she turned.

"Bob!" she gasped, "what. . . how long have you been there?" She sat, poised provocatively with hands on hips, full lips pursed in a pout. . . "I wanted to surprise you."

"You have, you were exquisite, it was beautiful. I could not have been surprised more," he said, proudly. "You've been practicing ever since the first day I bet."

"Well yes, did you like it ?" There was a certain pleading in her expression, "I mean was it really good—or are you just saying that?" She fluttered girlishly then—the defense mechanism giving way to boldness.

"Yes, it really is very good. I stopped in before, and hoped to see you then, but. . . "

"I know," she said, demurely, "I went with Pops, and I was with Ardith and Dorothy. . . " When he allowed a subtle sniff she sensed he had caught the wafting aroma from the kitchen.

"It's bread pudding, do you like bread pudding?" she asked.

"Why yes, its one of my favorites, Mom used to make it quite often, from left-over bread. . ."

"Come on," she said, taking his hand, "I made it myself and just took it out of the oven."

"Where's Edith?"

"She's out in the garden."

"What an amazing woman, how does she find time and

energy to cook and sew and clean, and do all those things?"

"Here, now be careful, it's HOT. I'll get a glass of cold milk, too."

"Ouch, oooh," he grimaced, his face a mask of sudden pain.

"Dummy."

"Oooooh—aaah," he jumped up, still trying desperately to suck in some cool air.

"Here, maybe this will help," she said, sympathetically as she scurried about for a glass.

He gulped large swallows, sucking in air, his face a twisted and bewildered mask of pain.

"Oh boy that was hot," he gushed, gulping another mouthful of cold milk and holding it there.

"Dumb, dumb, dumb," she said, ready to tease again.

He finished the bread pudding and another glass of cold milk, but realized his stupidity had greatly diminished the pleasure he had expected. She was right, he thought; dumb, dumb, dumb!

Eight

"Robert Marshall, you gonna sit there and stare at that letter and picture till your boy comes over here?"

"Huh?"

"She sure was a pretty girl—so young looking and all—was she one of those flapper girls, like to dance the Charleston and all? She sure got that flirty eye—"

"It was such a long time ago, Odelia, I had almost forgotten—

and now it all comes back like yesterday. I wonder what her life was like after that—if she is still alive—yes, she liked to dance—the Charleston and the Peabody. She played a beautiful piano, and won some awards for her competition recitals. . . Isn't it strange, Odelia—?"

"Strange, how?"

"How a young girl can change so in just a short time, like one summer, or winter too I guess. Like maturing over night—one minute you see them and they're filled with jitters and silliness—the next time, all grown up, in body anyway."

"I know what you saying, Robert. A man sees things—the body and the flirty smile and such, and he forgets they still just a young girl inside. . . It's summer all right, the warm weather, makes them sprout with all that chemistry, like blooms into flowers."

". . .and some men just plain fall under their charm, helpless and foolish, like a spell is cast, and without ever knowing it."

"Seems they plan it that way. It's part of their captivating charm—and mystique. They born knowing how to use it too, some more'n others—cause they got to test this new power they got over men."

"Makes some men do foolish things too—they turn weak, and act strong, and they get drawn in, some do anyway. . ."

"And some just plain fall in love."

"Some fall in love."

"You right about that too. It's part of that charm they born with, like a mystique, and some men are helpless. They born with that too."

Then he inched the photo closer, like it was a window he could see into. . .

"You got a lot to think about—you go right ahead an study that letter and pictures so you and him have a lot to talk about."

"I wonder if he looks like me—and if we should shake hands or if we'll embrace. I hope we don't just stand there looking at each other. Strange, isn't it Odelia, how the Lord works His ways for us all—I can't count the times I have thought of looking for him when I was in different cities, hoping to find him, just the way he found me, not knowing what name he's going under—ironic isn't it—across from here is Milton Street—and Milton Park, and his name is Robert Taylor Milton—who would have guessed it? And all I needed to do was check in Delaware. In time I put it all behind me, and forgot—"

"Well he be here soon as he gets through all that roadwork—then all your questions be answered. I got iced tea and hot tea ready and some iced cold lemonade, and cold milk, whichever he likes."

"And sugar cookies—I smell them baking. Odelia you are a wizard—you think of everything."

"Sugar cookies just the way you like them with toasted edges, fresh and hot out of the oven—if he be your boy he like hot sugar cookies with ice cold milk."

Even before she was through the door his focus once again concentrated on the photo and sitting there in his wheelchair he slipped away—back into that other life of long ago—when things were simple and the future looked bright and filled with promise, and he could do no wrong.

---

*T*he Glen, as it was called, was a grassy knoll overlooking a large hollow in the ground near Stuyvesant Hall, surrounded by big oak and maple trees. With summer gone and fall on its way soon the leaves would be changing colors and the warm fall foliage with its reds, oranges and browns and yellow golds strike a note for the new season. The glen was usually a popular place to watch and study the stars on perfect nights like this. In the winter, youngsters often gathered to ride their sleds down the sides to the bottom.

Strolling and laughing together, they recalled how Bob had burned his mouth on the bread pudding, and though it was not funny to him, Mary still found it difficult to conceal her amusement. She had given him a hard time at first, pampered him with sympathy and compassion thereafter.

"I'm sorry," she said, trying to sound even more sympathetic. "But if only you could have seen the look on your face. I am truly sorry, but I just can't help it, if only you could have seen."

The reminder seemed to make it smart all the more as he tried to change the subject, still remembering how difficult it had been to eat at dinner time.

He recalled that, after dinner he had gone to his room to finish arranging it. Soon there would be classes and studies and his hours would be filled, especially with his trips to Columbus.

Mary helped Edith with the kitchen chores. When he came out of his room, they had finished, and for a short time they sat at the piano while she played and he sang, or tried to sing. A little later Edith joined them and when they had noticed dusk upon them, he suggested a stroll to the glen.

Sitting down on the high grassy knoll above the hollow, it seemed to be their own private spot, for this night there were no others about.

Bob chuckled as he related how Joe had shown up late again, and had busted through the screen door just as the others were eating. "I wonder how much longer that screen will survive?"

"Mom had it fixed several times already. . . once when it was latched, Joe went almost through it from the inside, Mom would have thrashed him right then, but decided it was easier just not to latch it anymore."

"I guess so," he agreed.

They sat quietly for a time, then Mary broke the silence, "That was really neat, I mean when we were singing. . . how do you change your voice like that, I mean a four octave range is rare isn't it? And your resonance is so strong and smooth through the full scale. It seems so natural; I've never heard anyone with that kind of control before. It really is powerful, and then your bass is so low, especially when you sing the chords in *Deep River,* and *Asleep in the Deep.*"

"Just practice I guess," he replied modestly. "My father had a good voice, and when he was alive we used to sing and practice a lot. We still do when we're all together, but not as much now. I think I learned a lot the year I went to Montpelier Seminary."

"I wish I could sing like that, I mean rich. . . and of course in a woman's voice like, soprano. I don't have the range though."

"You have a beautiful voice, with a gentle, soothing quality in the mezzo-soprano range."

"Do you really think so?" She looked at him with renewed inspiration. "I'm not so sure though—I have tried, but then I always crack in the contralto range, especially when I laugh."

"You know what?"

"No, what?"

"I wish I could play the piano like you do. How did you learn? When did you start?"

"Ten years now."

"Ten years, that's a lot of time and dedication. Well, it sure shows."

"Yes, well almost ten years. I started taking lessons when I was six years old, and I had to practice every day."

"Did you take lessons at school?"

"Oh no. Mom had a tutor come in. A Mr. Bowers." She paused, then continued with a soft smile, as if guarding against the contralto crakle. "I joined the Glee Club my first year in high school, and played in the band also."

"A marching piano."

"No silly, the coronet," she added, with a certain pride. "Sometimes."

"Oh you play the coronet too," he said, with that sheepish grin smeared over his face.

"The English horn," she said, nodding ever so slightly. . . "and the French horn. . . and the baritone," then looking into his eyes, waiting for the surprise to show.

"Anything else?" he asked, still a little stunned, recalling all four were three fingered instruments.

"No, but the school took state championships, two years running, and this will be our third."

"Then you learned in school?"

"No. . . I already knew how." She waited, daring to enjoy his astonishment. "I learned from a boarder. Mr. Farley was his name. He had played with the Ringling Brothers Circus for years, and lived at the boarding house. Oh boy could he play, like peaches and cream," she said, closing her eyes for an instant as though she could hear the sounds again. "Well anyway, when I started high school I already knew how to read music, and I could play the horns so I just took what was left over. There; you see?"

"I'm impressed—very impressed."

"Once when we played out of town, in Worthington at a football game, it had been raining and there was so much mud, it was over our ankles in places, and we were marching and I was playing the Baritone when a football hit the horn and knocked me down." She started to laugh. "It wasn't funny then, like you and hot stuff, but I was all muddy, and for a long time I had a big swollen lip. . . right here," she said, indicating her lip for inspection.

He leaned closer as if to examine it. "It's all gone now," he mused.

"Naturally, silly."

Side by side they lay on the their backs looking up, as darkness overcame light and a jillion stars flickered on.

Bob pointed. "Look there," he said. "The North Star—see. Isn't it strange that for thousands of years people were aware of the stars, and worshiped them, and learned to navigate by the stars. They didn't know of the stars as we do today, that there are other suns existing far out in space. They thought that the stars made the outlines of animals or persons in the sky. They called the shapes Constellations. The Ancient Greeks thought that one group of stars looked like a winged horse, so they named it *Pegasus*."

She had been following every word, and when he paused she raised on one elbow, caught between reading words, thoughts, and watching stars.

"Other groups of stars were named after animals and persons, and these animals and persons became legends and spawned folk tales that have come down to us over thousands of years."

"Are you making up these stories?"

"Oh no, its in books. . . encyclopedias, anyone can read all about it, and in the Bible too."

"Oh yeah, like the Star of Bethlehem."

He paused to glance at her, then went on; "the Bible tells the beautiful story of the *Star of Bethlehem*, that guided the wise men to the stable where the Baby Jesus lay in the manger."

"Tell me some more, another story," she said, eagerly, squeezing his hand for attention.

"From early times man has often used the stars as symbols of high ideals and great hopes. They are often used in mottoes, and in poetry. Poetry and music show the mystery and beauty that stars have influenced on literature. . . and. . . "

"You mean like *Twinkle, Twinkle, Little Star, How I Wonder What You Are*."

"Exactly. The Bible speaks of Christ as the, *Bright and Morning Star*, and—"

"Oh yeah, I remember, when they built the Tower of Babel so

they could reach the heavens, and when Jesus went into the wilderness, and the devil tempted him, and he had the heavens as his companion. The stars, the moon and the sun were his only companions, is that it?" Her voice dropping to a new softness; "and when Jacob walked in the desert and mentioned the stars by night. . . "

They were both quiet for a long time again as they gazed upward, lying there side by side on the grassy knoll. She was still clutching his hand until he spoke again as though in a whisper. "It was the Indians who had some of the most beautiful legends—for example, the Blackfoot Indians believed that every star was once a human being, and when a person died his spirit rose to the heavens and became a star." He pointed with his hand as if measuring the distance in comparison, then paused to turn and find her eyes waiting on his. He knew then she was captivated by his every word. . . That also was the first time he consciously realized the power of his words over another person. After a short time he resumed, "One of their legends tells how the North Star came to be. The Morning Star came to earth and chose an Indian girl as his bride, he took her back to the heavens, where they lived happily, and she was allowed to do almost anything she wanted."

"*Almost* anything," she glowered.

"*Almost*. . . but she was warned against digging a certain turnip."

"Who would want to dig a turnip, up in the heavens anyway?"

"Well according to the legend, she did, she disobeyed, and the turnip she pulled up made a hole in the heavens, and she was returned to earth and her child became a star that was used to fill up the hole that she had made. This star-child must always stay in place to fill the hole and can never move about as the others do. That is why the North Star never moves, according to this legend anyway."

"That's beautiful. . . and sad too. . . I promise not to eat any turnips," she vowed.

Then there was another pause, each waiting for the other to say something first.

"Would you like to see the stars close up?"

"Sure, that would be the berries, but how?" she turned

quickly to face him and cooed, her eyes wide, half with caution and half quizzical with that schoolgirl charm breaking out again.

"At the Perkins Observatory, near Stratford, I'll see if I can get us in. I know the guy, a student who works the door. I've gone there myself several times, and I'm sure I can arrange it."

Rising to his feet, he brushed off his pants, reached to take her hand and pulled her up.

It was an aimless stroll hand in hand back to the house on Liberty street, to rush would have broken the spell.

A gentle tuneful melody reached them at the door, and as they approached the tempo quickened. Bob wondered what the name of the familiar song could be.

"Therese. . . Therese, that's what Mom still calls it. That's what Beethoven named it originally. Later it was changed to *Fur Elise.* Mom sort of treats it still in her own way though."

"I knew it sounded familiar." For the moment he thought of Claire. It was one of her favorites also—but he never heard it played in quite that tempo before.

"It's one of Mom's favorites—mine too, and the *Volga Boatman,* and *Moonlight Sonata.* Sometimes she jazzes everything up to suit her mood. I'd give my eye teeth if I could play like she does, but she always insisted I learn the proper way, by reading notes and I always had to play the classic's, you know, like Beethoven, Mozart, Tchaikovsky, and Liszt. . . Chopin. Those guys, you know, with long hair and sad faces, like they just lost the only love of their whole life."

"That's not bad company, I'd say."

"But Mom never took a lesson. She can hear a tune once or twice and play it her own way." Mary dropped her voice to a gentle softness so they could still listen. "She taught herself to play when she was a young girl."

"Remarkable. How she can play so soothing one moment and then take your breath away in another instant, yes soothing, and easy on the ears, like Vermont is easy on the eyes."

"Grandma doesn't play at all, Aunt Violet plays the organ, of course you already know that, and Uncle Jess, he plays the Harmonica and calls square dances sometimes. He's the one you met on the electric train with Pops."

"Pure, raw talent then," he said, reaching for the door at last and nodding his head in obvious astonishment. "What's that?" he asked, alerted to the sudden change in the tempo.

"*Tiger Rag*... Mom likes to play Ragtime too, *Maple Leaf Rag* is another of her favorites."

Lying in bed later that night he could hear the gentle relaxing sounds of *Onward Christian Soldiers* while in his mind he hummed the words. Unbelievable, he thought, such a magical touch, truly magic, and with his eyes closed he visualized her sensitivity and dexterity in her gentle, but commanding persuasion over the ivory keyboard. He remembered how enjoyable it was to watch her hands and fingers as they would dance over the keys.

Before long he relaxed into a deep sleep.

Rounding a curve, they could see the outline of a partially hidden, large domed structure. Perkins Observatory loomed directly in front of them as they maneuved into a parking place.

The past week had been a busy one with choir practice on Saturday and church on Sunday. Classes had started on Monday and he had been busy trying to catch up ever since.

At the door Bob introduced Mary to Rich.

Inside he guided her to the back row seats.

Professor Barrows was a rather short, lean man with thick gray hair. He was explaining some of the technicalities of the telescope and he often removed his spectacles to reveal small eyes pinched close together as he talked.

The Professor went on to explain about the stars and their groupings. He talked about the sun and moon and why the moon seemed to change shape, and the earth's rotation around the sun and how in ancient times people believed the earth to be the center of the heavens, and how the sun and all others revolved about it.

He went on further to explain the distance between earth and other celestial bodies and how they functioned.

Mary reminded Bob in a low voice that the professor was explaining some of the same things he had told her on their second visit to the glen and how fascinated she had been. "You tell it better," she said. "He looks like he going to fall asleep."

The professor was saying that the North Star is situated directly above the North Pole Axis, and that's why it never seems to move, as all others seem to be moving around the earth. Actually, he said, it is the earth's rotation that makes the stars seem to move.

After a short question and answer session, individuals were invited to come up and look through the telescope.

"Did you like it?" Bob asked when they were leaving. They stood outside the large domed building to gaze upward, searching so as to identify those elements they had just heard about.

"He was a ferrety little man, but he really knows his business about details and statistics," she conceded.

"Like Edith knows pies, and baking, and the piano."

"Yeah, like a farmer knows weeds and crops."

"It was so interesting to hear about it all again, even though it was mostly the things you had explained up at the glen. Do you come here a lot, you must, to know so much about it, the stars and astronomy and all."

"I come when I have time, about five or six times now, I think," he said, and he watched, her eyes light up with excitement. That was her, the way excitement glows. I would like to kiss your smile, he thought.

"What were you thinking?"

"When?"

"Just now. I could feel the wheels turning. Tell me."

". . .a little thing. It's nothing now."

Driving down the winding tree lined road they sat quietly. He was thinking about the touch of her hands, and how they felt and how thrilled and alive she had been when they had strolled around and talked of the stars and then of their classes.

"You know, I've been thinking about your piano playing, thinking maybe you could accompany me on the radio. Maybe we could even sing a duet, and well, how would you like to try out?"

"Do you think I could?" she cried, as she jumped, and shifted one foot under her, then turned to face him with eyes bright and flickering like a thousand Christmas lights. "You're just teasing, aren't you?" Then she added, "what about Angela?"

"Yes, I am serious. I wouldn't tease about a thing like that.

Besides Angela is having trouble juggling her classes as it is." He started to say that Angela doesn't like the tension. "I think we could make a good team. We have already been playing and singing together. . . of course we'd have to practice a lot, and I'm sure they're planning to increase my time, and maybe we'll get to do a recitation on Bible history, The Parables and the Travels of Paul. Who knows what it could lead to—"

She studied him there for a long time, speechless—yet her body waiting to leap into motion, like a spring all coiled and waiting to be sprung. He knew she would have believed anything he said. There was guilt of a sort there too, for exposing her vulnerable innocence.

"I can't wait to tell Mom, she'll be so happy, I just know she will. . . " She cooed, as the sparkle in her face danced about anxiously. "And Pops, I'll make him proud too." Suddenly she moved over to him and snuggled close. "And you too, we'll be great together, you'll see. I'll make you proud too. We'll have to go to Columbus—and maybe we can go to a dance contest—there's one coming up soon—lots of Flappers there dressed in the latest styles and we could dance together. . . "

He started to say: but I don't know how to dance. . .

As if sensing his dilemma she went on, "but you have so much rhythm and you're so easy on your feet—you can learn fast—I'll teach you how—they do every dance there is, the Tango, Quick-step and Cross steps, and the latest is the Peabody, it's a Foxtrot—and the Lindy Hop and the Charleston. When Ardith and Dorothy and I feel real silly at her house we even do the Hoky-Pokie—that's for kids—but it's such silly fun—all you have to do is grab me by the waist, wriggle about like a slippery slush—somebody said that, or wrote it, I think. But it's true—and they do Ragtime dances—Ragtime is Mom's favorite, on the piano. But there's all kind of dances, like. . . the Bunny Hop—the Shiver—the Kinkajou and Hug-Me-Close."

When he parked the Franklin there was no holding Mary back. She burst from the car almost before it had stopped with an aura of energy flooding about her.

"Hurry," she called back impatiently. She had started ahead, then turned back to take his hand, urging him to run with her.

The light in the kitchen gave them direction and they hurried to find Joe and Edith sitting at the kitchen table laboring over

Joe's homework.

"Mom, Mom guess what?" Mary cried out, "Bob wants me to be his accompanist on the radio. Of course I'll have to practice more, but I can do it, and we'll work as a team; radio is the rage of the future..."

Even Joe had snapped up from his boredom.

"Well yes, sure you can child," Edith said, finally recovering a measure of composure "Is this true Robert?" she asked, watching for his reaction.

"Yes, I've been thinking about it for sometime. Mary already knows most of the songs and she learned *Juba Dance* so fast. Of course I'll have to check with the station manager at W A I U, he knows Angela has to be replaced, and he may just accept my word; he'll want an audition..."

"Bob says maybe we can sing a duet and his spots may be increased so he can do some recitals on Bible History," Mary added.

"Well I don't know. This is so sudden—I suppose it's all right," Edith said, still weighing the uncertainties. "Come sit down and tell me more about it—have some fresh baked cobbler and a glass of cool milk."

Joe lurched upright; "I'll take some."

"You've already had yours, Joseph."

"Yeah," jibed his sister. "Pay up. Do your homework."

"Sounds good Mrs. Swaren," said Bob, scooting his chair to the table.

"Why are you so excited little sister, you've been on the radio before with the school music class, and with the band," Joe retaliated.

"Yes, but that was different. I was with a group. Anyway I'm not your little sister, I'm older than you," Mary shot back. He knew it always irritated her when he called her *little sister*.

"You may be older, but you'll still *littler,* little sister."

Mary shot him daggers with hooks, and decided to change the subject. She felt too mature lately for any such childishness. Anyway, boys were so infantile; and brothers beyond redemption.

She took a deep breath and spoke calmly in a reserved tone as though suddenly overcome with dignity—the girlishness fading temporarily. "We can start practice right now, it's not too late—how about *Amazing Grace,* I know that's one of your favorites and *A Walk in the Garden...* and *A Closer Walk With Thee."*

Edith interrupted. "Mary, its bedtime, and don't forget young lady, you still have school tomorrow."

"I know Mom, but Tuesday afternoon will be our first day and we have to be ready," she argued. Sleep would not come easy this night.

"Have you forgotten something?" her mother reminded, giving her a long glance which had become her trademark with Joe. "School, classes, studies?"

"Oh!" Mary exclaimed, putting a hand to mouth. "Classes, oh well that's no problem, two classes, typing and music. I'm sure I can get permission. I can make both of them up."

"Anyway—we have until Tuesday. That's four days, and plenty of time, especially with the weekend," Bob said, confidently. "We'll only be doing four songs at first, and we can start with ones we already know."

Later when Bob had gone to his room he could hear her in the bathroom above, singing in the bathtub. The vision of her lingered there for a long time.

They had parked the old Franklin and walked a block down High Street, then turned a corner and hurried toward the river. It was a crisp breezy afternoon. The radio station was on the third floor of an ancient looking, cut-stone French provincial building with a Mansard style roof.

Bob was explaining how the studio overlooked the Scioto River as it wound a twisted path through downtown Columbus.

He realized Mary was a little nervous, even though she appeared a picture of confidence. As they stood alone in the elevator he took her hand affectionately in his to offer reassurance.

"Don't worry—he'll like you, especially when he sees how pretty you look... as though you just stepped from the cover of a fashion magazine." He inspected her from top to bottom momentarily—nothing out of place. "He likes that."

"I sure hope so," she said, her damp soft hands betrayingly squeezed his back.

At the third floor door with the frosted upper glass and the letters W A I U on it Mary suddenly froze, then took that last deep breath. Bob opened it for her.

Inside they were greeted cordially by an attractive young woman who immediately recognized Bob. She left the office, then returned to tell them Mr. Clark would be with them in just a moment.

"Robert, how are you?" he said, warmly, and offering his hand, they shook hands, then he turned to look at Mary. "Sooo, this is Mary. Beautiful." Nodding agreement as he glanced casually at Bob and putting his arm around her shoulder, he took her hand in his. "Very nice, and she plays and sings too. Where did he find you, pet?" His office door was open and he steered her in. "Come on in dear, you really are blooming you know."

The medium sized office was warm in woodwork with a rich wooden desk and some comfortable leather chairs. Behind the desk, a window framed a view of the river, and if you glanced sideways at its corner you could see the downtown bridge.

"So, let's see," he said, studying his pocket watch. "We still have almost twenty minutes. I suppose you might like to relax and tune up a bit before we go on the air."

"I think that would be a good idea," Bob nodded his agreement.

All three were sitting, facing each other, as Ron turned to Mary again. "Robert tells me you have been on radio before, Mary," his voice more business like now.

"Yes, Mr. Clark, that was with the school band," she said, with reservation.

"With our neighbor station W S M, I would venture a guess," he smiled back easily, then added, "call me Ron." It was a disarming smile, and Mary was impressed.

"Yes, it was last spring, and the year before too," she replied, with growing confidence.

"Very well, I say lets go into the studio now and you can use what time is left to familiarize yourself with our piano," looking to Bob and rising to his feet, he asked, "what songs have you chosen for today?"

"I would like to start with *Amazing Grace*, then, *A Walk in the Garden*, and if you want more, we are prepared to do another. . ."

"I think we may have only enough time for three today, but we shall see."

"We're prepared to do several. . . *Deep River*, or *I Love To Tell The Story*, if time allows."

"Excellent, I can see you've come well prepared."
Through a different door they went into another room.
"Make yourself comfortable my dear," he said, indicating a polished grand piano. First, let me make sure the sound is turned off. Then you may start your warm-up."
Mary touched the open lid, then the keys. "Wow; a Steinway," she cooed. "Why didn't you tell me? They're the best."
She sat on the stool carefully and studied the keys while Bob stood close by with his hand resting lightly on her shoulder for reassurance.

The wind had picked up and clouds were beginning to form as they were driving home in the darkened night. They sat quiet, and though the night air was a bit chilly it felt warm and cozy to have her feminine body snuggled close to him on the car seat.
They had gone to a picture show after leaving the radio station. He smiled a bit, remembering Mary's satisfaction that everything had gone well and Ron had seemed so pleased.
In the theater, they had touched and held hands and looked longingly into each others eyes. One occasion he had raised her hands and pressed them to his lips and brushed his face with her smooth, delicate fingers, while slowly she had drawn even closer, she fit there like part of him, dear and intimate.
"Looks like rain, maybe we'll get some by the time we get home," he said seriously, looking straight ahead into the dark night.
"Do you think he liked us?" she asked.
"Who?"
"Ron, you know, at the radio station."
"Oh yes. . . he wants us to come back again. When you went to the ladies room I mentioned how well you play *Juba Dance*, how you vary the tempo, starting slow, then the crescendo for a finale. I told him of the others, the classic's and he wants you to do a solo. He says you're a very talented girl."
"Really, he said that, that he thinks I'm talented?" she said, as she jumped to put one leg beneath the other. "You're teasing. . . not just saying it to help my confidence?"
"No, not at all, and I told him we were working on a duet also."

"Oh, I don't know, I'm not so sure," she said, uncertainty creeping into her voice again.
"Not sure of what?"
"A solo. . . I don't know if I can. . . I was so nervous. I'm just not sure I can, playing is one thing, but singing?"
"Sure you can. Even Ron remarked on how calm and collected you were."
"Oh you're the one who is always calm and collected. And in church you're always so composed. Naturally, I mean. You're so. . . natural and I'm nervous, at least on the inside and I feel like it shows, like pins and needles."
"Well if you are nervous, it sure doesn't show. Even Ron congratulated you on how well you did, especially for a first time."
"I know. . . but I thought he was just being nice, and he probably compliments others, Angela too."
"Not everyone. Yes he did with Angela, but he wouldn't have if he hadn't meant it. He doesn't waste time pampering anybody."

"Well here we are, home safely to Delaware again and just in time for the rain." He pointed to raindrops splattering on the windshield.
In front of the house at 16 South Liberty Street, he turned off the headlamps and withdrew the key. They sat quiet for a few minutes watching the raindrops fall in the light from the corner street lamp, like silver pellets on an aimless journey.
Sensing her closeness he reached to touch her hand. He turned to kiss her gently, barely touching, then held her there for a moment. It had started as a gentlemanly impulse. She had been waiting, poised, with eyelids ready to close when the rapture took a grip he eased back—giving way to some hidden and evasive sense of loyalty, like a sign-post that spelled 'guilt.'
"What was that for?" she asked softly.
"Oh. . . I don't know," he said, retreating again, "but we'd better hurry or we'll get soaked."
At the front door they paused to listen to Edith working the keys to *Tiger Rag*.

Nine

Arthur Brown was talking about Korea and how it was there: "Say you was in France; you were lucky. I remember how it was in Korea—sure wish I could have seen France, the Riviera and sunny beaches—remember I'd dream on that lonely hill at night. Oh, you had your buddies, but it was cold, cold as ice, and gray and black as everlasting night. The gooks didn't seem to mind it like we did. They just kept on coming, out of the night, and nowhere. Over one worthless hill after another, bundled in rags and no weapons. Thirty caliber carbines was almost worthless against all that padding. I remember how they'd pick up a weapon, anything from a fallen comrade and just keep climbing those hills, coming at us, body humps all over the place to hide behind when we'd drop the flares. I remember they paid no mind— all they wanted was a weapon in their hands and to get at us. You could hear them breathing, and smell em, like old stale rags and piss, like silent ogres. And we'd shoot out more flares. They never saw so much light over there until we showed them flares. . . Yes sir, I'd of changed my place any day for yours—Paris, and the Riviera. You ever get to the Riviera?"

"Huh? . . .no, I didn't make it to the Riviera. Wish I had though. Guess I'll never get another chance."

"Man, if I was in France I'd head straight for the Riviera. Someday, I get there."

"Some of the guys went there, came back and said they liked it better in Spain, so I went to Spain a couple times. Then I was transferred to Leon, a base north of Paris. I loved Paris. When the time came I wanted to take my discharge and stay there."

"I heard there was a lot of money made on the black market in Europe, cigarettes and stuff we could'a used back then. Korea was a black market hell; corruption was rampant. I remember how guys would collect rations and pedal smokes in Seoul for a night with the whores, and blow their whole month's pay; come back bitching and gamble themselves into debt, waiting for the flares and them gooks to come climbing up the hill after us. What you do in Paris?"

I was remembering things too. Like when Mom told me about how my Uncle Joe and my father played basketball together. Man-to-man they called it. We call it one-on-one now. And then as if Arthur Brown's words triggered other past memories I switched to France. "I was attached to O S I then, because I had a photographic memory for numbers and nomenclature. It's called C I A now. I wanted to, or rather thought I wanted to become an agent back then. I was assigned undercover to investigate black marketeering in military supply depots. Somewhere along the line I awakened to the fact that O S I agents were no different from the unsavory characters they were trying to snare. So—I turned to selling cigarettes on the black market—to locals who had little money and could ill afford them. I never did understand the craving for American cigarettes. I felt dirty and gave that up too."

I drifted back then, to a time when Mom told me about an incident at the radio station where she and my father performed live. She had smiled at first, and laughed till tears flooded from her eyes. There was so much joy in that simple memory; I almost felt like she was there again. The station manager had uncaged a canary during a performance. She called it a little beast and a nuisance because it persistently fluttered about tweeting and singing its heart out, landing on the keys, and the soundbox, and finally on her shoulder. She tried to shoo it away and in the process wrecked the performance. My father sang on undaunted during the whole episode while the manager and his assistant chased it and even crawled around beneath the piano at her feet, trying to catch it. They laughed all the way home about it, wondering what Edith would say. She was wiping away the tears when she finished telling it. I wonder if Robert Marshall ever thinks about such things. . .?"

Arthur Brown blasted a guy with his horn, cranked his wheel to the right and shot through an amber light; close call. I wonder if he was taking a chance for my sake—save me some time on the meter and maybe get a ticket for himself. "Yes sir, I remember those cold nights all right, and the Riviera. Pity you never got there. I would have gone there first thing. I'd still be there, driving a cab most likely," he was saying.

We passed by a play-ground where kids were shooting baskets; some others in a corner seemed to be shooting dice, and a fight broke out, and then we passed them by. I remember how Mom's face lit up with joy when she told me about Uncle Joe and my father playing basketball back in Delaware. It must have been a happy time for her because her face broke out in happy tears, and she laughed. They played several games for the Swaren House Championship, see-sawing back and forth, and Uncle Joe taunted Bob by calling him Old Man College, and then there was the day Mom sat nearby with her two girlfriends and watched. They had called him the *bees knees* and he had flushed, and she said he had looked so stunned like it was a disease. "I'll never forget that look on his face," she said, her face filled with fond memories, and then the sadness flooded over her again. I wonder what Robert Marshall is thinking at this moment. . .

---

*O*delia Bright was humming a tune in the kitchen, something between Gospel and Soul, clanging pans and scrubbing to get things all cleaned up again, moving about between stove and sink, when Robert Marshall called out to her. She didn't hear him but it made no difference anyway. He was half speaking in a conversational tone and the other half to himself. . . "You know Odelia, how I used to have a memory for fact and figures—now I can't even remember my own phone number."

"You doing all right, Robert. You remembering the Lord's work," she called back.

"I was thinking of a sad girl named Loretta. I had all but forgotten her, but there are times she haunts me still. I had no words to console her or her mother with, and I wonder about the Loretta's of today. What would I, could I say to them to help now. I look back on the Loretta incident as a personal failing, because there were no answers. I have prayed for the Loretta so many times, and for the answers, if only for my own salvation.

"And then I remember Mary and how soothing it was just to hold her hand, and to have her sitting or lying close to me." For an instant he fondled the envelope as though it made him feel closer.

"There was a little thing I had all but forgotten until this moment; when we played at a radio station one time. A friend of the manager loaned him a canary, in a cage mind you, and told him it would sing better if he released it during our performance; for good affect, to compliment the piano. He pulled the stunt as a surprise on us and poor Mary was dumfounded. I thought she might desert her piano—she called it a vile little nuisance, and a beast, and claimed it wrecked the performance. Ron Clark was beside himself with pleasure over her gritty charm. I think he may have had some other tricks up his sleeves too. But Mary would not have allowed it. She laughed to tears all the way home, telling her dad and uncle Jess about it. She was scared to death at Edith's reaction though; her family and friends had gathered at her home to listen to the broadcast. . .

"I remember playing basketball with Joe while the three girls watched and poked fun at us from a respectable distance. Those were good times, shooting baskets with Joe. Later I played basketball with Mary; I rolled on the ground doubled up because she was so comical and filled with joy. She stunned me Odelia, and dazzled me, dribbling about, shooting baskets, and I'll bet I looked the fool to her then. She stomped me and promptly declared herself the Swaren House champion. Joe was crestfallen; he had relinquished the title to me, only to have his sister win it back. He declared it was a fix, and challenged me after that. I wonder if she ever told our son about those times, and I wonder what he is thinking right now?"

"Ardith says you're the *bee's knees*," Mary said, searching his face for a flushed reaction; she often did that; said a goofy thing to draw attention.

"What!" He looked surprised. *"The bee's knees*, I don't think I've heard that one before. Sounds pretty bad. Where did I catch it?"

"Silly, you know. . . the *bee's knees*, spiffy. Dorothy thinks you look real spiffy, in knickers and your polo shirt. . . a real collegiate. You know, a classy guy."

"I don't think I have been called that before, *spiffy*. . . or the *bees knees*," he chuckled. "How do they know so much—? and what do I do to get rid of it?"

"She should know, after all, she is dating a guy from the college."

"She is huh?"

"He's a freshman, from Pittsburgh. They just met a week ago. I don't think they're serious or anything like that, not yet anyway."

Crossing Williams Street they strolled casually towards the boarding house.

"Did you know Pops raised the roof on our house?" she said, pointing to the roof and her bedroom window.

"Raised the roof? . . . how did he do that?"

"I'm not sure exactly. It was about six. . . yes six years ago, when we were all still living together. He did something to prop it all up, and then he built on the whole second floor." She gestured upward again with a wave of her hand. "Where Joe and my rooms are. He added the bathrooms then also."

"Did Ross do the room downstairs where I'm staying too?"

"No, Mom had Mr. Miller do that. They don't see each other much anymore," Mary said, sadly. "I see Pops almost every day and once a month he gives me an envelope to give to Mom."

"You know, that reminds me, you said you can get a pass on the Interurban anytime and. . . "

They lingered in front of the house, each as if waiting for something to happen—her eyes wide and expectant; studying him there. "Are you going to tell me what you're thinking; I can feel the wheels turning."

"Well, for one thing, the old Franklin is about done this time, I think. I worked on it, but I'm not sure it'll start again, and even if it does, it might quit while we're in Columbus. So, maybe we should plan on the Interurban."

"You want me to get a pass?" she said. "We'd probably have to catch the two o'clock. . . and come back on the last one at five. We might be rushed a little though."

Bob nodded agreement as he opened the door.

"I was thinking we could practice some now, but maybe I better help Mom with dinner; then we'll practice later on; she can play while we try a duet."

When dinner was over he sat beside her, watching the magic in her hands as her fingers would glide gently over the keys, then they quickened as she picked up the tempo. The *Juba Dance* was getting a special rendition.

They were barely aware of Edith's presence when she sat down in the overstuffed leather chair, raised her tired ankles and feet onto the matching otterman and closed her eyes. Bob glanced over to see a soft smile and certain delight grow on her face, the pride of a mother's pleasure in the long and dedicated efforts, and for an instant he wondered what thoughts crossed her mind, or was she merely enjoying the moment.

Mary paused when she finished, then continued with *Moonlight Sonata*. After that she started by teasing the keys with a bit of *By the Waters of The Mini-Tonka* .

When she finished she gazed into his eyes, and it seemed even though their bodies were not quite touching, the temptation was there, like a smoldering ember, waiting and eager to burst into a lighted flame.

The spell spent itself, as they looked to see Edith still sitting, restful and smiling. "Play another one for me, honey?" she said, in a soft voice.

Intuitively, Mary turned the pages and placing her hands at the keys, once again she started gently. This time he knew the tune even as he read it, Beethoven's *Fur Elise*.

Bob explained to Edith: "Mary will play her rendition of *Juba Dance* first. . . I'll sing *I Believe*, with her accompaniment of course. Then we'll do *Just A Closer Walk With Thee*. We have more requests for that than any other."

"We've been practicing *In The Garden* as a duet," Mary

added, "but I can't seem to hit the high notes."

"Ron wants us to stay with the hymns and still work in a classical or even a popular piece, or a folk song at some time later," Bob said.

"Why don't you let me hear what you want to sing, maybe I can play, and you work on your duet."

Mary turned to the selected pages and started with a few bars, then looked up, giving the signal to Bob that she was ready.

>   I believe for every drop
>   of rain that falls. . .
>   a flower growwws. . .

"That was beautiful Robert, what a rich voice you have," Edith nodded her approval, when they had finished.

"Let's try it again," he said, "I think I can do better."

"Sure sounds good enough to me," Mary said, "I don't see how you could possibly do any better."

"Mom, it's your turn to play something now," Mary rose to offer the bench.

Edith struggled to push herself from the big leather chair as Bob hurried to lend a hand.

In front of the piano she sat down and proceeded to arrange herself comfortably, then gently touched the ivory keys as if testing for their response. "How's this?" she smiled.

When she finished she signalled for an encore. Bob suggested they try it once more, "And this time Mary, try to go one note higher on. . . *The Voice I hear.* . . "

"I'll try," she said, weakly.

After going through the tune again, Bob said, "on *He tells me I am his own*, try to hit one note higher.

"I can't. I've tried and tried until my throat hurts, and I. . . just can't."

He looked at her then, uncertain. "I think we have practiced enough for now. Maybe we could go for a walk in the glen before bedtime." Edith continued playing when they left.

Later that night lying in bed Bob wondered if he had pressed Mary too hard. It had always seemed so easy and natural for his sister, Aileen. And *In The Garden* had always been their most popular request, whether performed at church or at the Waterbury radio station. After all, he concluded, Mary had tried and maybe it just wasn't natural for her.

As he started to doze off, he heard the sound from the piano again, something that sounded familiar; a tune without a title, and yet he found it very soothing.

At last it felt good to sit back. . . to relax and watch the scenery go by. The trees on the distant hills were already preparing for their rich fall colors and occasionally a close one flashed by as the electric train approached the Glen Mary Trestle, he watched the blackbirds and starlings flitting about and a single crow or raven being tormented by the smaller birds.

It had been a hectic morning. He had risen early to deliver donuts and rolls. It seemed he had to rush from the very beginning. He recalled what his father used to say: "The harder you run the behinder you get." Having been late for his first class, owing to a lack of proper change when selling the donuts and he had arrived just as class was letting out, so he had to rush across campus making him late for the next one. . . and so on.

After cutting short his one o'clock class, he had hurried home only to find Mary late and anxiously hurrying about. They ran all the way, the three blocks to the Interurban Station at the corner of Sandusky and Williams Street. When they spotted Ross on the car step he motioned for them to hurry.

Both had sat quietly for a while.

"What a morning!" Bob said, with a sigh of relief. "You too? The whole morning was like that?"

He turned to see her looking down at her feet in a quandary.

"What are you looking for?" he asked; puzzled.

"Oh. . . I just wondered if I had both shoes and stockings on," she said, blushing a little.

"You're goofy, you know that don't you, but I. . . " realizing he almost said, but I love you anyway. Another time it could have meant a sisterly affection and unworthy of a second thought, but just now it took on a deeper meaning; like a commitment and it just hung there—like he had just swallowed a rock. For that instant they were held there in the sway of each other's emotions.

"But what?" she demanded. "You started to say something else?"

He said nothing, but took her hand in his own and gave it a reassuring squeeze.

Suddenly, both saw her uncle Jess working his way toward

them and collecting tickets as he came. "Close call eh?" he said, accepting Bob's ticket and Mary's pass.

"Hi Uncle Jess. We had to run all the way."

Ross turned to glance back and Bob caught his eye for a second. Bob wondered if Ross had understood their tardiness, considering Ross's affinity with the clock for punctuality.

"What are you thinking about?" she asked, curiously.

"Oh nothing really, just Ross. . . "

"What about Pops?"

"I wonder. . . I bet he's an awfully good poker player."

"How did you know? He plays almost every night."

"Well. . . I guess that shouldn't surprise me."

She sat quietly for a while and Bob was sure he could feel the wheels of thought turning inside her head.

"How do you know about poker?"

"Uh-Oh," he groaned. "I played a little, once or twice."

"You, played poker. . . you the preacher?" she said.

"When I was with the circus, last spring," he said modestly.

"You—with a circus. . . what other secrets do you have? A girl, a woman maybe; was there a woman?" She leaned forward searching his face for the truth of hidden secrets in his past.

He avoided her eyes, yet for a mere instant he thought of Josette, and Blanchard, and the others.

"Well, come on, are you going to tell me or not," she pressed on, as if there remained any choice; she must know all the details.

"It seemed like such a long time ago, I had almost forgotten," he said.

"So that's where you disappeared to?"

"Once. . . when I went ahead to work with the roustabouts, to set up tents at the new location; sometimes after a long hard day they would spread a blanket on the floor or ground. . . and sit around in a circle. Some shot dice, but most played poker. And I watched for a while, it looked easy like a way to pass time. I didn't think of it as gambling at the time, and they kept inviting me to sit in. Something about new blood."

"Well, go on. . . "

"I drank a little. . . and got a little woozy," he said, rolling his eyes and head around. . . "and lost all the money I had with me. The next morning I had my first hangover. Moonshine they called it. Ugly stuff. Some called it poison, and rightfully so."

"*First!*" she said, still prying.

"So, I figured gambling and drinking just wasn't for me."

"You said *first*, did you play again?"

"Well, yes, Jolly said. . . Jolly was the clown and a good friend, and he convinced me that you can't loose all the time, and you have to play again to get even. He said you get used to the drinking anyway."

"Jolly—where did he get a name like *Jolly*?"

"No one knew his real name. Everybody had called him Jolly for so long, cause he was sooo— jolly. And no one could remember a time when he had been called anything else."

"That's odd," Mary said, thoughtfully.

"Sooo. . . I joined another game. That was later on, and I was winning. After winning most of the money on the blanket that night, I got a little nauseous and woozy again." He made a motion with his eyes and patting his stomach, then resumed his story. "I didn't want to pick up all that money before the game ended, poor sportsmanship, or something like that. So I let Jolly take my place, for a few hands, I thought."

"What happened then?" she insisted, her voice eager with anticipation.

"He lost it all. I went to sleep, and when I woke up the next morning, with another hangover, the game was still going on, with different players though, but Jolly was gone. When I found him he said he had lost it all. Luck changed, he said, to the other side, and he shrugged it off, looking so helpless and like the clown."

"He lost it all, really—how much was there?"

"I'm not sure, a few hundred, maybe. Some of the guys told me later that Jolly is always the loser. They didn't understand why, but he just couldn't win, no matter what." Bob made a gesture throwing up his hands in dismay.

"A few hundred—*dollars*! Some friend," she said in mock-dispirited voice. "Poor guy."

"So, now you know my deepest secrets, and failings. That was the end of my drinking and gambling."

Mary tried excitedly, to explain what happened at the radio station when they returned that evening.

"Well come on child, tell me," Edith urged her impatiently.

"Well. . . it was that darn canary—cause the cage was left open."

"Canary?"

"Yes, somebody turned it loose," Mary gulped. "Well. . . anyway they said it got loose. . . somehow—likely story!"

"Ron said it got free, but I'm sure he or that other guy, Larry, must have turned it loose," Bob tried to tell her, his expression somehow lacking serious conviction.

"Yeah—sure, he turned it loose all right, cause he said the owner told him the bird would sing better if it was out of the cage, and he thought it would be a good idea, you know for the sound affect," Mary explained, and she looked serious for a moment. . . then, as the humor gripped her she smiled and continued. "He was a cute little critter, but he kept flitting round my feet," she made a fluttering motion with her fingers. "Then he flew into the sound box, all the time making those tweeting noises, then on my shoulder, no, no. . . wait. . . before that he flew around the room, and then he came back, and sat right in front if me. . . and Bob, he was so serious. . . he just went right on singing like Mister Calm. I don't think you ever saw him—did you?" she pointed an accusing finger at his face.

"I saw him all right, but I couldn't figure out why it was disturbing you."

"Well!" she inclined her head, striking an ingenuous pose, placed her hands on hips and leaned toward him. "Well. . . he was right there, in my face. . . and he hopped down to the keyboard, right next to my hand," she showed her hand. "What did you expect me to do. . . do just like you, just ignore him, playing dead-pan, huh? "

At first, he said nothing, grinning like a Cheshire cat, then smiled easily. . . "if only you could have seen. . . " he was trying desperately to remain serious. "You were sitting there, surprised—so sweet, and girlish, with it on your shoulder. I'd have given anything for a picture."

"Sweet and *girlish*, huh, I can show you, girlish."

Edith blinked, then blushed a little and coughed a strange noise to call attention to her presence.

Both looked to Edith, then cracked a smile as they returned to the humor of the situation.

Walking east on Williams street to Sandusky Mary was telling

Bob how she told the story of the canary to her friends at school and how they got such a kick out of it.

Bob recalled how Joe had challenged him to another game of basketball to determine the real champion of Swaren house, and indeed all Delaware since he was considered the best in town. Instead, Bob had declined, preferring to walk in town with Mary. Joe, in turn accused him of being chicken-hearted and promptly declared himself champion again by default. When Joe dashed off to the park in search of more suitable prey they told Edith they might even go to a picture show.

"I don't see how you can be the basketball champ of *our* house anyway," she said, in a challenging tone of voice.

"Why not?"

"Because you haven't played everyone there yet."

"Oh, who else is there?" he asked, looking at her puzzled.

"*Why me*... of course, you haven't played me yet."

"You, ha ha."

"YES... me, this is my fourth year on the girls basketball team, and we won the championship all three years running... and we're going to win it again this year too." Her words poured forth in a flood of youthful confidence.

"Well, Joe may have something to say about that, but if you're issuing a formal challenge I guess we'll just have to set up a tournament then."

"Okay, then we'll see," she countered, "But it's only fair that I should have a handicap, say eight points..."

"A handicap now... well we'll have to see about that. Anyway, a champ doesn't have to grant handicaps—"

They turned south on Sandusky Street and passed the creamery. Bob stopped to peer in the window. "Let's have an ice cream cone."

When they came out, cones in hand he said, "want to go to the cemetery and watch for birds?"

"Okay by me."

Usually, they walked down Liberty Street a few blocks and through a wooded area, then entered the rear gate from London Road. This time, while strolling down Sandusky, they were at the front gate. Licking ice cream requires a casual pace in order to get the full enjoyment, and inside the grounds they found themselves up to old tricks, like looking at the names on tombstones and searching for the oldest dates of demise. Off to the right was the partial remains of an old wooden fence bordering the grave-site area, and then beyond, to the rear, the woods and lush foliage where the trees were already beginning to change colors where evening light filtered through like a solemn and vanishing sunburst.

The day had been a bright warm day and they could see the birds, hear their song, and they watched them flit around from place to place.

Taking her hand they stepped easily to the unbordered woodsy area at the rear, quietly and hopefully to get just a little closer and so as not to alarm the creatures. She looked up to him with eyes ready to be kissed, a speck of ice cream still on her lip. "Oh," she tittered, and wiped it away.

"Look there, Mary," he said in a low voice, "a meadowlark, they live in the grassy fields and meadows. Can you hear its tuneful whistle—? They're one of the first birds of spring, but not a true lark. They belong to the family of blackbirds and orioles. They're about the size of a robin, but with a little heavier bodies," he whispered. "You can often hear their song while they're in flight. . . and sometimes you can hear the skylark's song when it is completely out of sight—high up in the sky. One of Shakespeare's famous songs goes:

"Hark! hark!—the Lark at Heaven's Gate Sings—"

They listened and watched quietly for awhile, then walked on.

"What's the rest of the poem?" she asked, in a soft voice.

He said nothing, but listened. . . then stepped easily into the thick green foliage, watching with ears alert, listening. . .

"Do you hear that. . . that weak, shrill sound?" he whispered. He had stepped ahead and now, he reached back for her hand, easing her closer to him. . . "many times, on the farm we. . . George and I heard the sound, but could not see them." He eased her in front of him and stood close behind until pressing his body against hers with one hand on her waist, pointing slowly with the other. . . "They're a tiny bird, sometimes only four inches long—build their nests high in the treetops. They dart around constantly, always singing their musical song. There is another one, see?" He drew her closer, pointed, and with his lips in her hair. "There are yellow throated vireos, and in the tropic's they're called greenlets, because of the greenish color, but. . . this one, see it there, this one must be a yellow throated vireo—you can tell because it resembles a canary—and from the way he's carrying on, he must be serenading a winsome female nearby. There, a little above him, almost hidden—not so brightly colored though." He was even more aware of her closeness now and could smell her clean soft hair and his mouth was so close to her ear—she smelled clean and fresh like outdoors and kitchen baking; he thought he could almost taste her flesh and wanted to. "It sings a conversational song and repeats the notes, as if it were talking to a congregation. . . Sometimes it's called the *preacher bird*, because its song seems to relate a message." He felt her tremble and go slack then; her nubile body leaned against his own so that he drew her closer as they stood quietly absorbing the musical bird-sounds, caught in the sway of their own passions.

"Is that what you are," she said at last, "a *preacher bird?*"

Turning her around, their eyes met, then they embraced tightly, kissed gently, then he released her backwards a little as if straining to withhold himself. She looked into him; a vulnerable look more than he had ever seen before, and there was something very fragile and wanton in her face also; womanhood yielding to forbidden passion, emotions overwhelmed, an irresistible weakness in her touch. They stood silent that way for a time, eyes and body revealing all their words failed to express. There were no words, no promises, no commitments. Both were eager to accept natures gift when he settled her gently there on to a soft bed of lush foliage.

When at last they rose to put themselves back together a certain shyness came over them so that they turned away. For that time there seemed a great space of forbidden silence. Even the birds seemed silent. The sun was already setting when they walked away, aimlessly, hand in hand, quietly and alone in their closeness.

"What was the rest of it?" she said.

"Rest of what?" he asked, working desperately to sort out the emotions at odds inside himself.

"The poem. . . about the Lark, how does it go? Hark, hark, the Lark at heavens gate sings. . . "

"Another time, I'll tell you another time," he replied at last.

On Sunday morning, snuggled tightly in her bed, she lay

there, awakening slowly. She glowed with a happy smile and then. . . she was aware of the sounds of the carillons playing. Early morning light wakened the soft colors of her chamber, while through the partially opened window the bells chimed from the tower at Styvesant Hall. Every morning they played, yet this morning they seemed to hold a very special significance.

Rising slowly to sit on the edge of her bed, she stretched, then standing, she stretched again. She was wearing a white cotton gown with small floral prints that she only recently made herself. As she twisted and yawned her gown pulled well above her knees. Gliding smoothly to the window, she opened the window all the way and leaned out to luxuriate in the soft sunlight—she reached outward as if to gather in the enchanting bell sounds. Through the treetops she could see part of the bell tower.

The *carillons*, she thought, the call to worship and still the sounds continued. . . floating in and among the leaves, dancing softly and gently. What a morning of joy, she thought, and listened. . . watching as the life of early morning arose and the sounds continued, gently. . . to permeate the atmosphere as far as she could see. The sounds even seemed to ooze from the very old stones of the elegant college buildings partially visible through the treetops and across the dividing park grounds.

Still leaning out of the window, she stretched again, running fingers through mussed hair.

Back in the room anxious fingers explored her body and guided her hands over her breast, and down her sides slowly, pausing sensuously over her thighs and buttocks. Her feelings seemed at odds. Touching herself again with new sensations, and then scratching a little, she moved to stand in front of the mirror. She folded her arms and smiled a sensuous smile at herself, wondering who she was, at the same time dragging her fingernails across her arms. Then for an instant. . . she scratched, imperceptibly at first. . . then at her waist, suddenly startled, she dug fiercely at her buttocks and thighs.

The mirror revealed red stinging welts on her arms and raising her gown she glared as still more of the red monster splotches appeared.

She put her hands inside her panties first, then lowered them to inspect the extent of reddened splotches. Turning sideways, she saw what looked like a hand-print in red and scratched; immediately it worsened. Raising her gown to reveal breasts. She stood there paralyzed and shocked, witnessing an evil attack her whole body.

"*Mother!*" she cried out hysterically, "*Mother!*" then racing to the door, she opened it and yelled again, "*Mother*," come here, hurry—please."

Edith rushed to the stairs, but not before a pan clanged to the floor where she left it.

"Child. . . what is the matter?" she said, upon entering the room, puzzled and searching for signs of a catastrophe.

In tears and silence Mary offered her hands and arms as evidence, as she stood trembling and horrified.

"What is it?" Edith insisted, as she came closer for examination. "What happened, child? Where did you. . ."

Mary dropped her hands to raise the garment slowly and indicated modestly to her thighs and legs.

Edith raised the gown further to consider the evidence.

"God's punishing me!" Mary said, pathetically, fingers tensed, not knowing where to scratch next.

"God does not punish this way child," Edith declared, thoughtfully. "This is something you've done to yourself. . . where have you been? What did you eat?" she asked with her eyes wide, searching for some clue. "I think it must be some kind of rash, poison ivy—or sumac maybe. Where did you get it?" she demanded, yet not sure she was ready to deal with her innermost suspicions.

"Maybe. . . the cemetery. . . we walked there, to watch the birds. . . and I had to go to the bathroom, the bushes maybe," Mary said, embarrassed.

"The bathroom—your whole body?" For a timeless interval the mother stood there, her eyes fixed on what appeared to be a reddish hand-print. "Well come. . . we'll bathe you in Epson salt water, Lordy, I hope that will help the itching. I'll send Joe to Doctor Leiberman's to see if he can come."

"I don't want anybody to see me like this. . . what will I do—church and school and I just can't let anyone see me this way."

In his usually cheerful mood, Bob bounded up the back steps and carefully opened the screen door often abused by Joe. He had been humming and whistling a medley of tunes as he greeted Edith warmly. Placing the empty basket with it's red and white checked cloth in the corner where it usually sat when not in use, he proceeded to empty his pockets of change and odd bills on the table.

Edith was always glad to see him, and often they chatted while he had a glass of milk or some cocoa and ate breakfast. Other times he had left early with the large basket of fresh pastries and didn't return until after afternoon classes, always with an empty basket. "Is Mary getting ready for church?" he asked.

"She isn't going today," she said, guardedly.

"Why not?"

"She doesn't feel good."

"Doesn't feel good?" he asked, remembering how cheerful she had been when they had walked home, and had parted after sitting on the front swing for while before bedtime, even then he had wanted her again. Edith had been resting in the leather chair with her feet on the otterman. And they had disturbed her only to say goodnight.

"What's the matter. . . is there something wrong?" he asked, suddenly sensing her apparent detachment.

"Yes, but she doesn't want to see anyone."

"But why? What's wrong? What happened?"

Edith said nothing.

Launching himself up the stairs three steps at a time he knocked at her door; "Mary," he called, anxiously.

"Who is it?"

"What's wrong?"

"Go away. . ."

"I have to talk to you. . ."

"I don't want to talk to anyone."

"Please. . . you must. . . if you don't, I'll come in anyway," he threatened and waited until he heard footsteps coming.

The door opened a little, and her sad face looked at him.

"What happened? Did I do something wrong?"

She opened the door a few inches more to show a hand, then an arm.

He studied them, then looked at her neck and there was scattered splotches. "What is it?" he asked.

"The cemetery... maybe... poison ivy."

"Oh my God!" he exclaimed, inclining his head with his expression betraying a lighted notion. "Oh God forgive me, of course... poison ivy. I'm sorry... Mary please," he pleaded. "It's my fault, I should have known," he said, as he envisioned the bed of shiny green leaves. "Oh Mary, I'm so sorry—I didn't think..." he wanted to hold her and somehow wish it away, but felt guilty and helpless.

"Where else?" he asked, tenderly, directing his eyes to her breast.

She nodded yes.

"And your body?"

She nodded yes.

"Your legs?"

"Yes." she sighed.

"And your—?"

In the process the door had eased open further. His gaze fixed on her standing there poised in the cotton gown with the light streaming through from behind.

"And your, that too?"

"Yes, everything."

He looked pathetically guilty and hated his complete helplessness.

"I don't know what happened, I've never been allergic to it before—are you?"

"No, I guess not. I've been in it, but I have never gotten it."

A full week had passed before Mary left her room while anyone else was present in the house except Edith; all because of those horrid purple splotches from the medicine Doctor Leiberman insisted she must use.

On one occasion Ardith and Dorothy visited her bringing news from school and lessons. In her room, they sat together ceremoniously as if in a ritual while she swore them to strict secrecy about her affliction and the circumstances surrounding it.

Bob was busy too, digging into his studies with a new resolve. He seemed possessed of a guilt born from betrayal of a trust—and he wanted or needed to repay the debt somehow. Edith was unusually solemn and the hurt bore down on her shoulders like a burden, but she spoke no more of the incident.

On Thursday afternoon he went to Columbus and upon his return he explained to Mary through her slightly opened door, that he had a short but amiable conversation with Ross and had spoken with her uncle Jess again.

He told her that their program proposal at W A I U had been accepted with enthusiasm, and after talking with Ron, he wanted them to hurry back as soon as possible. Bob had continued to explain, that he had told Ron that she, Mary, had stumbled into some poison ivy and her hands were covered with a red rash. "Just hands?" Mary had managed to sound somewhat amused; a sign that her spirits were returning to normal.

Bob had gone on to explain that calls had come in requesting them for more performances, even inquiring of their availabilities to other stations; some for private clubs and schools. The pay he had said was small, but it could be just the beginning; leading to bigger opportunities. If only he had dependable transportation, maybe he could work on the Franklin again.

Day by day, little by little she had escaped her self imposed exile as a new eager vitality filled her mind and body. She sat each day by the window and watched it rain cold drops and counted the leaves one at a time. It had been almost three weeks now. Most of the dreadful purple splotches that had replaced the itching red rash had dried and gone away. On a few nice days recently, she had even ventured outside to scamper about among the fallen leaves with a rare childish abandon—the Mary of old was back to normal again.

By Thursday she decided it was time to return to school.

Soon they resumed walking together again, kicking at fallen leaves, and holding hands as in weeks past. Always they steered a course away from the cemetery. Neither knew if it was a conscious decision or not, nor did they mention it again.

After church the following Sunday they walked across town, and turning East on Central Avenue, they soon stopped on a bridge and tossed pebbles into the water below. Facing Mingo Park and a widening of the Olentangy River that formed a small lake at it's banks they joked about a family and their young children at play while nearby the father fished. They decided to go on to Lake Street and then to Greenwood Lake where they could wander through the woods along Greenwood Creek.

At the gate, they pause to look around briefly and when certain no one was watching, they laughed childishly while Bob pried it apart so she could squeeze through. Inside, they trotted down the pathway toward the sound of babbling waters.

Later they wandered aimlessly beside the meandering stream of crystal clear rushing water as it broke over time worn rocks and made hushing sounds fed by the roaring sounds of a waterfall a little farther on. A silent and ominous mist formed at it's base. Across the waters and visible through the barren trees stood the remains of an ancient looking dilapidated log cabin, long since abandoned.

Standing there quiet and holding hands, they listened to the woodsy sounds.

"Someone must have lived here years ago. I wonder who they were and when, and what it was like?" He spoke softly in a whisper. "Let's make a vow—we'll place our hands together in the cool waters, and you repeat after me. . ."

"Okay," she agreed.

"As we join hands together in these sacred pools, and under God, so do we also join hearts and vow to love each other forever and ever, and forsaking all others till the end of time. . ." He paused for a moment while sunlight broke across her face and the old fragile vulnerability returned—eyes that were starkly sexual and missed nothing, but offered everything. "Now we'll say it again together."

After repeating the vow, they walked in the woods hand-in-hand, watching an occasional leaf flutter to the ground as they kicked through the heavy ground-cover already collected beneath their feet. He picked up a very special russet colored maple leaf, large in size and handed it to her.

*In the pitch blackness of night at lover's lane they sat alone in the Franklin, where just four days ago they had watched a man and his family play, tossing pebbles from that very same bridge. In the distance they could see the belltower of Saint Mary's church through heavy drifting clouds. Occasional lights from the distant shore reflected across the dark water and a dim glow appeared from scattered dwellings on opposite hills.

Bob recalled the events of the week briefly. . . on Tuesday afternoon and again on Thursday they had left school and hurried to catch the Interurban to Columbus for their performances at WAIU—a hasty pace for a busy week.

The opportunities to perform at other locations had motivated him to try working one more time on the Franklin.

As they sat quietly together in the front seat, huddled close, her face nestled in the nape of his neck; he kissed her hand and drew her close.

They laughed about the front seat being such a frustrating place, what with a shifting lever, and the pervasive steering wheel, and the dashboard.

Together they eased her body onto his lap slipping her dress over her head while he fumbled with her bra. Sitting face to face as he pulled her close. He put a blanket around her back to help warm her from the cold as they cuddled.

"Oh no. . . !" she cried, in sudden alarm. "Behind us, another car." Briefly, she watched the headlights filter through the steam covered rear window.

He strained to look into the rear view mirror, but Mary's head was in the way.

"He has a spotlight," she gasped helplessly as a light-flash lit up the interior. "It's Charley Van Houser—oh no, he's a friend of Pop's. . . and he knows Mom, what can we do? I can't let him find me this way. Pops warned me *never* to come here to lover's lane."

Immediately, his hands clinched her buttocks. Without reservation he tossed her over his shoulder into the back. "Here's the blanket, hide on the floor and cover up," he said, in a frustrated voice, trying desperately to get himself together.

"My dress," she squeaked.

"Here, cover up."

A man in a uniform with a shinny badge pinned to his coat flashed his flashlight in Bob's face.

"Roll down your window," he motioned.

Lowering the fogged window, Bob raise a hand to shield his eyes from the brightness.

"What's your name?" demanded the voice in a definite tone of authority.

"Robert Marshall."

"Do you have any identification?"

"Yes," he said, reaching for his wallet.

"Vermont huh?" said the officer. "—college student?"

"Yes, at Wesleyan."

"What are you doing out here?" he demanded, flashing his light around, searching the interior for some hidden clue.

"It's peaceful, and I like to sit here alone, and watch the lights reflect on the water."

"Alone?"

"Yes," he lied.

"We don't like to see anyone hanging around here very long at night. So you better move along," he said, sweeping his light around the interior one last time.

"It's safe now," Bob called back, as he turned to witness a curious peek-a-boo face over the seatback with a blanket draped over its head.

"That was close," she sighed.

He nodded, in visible frustration.

She climbed back into the front seat and he smiled a little at her as they sat quietly spaced apart for a moment. She was dressed again, but had left the blanket in the back.

"How did you do that?" he asked.

"Do what?"

"Get dressed so fast?" he smiled a wan little smile. Then turned the key and with his foot pushed down on the starter. It ground away. . . but nothing happened.

"Maybe it's flooded," she said in a small voice, as she watched him pull a thing she guessed to be the choke.

"We could smell it, if it is. . . flooded," he said exasperation creeping in his voice. "I've changed everything else or at least worked on it; the gas pump, the carburetor. That's probably it. Or, maybe the gas line. Maybe it just wants to die in peace."

Finally, grinding to a halt again, it found silence and rest.

"Now the battery's dead," he said solemnly, "peace at last."

He opened the door and reached for her hand as she slid across the seat.

With hands on hips, he stood there momentarily starring at the impotent object he had had so much hope for.

Mary wondered about his temperament. She had never heard him raise his voice except to sing. Sensing the tension build she waited nearby with arms folded tightly, braced against the cold night air. If only she had thought to bring a coat or sweater.

In a final gesture he kicked the rear tire once, then said, "I guess we'll have to walk."

A dozen steps later, he stopped to look skyward and tested the first warning droplets of rain. He turned to find Mary huddled beside him, arms crossed, body shivering in the cold night air.

"Wait here," he said a little harsher than he had intended, then hurrying back to the silent hulk and opening the door he removed the blanket, shook it out, then hurried back to wrap it around her shoulders. He held her tightly there while rubbing her back to warm her a bit.

They hurried along Lincoln Avenue with heads and bodies bent as the rain poured down in torrents, hesitating only to cross at Sandusky Street. The streets were bare of civilization as a single automobile drove by, splashing as it hurried on it's way. Together they ran, at the same time searching for some shelter until they finally stepped into a doorway next to a shop. Waiting together in the shadowed doorway she opened the woolen blanket and moved close to wrap it around him so they could huddle together.

She stretched on tip-toes, kissed and clutched him tightly for long moments, still it poured and lights glistened. . . and they were alone.

"I need you—I want to be alone with you, in a bed. . . and I want to smell you and taste you. . . and reach deep inside—" he spoke softly into her ear, while nuzzling her wet hair.

"I know," she said, softly, trembling. "I know. . . and I want you to do anything you want with me—anything. . ." And still it poured down buckets until they made a break, turning west on Williams Street and after a few blocks they hurried up the steps at 16 Liberty Street.

Then they stopped, each exhaling a great sigh. Shelter at last. Looking back and pausing for deep breaths, he removed the soaked blanket and studied her as moist droplets trickled down her face from stringy soaked hair.

"Tomorrow," he said; "we can go to Columbus for a picture

show, there's a little hotel, the Chittenden, we could go there after..."

She watched his face as the words came slowly, with sincere effort—words that came with a burden of difficulty, and yet heavy with pent-up emotion. "There's a dance contest that afternoon in Columbus—I could tell Mom that's where we're going—and wear the dress she just finished—we'd miss the five o'clock Interurban back."

He nodded slightly, holding her eyes, then kissing her hands and lips gently.

They shook off what they could of the wetness before entering.

"Lordy, sakes alive," Edith exclaimed, her voice pained with alarm. "What on earth happened to you two?"

"The Franklin quit... and we had to run all the way home," Mary said.

"Well, gracious sakes, let me get some towels for you to dry off with. And I'll fix some hot tea and honey with a little lemon—a little something to ward off the chill. Don't want you two catching a death of cold. Not good weather to be out and about in you know..."

Five thirty in the afternoon was more like night that day when they left the theater and walked towards Chittenden Avenue to the hotel a couple blocks away. Pulling their coats tightly around them to protect against the chilly damp air, they went carefully, not certain if they should let known their pressing eagerness, and yet they seemed guarded too.

As planned they had caught the noon Interurban in Delaware and had gone to the matinee double feature with Charlie Chaplin and Buster Keaton instead of the dance. It had sprinkled from time to time, but nothing heavy yet.

Mary had explained that they were lucky, because every second Saturday and Sunday are days off for Ross and Jess.

Bob tugged her to a halt in front of a little cafe. They decided to go in.

It was small inside, Bob counted only six tables, and quaintly Italian with pictures on the wall of Milan and Roma and some old style sailboats, probably of Venice, he wondered. Candles on each of the tables provided most of the light. It was cozy and ever so inviting so they sat down by a window with red and black curtains and wondered also what it would be like to take her to those places in the pictures, just the two of them alone and together.

A little man with a dark complexion approached wiping his hands on a soiled apron and greeted them in his charming Italian accent. He flashed a polite smile and offered a one page hand written menu.

"How do you like'a spaghetti?" he asked.

"That sounds good to me," Mary nodded.

"Two spaghetti and meatballs. . . and salads, yes two salads," he said, accepting her nod. "And wine, do you have a good Vino?" Bob asked.

"Yes-a, we hava very good-a white, and a red-a, the best. . ." He seemed to hesitate for a moment, then shrugged it away with a discerning smile.

Bob showed two fingers.

The waiter turned and hurried away, only to return quickly carrying two glasses on a tray.

Mary blinked in surprise then leaned over to whisper behind a cupped hand: "isn't wine illegal?"

"Not to the Italians—they and the French are the only ones who have wine. I heard about this place from a student friend. He could have refused us but he didn't. He'll bring us two glasses and somewhere beyond the kitchen there is a mystery keg. I'll have to go and get it. They can't sell it, but it will be included in the cost of the meal. The Italians and French consider it food—a custom from their old country."

"Oh," she uttered, as if weighing the laws of prohibition against the desire to accept wine as food. . .

Bob winked and casually went in search of the mystery keg.

"I hope you like it," Bob said when he had returned.

"I don't know, I've never tasted it before." She sipped and made a funny face.

"You don't have to drink it if you don't. . ."

She sipped again, a dainty sip, as if taking time to fully consider the bouquet and held the glass there. . .

"I rarely drink it, but once acquired a taste for it in the past. And I thought this should be a special occasion," he said, releasing her hand and lifting his glass in a silent toast.

"It goes well with the music." He gestured to the victrola

where the little man had placed a record playing a favorite, no doubt from his home in Italy.

They glanced around, taking in the coziness of the little place and the empty tables, studied the pictures and laughed about some scenes in the movie. Soon the waiter came scurrying back with two giant plates they had ordered minutes ago.

Again he hurried off, only to return with salads and some dressing in a small bottle and another container of grated cheese and a basket of steaming French bread.

Both looked on in amazement. "This is enough food for a whole week!"

"I think the Italian's claim it is their bread really, and of course the French claim the same," Bob mused. "No matter who claimed it, it's still my favorite, crumbs and all."

The waiter bowed easily, then asked if they desired anything else. When a bell jingled above the door. A man and woman with two small children entered and were promptly greeted in their native tongue. Obviously they knew each other well and must have been regular customers and once seated the man went off with glasses toward the kitchen.

Mary took another sip and giggled. "It tickles," she declared, rubbing her nose.

The hotel room proved to be a small cramped affair with a single bed, a picture, a chair and a dresser with a mirror hanging crookedly. And in the corner, a wash basin. There was a single window facing the front street where curtains hung neglected. The manager had told him this was the last room and the bathroom was just a couple doors down the hallway.

He felt embarrassed, and cheap. "It should be better," he said, lamely.

"It's okay," she managed to say, trying desperately to hide her disappointment.

Across the room he felt the radiator for heat. "Colf as stone," he muttered, then he moved to open the window, hoping a little fresh air could relieve the stuffiness.

She went to stand by his side and they watched and listened to the raindrops falling slowly at first, then increasing so they made a tinkling and humming rhythm. There was no radio, but he looked at her and wondered who could ask for more.

"Well. . . at least we don't have to worry about poison ivy," she declared with a demure smile.

Swooping her up with his arms, she held on around his neck as he lifted her from the floor while they swung round and round until falling on the bed, embracing and eager.

Later he was lying on his back with arm around her as she snuggled close to his side with her head on his chest, they were breathing easy, huddled in the covers and listening to the sound of rain and wind. Sometimes it blew in the window, whipping the curtain about wildly, still it was cozy and they were together, and that's all that counted.

"Tell me the rest of the poem," she pleaded. She had asked him many times since the cemetery, but always he had put her off till another day.

"What poem?" he teased.

"You know the one. . . about the *Lark at Heaven's gate?*"

"Someday."

"I want to hear it now."

He smiled wryly, but said nothing.

"You don't know it, do you?" she teased.

He hesitated. . . feigning sleep and a snoring sound.

"Now. . . "

"Hark! Hark! the lark at Heaven's gate sings. . .
   And Phoebes' gins arise,
He steeds to water at those springs
   On chaliced flowers that lies;
And winking Mary-buds begin
   to ope their golden eyes
with everything that pretty is,
   My lady sweet, arise!
     Arise, arise!"

He finished the last line, glad he had taken the time, at last to look it up just two days ago in the library and commit it to memory.

"It's beautiful," she said, with easy surprise. "Tell me another one, with *pathos*, yes something with *pathos*."

"Tomorrow," he said, smugly, again faking sleep and a snoring sound; eyes closed—a twisted curl on his lips.

"Now!" she demanded, jumping up to sit on top of him in a

position of superiority. The covers fell away as dim lights reflected in to outline her body and betray a teasing expression. "Now! or I'll keep you awake all night. *arise, arise,* or I'll keep you up all night."

"Is that a threat... or a promise?"

You'll find out if you don't tell me something... romantic."

He watched, as her innocence changed to slow erotic movements; the young girl was no more. Then he spoke:

> "Half a league, half a league,
> half a league onward
> All in the Valley of death
> Rode the Six Hundred.
> 'Forward the light brigade!
> Charge for the guns!' he said.
> into the Valley of death
> Rode the Six Hundred."

He paused to see her admiring look, and body still poised and waiting... then continued,

> "Forward the Light Brigade!
> was there a man dismayed
> not tho a soldier knew
> Some had blundered."

Again he paused to see her awaiting his every word, then changing his voice to a deeper inflection, he went on to finish,

> "When can their glory fade?
> O the wild charge they made
> All the world wondered.
> Honor the charge they made!
> Honor the Light Brigade.
> Noble Six Hundred..."

"That's not romantic," she said, tickling his ribs guilefully.

"But it does have pathos."

"But *not* romantic," she tickled his ribs again, this time as though in torture, then added, "something romantic, now... or else."

"Tomorrow... I promise," acting sleepy again.

"Now... or no sleep!"

Watching her eyes dance with delight, he started again, but slowly...

> "How do I love thee,
> Let me count the ways.

> I love thee to the depth and breath and height
> My soul can reach, when feeling out of sight."

Again he paused, waiting for her reaction, and satisfied with her surprise he resumed his act.

> "I love thee to the level of every day's
> most quiet need, by sun and candlelight.
> I love thee with a passion put to use,"
> "And if God choose,
> I shall but love thee better after death. . . "

Both were still for a time, as though caught up in the rapture of their own emotions.

"Now, that was romantic," she whispered.

". . . And profound?"

"And it has pathos," she sighed.

"And now it's my turn," he threatened.

"Your turn; for what?"

"To keep you awake all night," he glowed, forcing her body over and spinning himself on top of her. . .

"You wouldn't," she refrained, shrinking into the pillow, "you couldn't. . . could you?"

"You'll see. . . "

Bodies stirred, still embraced and tangled, as they awoke. The rain had slowed to steady drizzle and the lights of night were gone. It was still morning though darkened by overcast.

Both peeked out, squinted at each other, pulled the covers over their heads and rolled about delirious while teasing about the night past. They made love again and lay close.

When at last they pulled themselves loose from the tangle of limbs he decided to check the hall, and with a threadbare towel-wrap explored first, then both stole away to the bathroom, just two doors from their own. Locking themselves in they bathed together for the first time.

When they were done he peeked through the door to consider the empty hallway and quickly the two darted back to their waiting room.

He had closed the window and they stood together by the old iron radiator, hesitant and tentative.

Somehow, new signals reached them and together they dove back into the bed to wriggle beneath the covers, only to play at love one more time.

Finally, deserting the covers again, they scanned the empty hallway, quickly bathed, returned to their room and dressed.

The rain had stopped, and now starved, their first priority was breakfast.

As rainy seasons come and go this one started no different than those of the past. Getting from one place to another depended on age old instincts—and a matter of timing disguised as luck. It was noon already, and Edith would be home from church. They wondered what she would say.

Though everything was neat in her kitchen, still she was nervously busy arranging things. She said nothing, yet her expression and demeanor demanded an explanation.

"We missed the five o'clock. . . " Mary offered. It wasn't a lie.

"And it started raining—heavy," Bob broke in, "and we. . ."

"We were standing in this doorway. . . and it just kept on raining and we were next to this hotel. . . so we had to stay there," Mary said, as if starting a confession.

Edith studied her, then shifted to face Bob also. The hurt shown plainly in her expression. She went on, her voice obvious in its disapproval. "You could have stayed at your aunt Ivalou's house in Columbus. She couldn't have been that far. . . You missed church."

"We started home as soon as the rain allowed this morning, and we stopped for breakfast," Mary said.

※※※※※

The Franklin was gone. He watched sadly as the last chance for independent transportation had been towed away for junk.

After their last afternoon class they met and walked to the station where Mary was to visit her dad, while Bob went on to meet the man with the tow truck.

She waited inside the interurban station as agreed until he returned in a cloud of gloom. He failed to catch the sheepish grin she was wearing as a hint of surprise.

It was cool even though the sun was out, and they walked on the sunny side of Sandusky Street.

"Eight dollars for the Franklin," he said, his spirit filled with remorse. "That's all it was worth, so ironic, all that work to make it, all that material, steel and rubber and glass, and now it's an impotent heap... eight dollars for the scrap metal. Of course I'll split it with Bill."

Mary handed him an envelope.

"What's this?" he asked, hesitatingly.

"Open it..." she urged, her voice inpatient.

"Where did you get this?" he asked, counting. "Two, two forty, two sixty... three, three hundred. Where?"

"From Pops," she answered calmly.

"Ross!"

"Yes... I told him about the trouble you were having—and how you arranged all those performances, but we couldn't go because the old Franklin just quit for good. The bank was right there next door and he took me in and made a withdrawal."

"But... I can't accept this," he indicated the envelope. "It wouldn't be right..."

"He said it can be a loan. You can pay it back later." She watched him; the wheels turning—

He hesitated, as if weighing the envelope and its contents, then spoke, mindfully. "Okay... It's a deal, but a loan. I'll tell Ross, when I see him, and thank him too."

They had stopped, and now they started again, with lighter and quicker steps. The sun shone a little warmer.

"Tomorrow; I can start looking for one... why wait for tomorrow? why not today? why not right now? Back on Sandusky, there's a place with a Chevy for sale."

He turned her quickly and they hurried back the way they had come.

Halloween passed them by with hardly a notice and Thanksgiving was just four days away as Mary curled snugly beneath the warm covers. She had not heard the Carillons this morning cause the window was closed tightly, and she was encased in her quilted cocoon against the winter cold. Outside white flakes floated in lazy flutters groundward. It had snowed off and on for three, maybe four days. She didn't care to remember how many. It seemed, after the first day somehow the charm and beauty had worn its welcome.

Wriggling beneath the covers and reaching out with one arm, she pulled her robe in with her to warm it before putting it on. Finally, she emerged like any critter from hibernation.

She darted to the window for a quick look, shivered and pulled the robe tighter about her body. A familiar odor reached her nostrils, wafting from the downstairs kitchen— *donuts!*

"OH NO!" she wailed. Covering her mouth, she ran to the door, the hallway and bathroom.

Standing in front of the mirror, she stared pale and languid and spoke to herself, aloud. "Oh my God, you look as bad as you feel." She had rinsed her mouth a dozen times it seemed, washed her face and brushed at her hair. It proved a futile effort—then the bed beckoned.

Back in her room, she wondered how she could make it downstairs; those awful donuts. The very thought made her nauseous again. Quickly, opening the window, she stuck her head out into the cold fresh air.

White snow crunched beneath her feet as she hurried along as though picking her way through falling flakes.

She had dressed and left the house without eating, explaining to her mother that she was late and had to meet with Ardith and Dorothy.

What would Bob think, and say? How would he react, if indeed her inner most suspicions were true?

With another automobile, their last two weeks had been busy and happy ones with several afternoon trips to perform at nearby localities, and now she felt the grip of a new anxiety.

In the distance she saw Ardith and Dorothy and called for them to wait. Steam gusts ushered from her mouth and nostrils; when she caught up she hesitated, not sure where to begin.

In a despairing voice she started, *"remember. . ."* and then she thought to herself how Ardith had told them; she felt sick in the mornings and had left home early without eating, and that her period was late and she had gone to her sister who was married, and asked for help. She told her sister everything and they were sure she was pregnant.

She tried again, her breathing easier this time; "remember when you told us about going to your sister?" she hesitated. . .

"When you got sick. . . and about your period. Well, I think it's happened to me too," she said quickly, as though spitting it out; then a tear followed.

"What—! Do you mean you're pregnant?" Dorothy choked, lamely; a little louder than she had expected.

Mary nodded and shushed her.

"How do you know for sure?" Dorothy asked in a low voice at the same instant casting a cautious glance to Ardith.

"I'm not sure," she cried. All three stood huddled in a cloud of breathing steam, staring at each other, searching for answers.

"I mean. . . I don't for sure, but my period. . . it's almost two weeks late, and this morning I threw up and. . . " Her voice trailed off, recalling how Ardith said she left home early because of food, and that the fresh air helped.

"What are you going to do?" Ardith asked, her voice weak and sympathetic.

"I don't know. . . I mean, I'm not sure. . . what to do next?" She spoke as though each of the words themselves weighed heavily and she gripped her stomach as the sudden recurring thought of donuts thrust her into renewed throes of nausea.

They stood quiet and teary-eyed, seemingly oblivious to the falling snow.

Dorothy reached to put her arm around her, then the other, as the three girls stood quiet, then wiped their tears and a forced smile appeared.

"I don't know whether to tell Bob, or what. . ." her voice faded off again as they started to walk, slowly, towards the school, each huddled tightly in their own dilemma.

"I just couldn't tell Mom. . . or Dad," Ardith admitted sadly. "Sis said I should tell Colin first. . . and then. . . he wants to marry me and we love each other. . . but there's his family. . . " She turned away.

"I think I'll tell Mom, and then maybe Bob, but I don't know yet for sure. . . But, I don't know how I can face Pops."

"You'll have to tell somebody," Dorothy concluded.

"Sis said I could go away. . . and then give the baby up for adoption," said Ardith, wiping the tears from her cheeks.

"I couldn't do that," Mary winced; "I could never give it away."

"Me too," Ardith declared, rather weakly.

"Well anyway, there's the bell, and we'll have all day to think about it," Dorothy collected them close in a lingering huddle.

He liked to walk anyway, a carefree time, crunching through new fallen snow bristling under bright sunlight. The air was crisp and clear now, yet by tomorrow morning every thing would probably be frozen, altering the scenery in an ever changing cycle.

Even though it was almost three years old, he considered it the same as new. The Chevrolet Tudor Sedan filled him with temptation to drive, anywhere, and new sense of confidence and independence. Still, he left it parked when possible to save gasoline.

He turned the corner at Liberty Street to see Mary coming to meet him. When he stopped before her, she took his hand and leaned close on tip toes to kiss his face. He was always shy about kissing or embracing in public, so his body braced a little, recalling how affection for men was considered a private affair.

"You look sweet and happy today," he said.

She blushed and squeezed his hand at the same time turned to walk beside him. "I have something to tell you," she said seriously, stopping then to search his face, seeking an answer without asking the question.

"Sooo, what's the question?"

Still she hesitated. . . "I think I'm pregnant," she said finally, like spilling it out all at once.

"Oh," he stalled, taking a tentative last step—he stopped there. It was a sort of stutter-step, and his mouth gaped open, like he had been struck. "Oh—" is all that came out, and it just hung there in a gasp with difficulty finding sound.

Both were quiet then, resuming uneasy steps—then a pause.

"So. . . " he said soberly, "I guess you'll just have to marry me."

"Are you serious? Really, do you mean it? You would do it just for the baby. . . you really want to?"

Lifting her in his arms, he swung her around happily. "Sure, I love you, don't you know, or haven't you noticed lately."

"Oh I love you too," she sang out, holding tightly, at the same time kissing him unceasingly.

"We're in public," he cautioned, settling her down gently, "you don't want to make a spectacle, do you?"

"Yes—"

Both stood still then as they returned to the reality of their situation. Bob thought of Ross. How would he take it? Edith would be hurt, and show it. Joe might not even understand. As for Ross; now that could prove a sticky problem; he would cross that bridge when the time came. But, Edith would be the toughest to swallow—like betraying a trust. Already he felt the lump swelling in his throat.

"What do we do next?" she asked.

"Tell Edith—I suppose. It won't be easy"

"We can ask her what to do."

"Yes, I guess you're right."

Edith was alone in the kitchen when they entered.

Bob went to her first, but Mary stepped in front of him.

"Mom— we have something to tell you." Mary spoke calmly, and yet with determination to present her thoughts in proper order.

"What is it?"

"We want to get married." Then with difficulty she added: "I think I'm pregnant."

A wounded expression soon replaced one that had started with joy as she regarded them closely for a long period. She also chose careful words; "I'm happy for you—so happy..." Then she added, "you had better see Doctor Liebermann. *You too, Robert.*"

Doctor Liebermann said it was really too early to tell for sure, but felt she probably was pregnant from what she had told him. In the waiting room Bob waited with a case of the jitters until she returned with the news.

In his mind Bob recalled Edith's words as they had left for the doctor's office, "I'm so happy for you." She had repeated it several times as if searching for other words and unable to find them. She had followed them to the door, wiping the tears from her eyes; "and, Lord knows we all wish you so much happiness."

For Robert Marshall the seriousness of their situation settled heavily, also the commitment he had not considered fully until this moment.

"What do we do now?" Mary asked in a small voice.

He said nothing as they trod cautiously along the path. In his own mind he was asking the same question.

"I figure we can drive to Newport. . . Kentucky, maybe day after tomorrow. It'll be quicker, and I hear you don't have to wait for blood tests. Then we'll stay one night in Cincinnati before heading home. . . "

"A one night honeymoon?" she asked.

He opened the door, lifted her in his arms, ceremoniously and carried her inside to let her body fall easily to the large bed. Glancing around, he noted the high ceilings above the double French doors that opened to the balcony, opened it to consider the view, crossed the room to a dresser to see if he could tune in W A I U on the dial.

Mary stood beside the French doors looking through at the city lights and the Ohio River, as more lights flicked on in the distance, then the bridge lit up like Christmas. She turned from the doors, and he from the radio. Both waited. . . each looking to the other for hidden signs, their expression betrayed what words could not describe; what now? She drifted over to stand by his side while they looked over the tops of other buildings and to the river below. For long moments he seemed lost in thought.

"Are you sorry," she asked.

"About what?"

"Oh, you know—getting married? like you had to?"

To escape the crisp, biting air he drew her inside and closed the door. "How could I be sorry, I have you." Together their eyes scanned the room, it was spacious and nicely decorated with Provincial furnishings, so different from the one in Columbus.

"Look." She cupped his face in her hands to hold his eyes and motioned with a subtle nod; "our own private bathtub." She crooked a finger and steered him in that direction.

For a moment his thoughts returned to the events of the day. They had left early that morning, driving quietly. It had been cold and she sat close, occasionally she had rested her head on his shoulder. The trees on the countryside were barren of leaves and he had noticed scattered patches of snow still on the ground and hills beyond. Dark clouds, like clouds of doubt in his head.

As if the mood demanded something to bring out the feeling

of spring resulted in a rare purchase. She wore the new soft yellow dress with lace collar and ruffles and belted sash Edith had bought only the day before. The color had reminded him of sunshine and she had worn one of those little round hats that seemed the style. She had a different hair-do and a new coat and white stockings. A disquieting concern hovered about her the whole day, and yet the happy glow was there too.

Driving through Cincinnati, he had decided on the hotel they would come back to. They had continued on to Newport, the sister city.

The Justice of the Peace had been a small roundish man with a bald spot on top of his head, and a little patch of wavy hair at the front that twisted in a curl like a piglets tail. His wife was a petite slender lady with dark hair and possessed a gracious smile.

It had been a smooth efficient ceremony and was over quickly with a simple gold band. By evening, they found themselves back in front of the red brick provincial looking hotel, still wondering how it had all been so easy.

"Are you hungry?" he asked.

"Yes," she answered. It was her eyes that did most of the talking, sometimes with gay amusement—at times with hidden reserve—just now they spoke of eagerness and desire—desire to please, and to let him know that all was right.

"Your hands are cold."

"I know. . . yours are warm."

"Cold. . . and hungry?" his eyes turned slowly to the bathtub, it seemed to beckon.

"Cold. . . and hungry," her eyes followed his.

"First, a hot bath. . . then dinner downstairs." Again without moving his head, his eyes glanced to the bed. . . she nodded in agreement. He felt that smoldering sensation deep inside. She had put it there.

He drew her close and started to undress her. . . very slowly. Beneath the surface there was a giggle starting—perhaps the playfulness of a young girl still lingered there also.

With a mere five days left until Christmas everyone was busy with shopping and decorating, and more shopping. In grand ceremony the tree went up the night before so Mary and Bob could help and see it one last day before leaving for Vermont.

Edith and Mary had been extra busy making candies and cookies and wrapping presents to take along, small things they had shopped for together, a tie, a handkerchief, and a scarf for Bob's mother.

It was Bob's last day at school and they planned to leave early in the morning. Bill was to meet them at the boarding house and together the three would drive to Ann Arbor to pick up George and a friend of his named Martha. Bob had written to George and made the arrangements.

Since the return from their honeymoon night in Cincinnati Bob had moved into her room and daily events whirled by at a maddening pace. He dug into his studies with a renewed determination. Twice a week they had taken afternoon trips to perform on the radio.

Mary decided not to return to high school. Among her friends it would have been applauded as daring and courageous—but school at this juncture served no useful purpose, Beside that, others had tried in the past, arousing moral dilemmas with embarrassing repercussions. It mattered little in the longer haul; she was soon to be a mother and wife of a promising preacher-man. The future was a bright road lit with unlimited potential. Not that she had scribed a plan or outline in stone—but it was there; a vague scenario born of dedication and blind faith. The only problem was that both unwittingly looked into the future through quite different windows.

Bob was out early scraping heavy frost from the windows before leaving. With no heater Bill coiled himself into a blanket in the back seat to catch up on his sleep, while Mary wrapped herself tightly in another and snuggled close to Bob for comfort. He curled one arm around her and drew her closer until she to dozed off intermittently. With any luck they would be in Ann Arbor by mid-day.

"Pops said we would have a white Christmas. He said he could feel it in his bones."

"Looks like his bones are pretty accurate," Bob conceded, "if only it will hold off a bit, for a day or two. . . anyway."

"How are you doing, brother?" Bill asked, popping his head up from the back seat.
"I thought you were asleep?"
"I was."
"I'm doing fine but looks like snow," Bob said, reflectively.
"Hm... almost ten o'clock," Bill said, studying his pocket-watch. He looked around, considered the location. "Looks like you're making good time though. How are you doing Mary?"
"Cold, that's all... I guess," she sat up, pulled the blanket tighter and turned to face him in the back seat... "I was just thinking about something though..." She waited a moment to secure their attention. There was a mischievous scheme brewing inside... "Bob says you are the poet, or that... you're the one in the family who likes to recite poetry."
Bill said, "what kind of stories has he been telling now?"
"Uh-huh—he told me some poems, and he said that you are the family poet, so I think we should each recite a poem."
"You have something in mind...?"
"Sure," she said. " Why not?"
Bill laughed.
"I know a Tennyson," she grinned.
"You never told me you knew any poetry," Bob said.
"I'll recite mine, if you two agree to do one too. It can be anything you choose."
"Okay by me," the brothers agreed.
Mary took a deep breath, exhaled, then started:
   "Sweet and low, sweet and low.
      Wind of the Western Sea
   "Low, low—" she held up her hand sensing Bob wanted to challenge her choice... then continued to the finish:
      "Sleep my pretty little one,
      Sleep my pretty one... sleep."
"You cheated," Bob said. "That was a song."
"Well it's a poem too, she said, sticking out her tongue. "Now it's your turn, so do something romantic."
"Okay, let's see," he said, pausing a few seconds to collect his thoughts.
   "Half a league, half a league," he showed a hand motioning her to wait.
   "Half a league onward,

All in the valley of death..."
With a wink he continued on to the final lines:
"Honor the charge they made!
Honor the Light Brigade,
Nobel Six Hundred!"
"How do you remember all that?"
"Ask Bill." He pointed a thumb over his shoulder. "He's got the real secret."
"Okay, how?" She turned to see he was thinking, gears turning. "It's your turn now."
"See if you recognize this one;
On either side of the river lie
long fields of barley and rye,
that clothe the world and meet the sky;
to many-towered Camelot;"
He paused—and the mental wheels churned on as he continued his recital as though there could be no ending;
"Out upon the wharfs they came,
Knight and burgher, lord and dame,
and round the prow they read her name,
The Lady of Shalott.
Who is this? And what is here?
And in the lighted palace near
died the sound of royal cheer;
And they crossed themselves for fear,
All the knights of Camelot;
But Lancelot mused, a little space;
He said, she has a lovely face;
God in his mercy lend her grace,
The Lady of Shalott."

"How on earth do you remember all that?"
"That's an odd story all by itself," Bill said, still smiling smugly.
Bob smiled too, yet offered no comment.
"Didn't Bob tell you about it?"
"No. What story?" she said, anxiously. "Tell me."
"It was a long time ago, when we were boys... twelve or thirteen I guess, and we made some wooden boats. All five of us, it was Bob's idea... let him tell it."
Bob said: "well, all five of us made these boats and

torpedoes, and we had a game in the horse trough, and we shot the torpedoes, but we weren't supposed to hit each other's boats. Anyway Bill got mad. . . "

"Bill got mad, you mean you got mad first," Bill broke in with a crooked look of amusement.

"Well," Bob said, calmly, "we were both a little excited, and someone thought we were going to fight. . . and. . . "

"Fight, you two?" she looked first to one, then the other, shocked. "But you two get along so well, and you never raise your voices. . . I just can't believe you ever thought about fighting."

"That was a long time ago, we were just kids and didn't know better," Bill chuckled.

"What does this have to do with poems anyway?" she asked.

"I was coming to that. Anyway, somebody ran to get Mom, and she separated us and Bill claimed he won the game and I claimed I won. So she decided to settle it. She said we must both learn a poem. . . of equal lines or stanza's and the one who could recite his first without a mistake would be declared the winner. I chose the *Charge Of The Light Brigade*, and Bill decided on an equal number of lines from *The Lady of Shalott*," Bob hesitated, then added, "in those days, I thought I wanted to be a general or an admiral when I grew up. And that's why I chose the *Charge of The Light Brigade*. The military mentality at work I suppose."

"We only had one book of Tennyson's poems, so we had to work out a system of sharing it," Bill added.

"Who won?"

They both chuckled again and Bill said: "you go ahead and tell her."

"On the second day, I was sure I was ready, and we all got together in the sitting room. I was certain of victory, and I recited first, I struggled, but got through it without a mistake. . . then Bill started, he recited the equal number of lines easily, but instead of stopping he finished the whole 171 lines of *The Lady of Shalott*."

"Then Bill was the winner," Mary considered them, the features and animation. For that instant she could see they were brothers, and yet so different otherwise.

"Not exactly," Bill smiled evenly. "You see Bob argued that we had agreed on 55 lines, and that's all that should count. . . everybody voted, and it was declared a draw."

"And that's how you learned to memorize poetry, interesting, still 171 lines, sure seems like a lot, and in only two days, seems like a lot to me anyway. . . pretty smart Mom too."

Two thirty in the afternoon they arrived at the college in Ann Arbor and it was later than they had hoped for.

With Martha and George, they made a hasty departure.

Bob decided to take the more direct route of side roads north of Lake Erie, through Ontario, Canada and on to Niagara Falls. Soon, it was evening and snowing heavily. They hoped to reach the little town of Marshalltown and had joked about it having been settled by a relative or ancestor.

At Niagara Falls they stretched and sprang loose like animals unleashed from captivity. The sky was clear and bright blue, and a silvery white blanket covered everything, rooftops of buildings and the few motorcars, some covered over like winter burrow mounds with telltale peepholes. Huge gobs of white stuff hung heavily from tree branches and bushes. Bill paused momentarily as if in meditation, and then to make a declaration; "Some say that here, more than any other place on earth, one can see the hand of God at work."

No one could have testified as to who threw the first snowball, but it only served to start a running, shouting free-for-all. Soon, they were racing and sliding and falling on the steps towards the view-point landing that divided the American Falls from the Horseshoe Falls. They used the sloping ground and steps for skating. "Look I'm skiing—no skis," someone shouted. Soon all were doing the same until they were lying breathless and exhausted.

Then they paused for a time to marvel at the great falls with it's steam rising from a wintry cover and the ominous powerful roar. Someone remarked how the old iron bridge spanning the gorge they had crossed seemed strained under the leaden weight of ice and snow, and that it felt an eerie sense as if ready to collapse when they crossed. (Two years later it did). Then a rainbow appeared, sweeping across the falls.

Later, they were driving again along a cleared stretch of

roadway where, at times high banks of snow shielded the snow covered fields of the countryside.
Someone said, "Let's sing something."
"What?" asked another.
"Oh. . . How about a round of, *Row, row, row your boat.*
"Everybody knows that one."
"Mary, you start, then Martha you come in," Bill looked at George. "George, how about jumping in next, then Bob, and I'll finish." Bill pointed to Mary like a conductor, indicating it was her cue;
"Row, row, row your boat,
gently down the stream
merrily, merrily, merrily, merrily,
life is but a dream."
Bill finished with the last chorus. "That's great, now again, and this time faster, increasing the tempo as we go."
"Let's do it again, that's fun." They all joined in until the girls became giddy and others tongue-tied and breathless.
"How many know *Dry Bones*?" asked Bob.
"Oh I've heard that one, how does it go. . . your neck bone connected to your toe bone," Mary said, laughingly.
"Neck-bone connected to your toe-bone, ha, I like to see that."
"Me too."
"I've heard it. . . cute, but I don't know all the words," someone else chuckled.
"Me too," added another and another.
"I'll teach you," Bob said. "When I signal, everyone repeat after me. . . ready?"
"Ezekiel dried dem dry bones," he chanted, and signaled with his fingers to repeat two more times.
"Now hear's the word of the Lord,"
"Ezekiel connected them dry bones,"
He signalled for two more repeats, and. . .
"Now here's tha words of the Lord,
Ya toe bone connect'd to ya. . ."
Bob went on alone with the verse, and as he continued to sing, he dropped his voice a note with each line. And finally, low, low, in the deepest hollow sounds, signaling the others when to join in until they had finished.

"That was fun, let's do it again."

"Yes, let's," cried another.

"Okay only this time I'll join Bob with the verse and you three can sing the chorus," Bill said.

Back on the road, they watched the winter scenery flow by. With the middle of the day upon them and other motorcars passing by with hands waving; soon they were waving back. Before long they were waving gaily to everyone, including those who just ventured out to enjoy the rare burst of sunshine.

Bob had been quiet, thinking deeply, and Mary sensed he was concocting something.

"How many know, *Wi A Hundred Pipers*?" he asked.

"I think I know most of it," Bill said.

"Maybe a little," added George.

Martha and Mary said they hadn't heard it at all.

"Let's try it," he said. "You'll catch on."

"The chorus goes like this;
   Wi' a hun-dred pipers an' ah,an' ah
A, like ahh, long, or aw. . . you do it twice, then back to the chorus,"
   We'll. . . up and an' gie them a blaw, a blaw,
   Wi' a hun-dred pipers an' ah, an' ah.

Emphasis on *hun* and the last *ah*. . . let's see Mary," he turned his head momentarily to the back seat. "And Martha, you two sing two choruses, then George come in on the third. Now on the first chorus you sing legato." He made a motion with his hand and head, mockingly, like Italian. "Sing smooth and evenly, then. . . when George comes in. . . increase the tempo, and then Bill and I will signal and we'll do the verse. . . oh wait, when you come in the second time; sing pianissmo," he said, sounding Italian again, "very softly, so Bill and I can increase gradually to *fortissimo*, you'll see."

"Wait—wait just a minute," Mary pleaded, as she waved again to another motorcar passing by "Let's open all the windows."

"Yes, let's. We'll sound like a motorcar victrola."

As they started, Bob waved his right hand like a conductor, emphasizing the *hun'* and *ah'* he and Bill filled in the rest of the chorus;

   "O it's owre the border ah'-wa', ah'-wa'

It's owre the border ah'-wa', ah'-wa',
We'll—on an' we'll march—to Car-lisle ha'.
wi' its yetts, its cas-tle an', ah', an' ah',
wi' a hun-dred pipers an' ah', an' ah'.
wi'a hun-dred pipers an' ah', an' ah',
We'll up an' gie them a blaw, a blaw,
wi' a hun-red pipers an' ah', an' ah'.

Pianissimo—
Wi' an ah', an ah'," Bob signaled verse.
"Oh! our sodger lads looked braw, looked braw
we' their tartan kilts an' ah, an' ah',
wi' their bonnets an' feathers an' glitt'rin gear,
An' pibrochs sounding loud and clear.

Four more lines, then chorus, then verse:
Oh! wha is foremost oh' ah', oh' ah',
Oh! wha is foremost oh' ah', oh' ah',
Bonnie Charlie the King oh' us, a' hurrah!
wi' his hundred pipers an' ah', an' ah'.

Four more lines, then chorus, and last verse.
The Esk wa swollen sae red an' sae deep,
but shouther to shouther the brave lads keep;
Twa thousand swan owre to fell English ground
An' danced themselves dry to the pibroch's sound
Dumfoun'er'd the English saw, they saw,
Dumfoun'er'd they heard the blaw, the blaw,
dumfoun'er'd they ah' ran awa', awa',
Frae the hundred pipers an' ah', an' ah'."

All joined in to signal chorus as he raised his hands up and up, *fortissimo, fortissimo,* and they rolled down the highway singing their robust chorus of the Hundred Pipers. Everyone joined in waving their hands as if conducting. Following his signal again, they all slowed, *legato,* then three more choruses; *pianissimo,* and finished with three *legatoes.*

At the end they shouted and waved to bewildered motorists.
"Even the words sound rhythmic and lyrical."

"I thought it was *giggles* and *cheers* instead of *glitter* and *gear*," said George, affably.

"Let's do it again," so it sounds like a band of marching pipers coming over the hill from a distance— and then fading away as they pass. . ."

"Yeah, let's do it again, like the Warsaw Concerto."
"Yeah, this time with giggles and cheers," laughed Martha.
Through one small town after another they sang and waved to the bewildered people on the streets.

Arrival at Uncle Henry Peterson's in Syracuse that late afternoon found everyone stiff with fatigue and it felt good to stretch again. The last of the sandwiches Edith had made for them were long gone and they looked forward to a good meal. Bob had written ahead, explaining that they would stop for the night and so they were expected. Also a good night of rest touched some with anxious anticipation.

Such good intentions however, often go awry when old friends and family get together after long separation. The men stayed up all night visiting, while Martha and Mary begged off to bed, only to be awakened by the late night chatter.

After an early breakfast, they were on the road again.

The road was icy. Bob was driving very carefully.

"This is like trying to balance on a greasy stick," said George.

They were watching a car about eighty yards ahead traveling slowly in the same direction and when their tires caught some ice, they started sliding sideways. Bob twisted frantically in the opposite direction till the wheels gained traction again, then straightened out. They were safe this time.

Suddenly, the car in front was sliding sideways, spinning a completely around for a time, even sliding backwards so the passengers faced them with starkly expressive faces, then it slid off the pavement coming to rest facing in their direction.

Bob had his foot poised to touch his brake. Bill warned: "don't hit the brakes!"

As they passed it by, two men and a woman got out and started to push while another woman stayed at the steering wheel.

In passing they tooted horns and waved to each other, wondering if they should stop to help, and satisfied they had not suffered the same fate.

As uneasy minutes passed they relaxed and soon were laughing again when suddenly they found themselves completely out of control again, helpless, turning, sliding sideways down the road. Bob cranked the steering wheel fiercely, first one way, then the other, the others joined in, feet pressing on the floor, hands grasping anything in front of them, dashboard, seatback and held on desperately and helpless as the Chevy seemed possessed with a mind of its own, or no mind at all. It turned round and round and slid uncontrollably. . . finally jolting to a halt at the road-berm. It snorted heavily in grand fashion as steel joints screamed like animals in pain, then choked a sigh of relief.

They stood there staring at the passengers of the other car as it approached and passed them by, honking, and waving back through open windows.

They waved and shouted: "Merry Christmas."

After much heaving and pushing they were back on the road once again.

Another half mile down the road the process started all over again with the same familiar car, pointing at them from the roadside. Rolling their windows down, they honked and waved and shouted: "Merry Christmas."

"At least you're on the right side of the road this time," someone shouted.

In the distance another car materialized coming from the opposite direction. As it passed them Bob honked and they waved. All but Bob turned to watch it slide out of control.

It was a day like that—a day on the road of laughs and cheers; of heaving and sighs. A day of taking turns in the ditch; sometimes you win and sometimes you loose.

After a while that morning, it seemed they had come to know the folks in that other car personally. No one had counted of the number of times each had passed the other. A sort of competition had developed to see who could get *somewhere* first, and who could shout the season's greetings the loudest.

At her home in upstate New York they dropped Martha off and crossed Lake Champlain on their way to Burlington, then on to the farm on Blossom Hill Road.

When they arrived at dusk the farmhouse and barn shone in

the eerie shadows of dirt-crusted headlights. It looked cozy and inviting with Christmas lights in the windows.

"Looks like we'll get to ski tomorrow," Bill said, straining his eyes against the dark to the downhill slope across the road.

Mary lifted her head and sat up to look around rubbing the sleep from her eyes. "Is this it?"

"That's it," Bob said.

"Oh it's beautiful. . . just like Christmas," she said, wiping her eyes all the while fussing with her hair and clothing.

They stepped out ginger-footed, and each taking an armful, walked crunching the crust of recent snow beneath their feet.

For moments Bob looked through the window. At the table sat Mother Marshall and Leslie and the other sister Aileen, who folded something in front of her.

George was first, and flung the door open, "*surprise*—!"

"Here we are ready or not," declared Bill, then they gathered embracing one another.

When they were done Bob turned her gently, "Mom, I have a surprise for you," he said. "This is Mary—my wife."

Mary stood just inside the door waiting. She had urged, even begged him to write and tell them, but he had insisted on making it a surprise.

Nervously she waited while they studied her with curious regard.

Coming from a family of many aunts, uncles and grandparents who lived nearby and who often embraced each other affectionately she felt alone and embarrassed at the sudden aloofness when she desperately needed a sign of acceptance.

Aileen came to her first and offered her an embrace.

It was a total surprise, and for that instant all seemed lost for words. For Mary it was a frightening period.

"I bet you're all starved, come sit. . . we have some hot cocoa and soup," the mother said, in words soft spoken and warm. "This is a happy occasion. . . a new member of the family," she turned abruptly, "Robert, you just wait till I get hold of you alone," she scolded, twisting his ear. "I can't imagine you not letting us know. . . but then I guess you always were one for surprises."

"John and Allen will be in any time now," the sisters said, eagerly hurrying about to arrange places at the table.

Mary looked to Bob modestly, wondering how and where to

start. She feared the expression on her face might betray her; *I need to go to the bathroom.*

Stomping noises reached her from another room and she heard some shuffling.

"Guess what? We have a *surprise*," the word surprise flooded out musically, like a chorus. Leslie caught them at the door and guided them to the table across from Mary. Both stood quiet, faces framed in bewilderment. The girls explained: "Mary is our new sister, Bob's wife, they were just getting ready to tell us all about it when you two clods came stomping in."

All eyes fell on Mary again. She looked to Bob for help.

They talked and ate and laughed. Bob explained how they had met last spring at church, and how he had stayed at her mother's boarding house, and they had gone to the observatory together and bird watching. . . and then they had performed on the radio together, and finally we decided we could make a good team. "So, we asked her mother." He reached to squeeze her hand reassuringly.

Then they waited quietly on Mary; ". . .we drove to Newport, Kentucky for a quick ceremony and a one night honeymoon," she confessed.

"And now guess what?" Bob said.

Their eyes quickened expectantly.

"We're going to have a baby. . . Mom you'll be a grandmother."

Everyone agreed. This night was cause for a double celebration, and Mary was grateful for Bob's explanation, all except the part about, "making a good team." Then she leaned over to whisper in his ear: "Where's the bathroom?"

Midnight passed them by when the old clock in the next room struck its ominous notes. They were still talking and laughing then and had discussed cows and weather and school. Bob had told of the canary incident at the radio station. Everybody pleaded with Mary to play her *Juba Dance*. She explained that she was too tired and sleepy and would certainly make a mess of it.

Earlier Aileen and Leslie had taken leave to prepare an upstairs room for them. It was a front, corner room, small, with some boxes of stored things stacked in a corner, but neat and clean. Mary glanced sleepily through the window to see the tree lined road they had driven on earlier. A bright moon hung there casting off reflections and shadows on the silvery slopes and the hill outlines beyond the valley of dark and gray haze.

Bob slipped into bed first and heaved a great sigh of relief. Mary came to bed and snuggled close with her head on his chest wrapped tightly in heavy comforters.

"We can take a bath tomorrow—together," she said, soft and wistful, recalling how on their wedding night, he had vowed they would always bathe together.

"I don't think we better here," he replied.

"Why not? We do it at my house."

"That's different."

"Why different?"

"Well, there's Mom. . . and my sisters here too."

"There's my Mom. . . at home too," her words flowed soft and slow from challenge giving way to curiosity.

"We never do it when anyone else is around, except Edith, and then she's always downstairs. . . but here, we'd have to go downstairs, and others would be there. . . and. . ." his words trailed off. Then he added, "it wouldn't be proper."

She lay quiet for moments, as if judging the weight of his words against thoughts.

"I like her. . . I mean your mother, she's really amazing, you know?"

"Go to sleep."

"Seven. . ." she muttered. "Seven children, in nine years. And then the farm. . . How did she do it?" Mary said, raising her head a little, as if looking to him for the answer.

"Go to sleep."

"Is that what you're going to do to me—? Keep me pregnant, with a baby every year?"

"You'll see, if you don't go to sleep."

"Promises. . . promises. . . and threats, and promises," she murmured, sleepily. . .

In the morning she awoke groping about the empty space next to her. He was gone. He had told her that night he would get up early and help with the milking the next morning. Glancing to the window and beyond to an overcast sky that threatened more snow, she wanted to roll tighter into the security of warm covers. "But alas," she said aloud. "One must rise to greet the day. Oh! So you think you might attempt literary genius this day, and per chance scare the clouds away. *Away, away,* ye o'clouds of gloom. Begone," she declared in a wily fashion, waving her hand like a wand while she stepped gingerly to the window.

She tossed clothes about from a suitcase, still muttering to herself, as if she had no idea what she was searching for. Ahh, some furry little slippers that made her feet look like fuzzy stumps. . . and a chenille robe. All of which were icy cold and did nothing to warm her much. She stirred around in an erratic circle, folding her arms tightly, forcing breasts to swell upwards, then stepping in front of the old oaken dresser and mirror, there to study her face and muttering lips.

"Bathroom! Where is that confounded bathroom?" Quickly, she grabbed some things; stockings, a sweater, stumbling to put on the slippers as she hurried downstairs. At home she never went downstairs in a bathrobe.

From the kitchen came the smell of oatmeal and cinnamon; no donuts, thank God.

Aileen greeted her as she stood in the doorway.

"Would you like something to eat now?" inquired Leslie from across the kitchen. "The men will be in for breakfast in a while, but you can have something now if you like."

"No thanks," Mary shook her head modestly. "Is this a good time to take a bath?"

Aileen reached for her hand and guided her through the doorway with a benevolent smile.

Her feet burned hot from the cold as she soaked luxuriously in the warm water. After bathing and drying, she combed and fussed with her wet hair only to wrap it in a towel at last. Gathering her robe and nightgown, she hurried back upstairs and exchanged slippers for shoes. Then she made the bed and proceeded to organize their clothes into drawers, placing her own and Bob's personal items on the dresser top. After fussing with the curtains and a table lamp, she went down to breakfast.

Nine they were, gathered round the table that morning.

"Are you ready to go skiing, Mary?" asked Bob.

She looked out the window. "But, it looks like snow—"

"That's the best time—when it's snowing," John added.
"But where?"
"Right across the road, our own mountain, or, well hill anyway," Bob said.
"We'll all go," Aileen declared. "We can clean up here first. You go ahead."
"I can stay and help too," Mary stalled, uncertain about this skiing thing.
"You just go ahead. We do it all the time and we won't be long. . . right Leslie?"

Mary went for more stockings and Bob brought her a pair of pants that were much too big. He tied them snugly with cord around her ankles, then she slipped into a heavy sweater and a heavy oversize old coat, finally donning a woolen hat she had knitted herself, and a pair of gloves, all of which made her look like a poor little beggar of a street gamin. She was ready at last, though hardly recognizable. At times she wondered if she looked more like some little gremlin as she stumbled and thumped down the stairs towards her first adventure on skis.

The brothers had already dug out some old wooden skis and poles and a sled.

Before long she found herself strapped and harnessed onto two slivers of wood attached to black, ugly boots that felt like buckets. Bill and George were already latched into theirs, grown men acting like nutty kids, sliding down the driveway and across the road. They made it look easy. Allen took off on his own with the sled, because there were not enough skis for everyone to use at the same time. They would have to take turns.

Just then Aileen and Leslie came out all bundled up and anxious to go, or at least that's the impression they gave.

"Just point the tips together—snowplow, like this. . . and squat a little like sitting down to a chair, and go straight ahead," Bob demonstrated for her. "The skis will do the rest."

She started moving, slow at first, then a little faster, but the tips didn't point inward like he promised, instead they seemed to have a mind of their own, like spreading her into a split as she gained momentum.

"*Snowplow*," a voice called out.

"I, I, I cannttt't," she cried back, just before collapsing spread-eagle in the snowbank across the road.

Bob hurried to help her.

The others thought it was hilarious. "Do it again!"

"What happened?" she sputtered, spitting out snow and trying to wipe her face and shake the clods from her body at the same time. She watched them bewildered, wondering why it was funny.

"I'm sorry Mary, but you looked *so* funny. . . and we just couldn't help it, we really are sorry. . . for laughing but if only you could have seen yourself."

"Are you okay, hurt I mean?" Bob asked with concern, trying to sound serious. "Do you want to try it again?"

"I think I'll watch for a while; later maybe. Besides, I don't think this is a very ladylike thing to be doing, for an expectant mother."

After digging her out of the snowdrift and unfastening the skis and poles, he helped her over the bank to the hill on the other side.

"Oooh no. . . I'm not going down that, this is nonsense," she exclaimed, all the while pointing and shaking her head.

The hill sloped downward about three to four hundred yards to where dormant trees waited at the bottom, their branches still heavy with clusters of snow.

The sled came chugging uphill tugged along by a figure, and two others trudged heavily, carrying the long sticks on their shoulders. She could hear their laughter in the distance and saw them, like work-horses snorting steam in the crisp winter air.

Aileen was busy strapping in the ones Mary had used while Bob had fixed himself into the ones Bill just returned. Bob gave her a sort of salute and took off gracefully, cutting a curved pattern; showing off.

At the bottom where trees formed together like a curtain-wall he came to an abrupt halt, teetered for a moment, then fell over. Then came the long hike back up to the top to share skis with the next person. They watched and played and threw snowballs. Mary tried the sled, which was more familiar.

Then it was her turn again.

I'm not going down that hill," she said defiantly.

"Traverse," Bob pointed. "Across the hill, like that. . . see, like Leslie's doing. It's easy and slower, you'll see—I'll ski along side of you and tell you what to do. You press down on the left ski—tilt your knee in, like this, so pressure is on the inside edge, and that'll make you go uphill and slow or stop. Always the *inside* edge, remember that—"

"We'll do it together, with me beside you on the downhill side, that way the slope won't intimidate you. . ."

"I'm already intimidated."

"I'll be right here next to you, just like dancing."

"We never got to dance—"

He looked at her for a long moment with that wry grin spread across his face. "We will—"

"Promise?"

"Promise."

"Ready or not," she said. Then, without warning she found herself upside down in the snow again. It was a sudden and mysterious thing; feet just flew into the air, and there she was upside down.

Again he was helping her up.

"I didn't do anything," she sputtered and struggled, her face a mask of white, like some hoary thing. From behind the mask wary eyes peeked through, bewildered. "What happened this time? I didn't do a thing, just standing there, and all of a sudden, *flop* . . just like that. . . *flop*."

He was having a tough time himself, struggling fiercely to maintain a straight face.

Moving slowly in the tracks someone before had left, Bob slid easily along her side, giving instructions, reassuringly. "Good," he said. "Now you're getting it. . . see it's not so hard." Then she started leaning, then more, and more, and over she went. "But you're getting the hang of it now."

After trying a few more times she came to stand gasping for breath beside Leslie while Bob struck off downhill with his brothers.

"I'm cold, and soaked," Mary said, starting to shudder, "and look, it's snowing a little."

"I'm cold too. . . and I'm ready to go in where it's warm," said Leslie. "Let these clods have their fun."

"And dry too."

Plodding over the bank and across the road, they hurried up the driveway, shaking to dislodge the clinging ice and snow.

In the kitchen Mother Marshall busied herself tending a pan on the stove. She smiled warmly and listened as the younger women described Mary's first ski experience. When they finished, she said, "I watched from the porch when you started out. . . and then I went upstairs to get a better view." She spoke softly with an easy manner. She continued stirring something in the pan. Her long graying hair was tied into a bun at the back of her neck and narrow soft face. Her bones and skin looked delicate, yet she was a woman who possessed the inner strength to manage a farm and raise seven children on her own. "Some hot cocoa to warm you," she said, pouring two cups.

Aileen had come in earlier, and now they heard laughter and stomping outside. One by one the men entered from a door to the woodshed and horse barn, where in years gone by the boys had played basketball and other games in the loft above.

Gathering round the old iron stove, they shed wet outer garments while rubbing their hands and feet and poking fun at one another. Mary said: "do boys ever grow up?"

Later Mary joined the girls at the table, making decorations for a Christmas tree. She had been told that tomorrow some of the men would probably go for a tree, and Aileen explained how they would use an old sled drawn by their one horse named Trooper, and go up into the hills out back where there are lots of trees. That's where we get the maple syrup from. Leslie explained how they would go up into the woods and draw the sap and boil it to make syrup. And sometimes they would stay overnight in the cabin. It's so beautiful up there in the trees, with a solemn stillness, and lots of birds too.

Bob went over to put his hand on Mary's shoulder. She was sitting at the table, stirring candied popcorn. He squeezed her shoulder affectionately while sipping cocoa. "A person can be close to God and nature up there."

She wanted to tell him: *I could use a rest.*

"How about a sleigh ride tomorrow? Looks like there will be a fresh snow cover on the ground by then. . . and there's someone I'd like for you to meet."

"But won't they need Trooper to go for a tree?"

"Oh, I see," he said, glancing around at the grinning faces of his brothers. "They've told you about old Trooper already?"

Allen chuckled.

"There will be plenty of time. We can go for the tree right after chores and breakfast, and then we'll take our ride. It's only a few miles, over the hill, and by two very quaint little cottages, then over a bridge. But it's a back trail. We walk it a lot in the spring and summertime... and in the fall when the maples turn color. That's when it really is at it's best. In the winter it's different, beautiful too, still different." His words sounded reminiscent. "You'll see. How about it, guys? We go for the tree in the morning?"

Mother Marshall said: "chicken soup with homemade noodles, good for the body and soul, especially in the wintertime and it's ready."

After dinner, the girls made strings of cranberries and popcorn and made colored paper decorations while the men attended to the milking.

Mary was already in bed when Bob came in. He undressed eagerly and dove beneath the covers, squirming to adjust to the sudden shock of cold, then, he reached to turn off the small light nearby and cuddled close.

He reminded her of another vow he had made on their wedding night; beds were made for lovemaking, and he considered it his inspired duty to christen every bed they should ever come to sleep in.

"I doubt," he whispered, "this bed has ever been used for lovemaking."

"'Over the hills we go, in a one horse open sleigh...'" John Pierpont no doubt intended his *Jingle Bells* to be sung in just such a setting; gliding along scenic wintry Vermont roads, or any wintry road for that matter, in an open sleigh pulled along by a jaunty horse to the tinkle of bells. He must have done it himself while conceiving and writing the tune. Together they cranked out the words merrily, however out of tune, with the jingle of sleigh bells, while Mary sat bundled in a sweater and coat with a woolen blanket wrapped tightly about her legs.

The morning had gone as planned the brothers returned with a scroungy looking tree, which everyone made fun of except Mother Marshall. Of course each of the brothers blamed someone else for choosing it.

Mary said: "who really picked the tree?"

"I'll never tell—"

Bob shouted encouragement to old trooper to motivate him while pointing to a small stand of trees in the distance, then a house with smoke puffing from the chimney on their right, a foot thick layer of snow on it's roof, and a picket fence where some of the tips poked through. On a bridge, he pointed to the busy creek below while old Trooper snorted great clouds of steam and fidgeted nervously.

"Claire is my cousin, and her family is very close," he explained. "You and she are a lot alike. . . we used to take hikes together and go bird watching. . . and she would play the piano, and I'd sing. Her grandmother would sit in the corner in her rocking chair. She'd rock slowly; she loved to hear us play and sing hymns together. When we finished, she would smile and nod her head, and say, 'that's very nice Robert, thank you'. She'd still sit there, rocking and smiling, a very precious lady; silver hair. . . and such a sweet smile. You'll see."

They rode quietly for a while and pointed to two small winter birds flitting about, and talked of the scenery and made fun of old Trooper's awkward gait.

"Well here it is," he said, at last pulling into a tree-lined pathway. They stopped. Trooper stomped and snorted a great cloud of steam as if relieved of a mighty burden. Trooper has a mind of his own she would soon learn.

"I'll go in first. . . and then come back. I want this to be a surprise," he said, tying the leather reigns to the sleigh. "Be still Trooper, REST."

Mary sat there, for what seemed like a long, long time, arms folded, and waiting impatiently. Trooper stirred. The sleigh budged a little. . . then a little more.

"Whoa Trooper," she called out, "be still—rest, *Trooper, rest*."

The beast snorted and stomped a front hoof defiantly, then took off in a gentle but determined trot.

"Whooa. . . whooaa, Trooper. TROOPER STOP!" she commanded. "Stop, go back. . . you dummy."

The words only seemed to fortify his stubbornness and determination as he continued steadily in the direction they had just come. She scolded; he continued defiantly. She heaved a clump of snow gathered from the floorboard; hand-packed and hard like a rock. She pouted. . . then as if finally conceding to a force beyond her control, she tried to relax and enjoy the ride and scenery. Obviously Trooper needed no guidance; most likely would have ignored any.

An hour later the beast slowed down a little to struggle up the driveway at the Marshall farm, and into his barn stall. He snorted and stomped triumphantly.

Allen must have seen them and came to help. He chuckled smugly and removed the harness. "I guess Bob forgot to tell you about old Trooper," he said. "We thought about renaming him *old lazy*, cause all he wants to do is stay here in the barn and eat and sleep, he doesn't like the winters anymore, or towing the hay wagon."

"He doesn't like sleighs either, I see."

He reached for her hand and helped her down. At first she pouted—then smiled a little smile.

"What's Bob going to do?" she asked.

"Walk, I guess."

"Serves him. . . " she replied, heading for the house and a place by the stove.

Inside by the stove, Allen sneaked close and gave her a surprise kiss on her cheek. She beamed a happy glow, with his handsome face and dark eyes he smiled back warmly. She remembered how, when they had been introduced, he had taken her hand and kissed it with a gentleman's flair.

It was dark when Bob plodded heavily up to the front porch, stomping his feet to shake the ice and snow off.

Snow had started falling just about the time he got to the bridge, and now he was covered head to foot, like a walking snowman. He removed his hat and jacket, shaking them vigorously.

A familiar sound reached his ears. Mary was playing a rousing round of Juba Dance with a vengeance while the others gathered in the sitting room, laughing and decorating. Tentatively he settled on the stool beside her with his back to the piano, waited and listened. His mother rocked quietly near the stove across the room. At the opposite wall a tapered tree stretched for the ceiling, neatly decorated while Leslie and George toyed with the finishing touches.

Mary changed the tempo to a giddy version of the *Waters of the Mini Tonka*, like burning off a head of steam.
When she finished he asked: "What happened?"
"You could guess."
He stared at the tree but said nothing.
"That thing in the barn... old *dummy*, he has a mind of his own, you know," she said, with a hint of irritation in her voice—"you could have at least warned me—"
"I should have known," he said, apologetic and humble. "When I came to get you, you were gone. I realized what must have happened... Are you okay?" he turned to look at her, his eyes warm with affection. "I worried all the way..."
"That helps."
His shoulders sagged noticeably but he avoided her eyes and said nothing more.
"Are you hungry?" she asked—relenting a little.
"Starved."
"I talked Mary into playing for us. She really is very good you know," Aileen said, interrupting like the peacemaker. "We've all eaten, but if you'd like something?"
They went into the kitchen where Aileen served him and Mary sat at his side.
Tomorrow would bring the joy of Christmas Eve; a day of great expectations; of Holy Worship in the remembrance of the birth of Baby Jesus. This would be a very Merry Christmas, also at night, the candlelight service of family gatherings, and the bells.

Outside the Waterbury Methodist Church it was late. An occasional snowflake fluttered lazily downward. They were grouped with so many others, waiting as robed members of the handbell choir, four on each side took their places forming an aisle leading up to the entrance. Then three members with lighted candles placed themselves on either side, and between the handbellers. On cue they started, a melodious tinkling sound filled the night air, even the very snowflakes seemed to ring with joy as the handbells sang out, and ushered in the flock to the *Carol of the Bells*.
When everyone was seated in their pews holding unlit candles, the handbellers entered to take a place in front of the

alter, where they performed, *Deck the Halls*, then *Silent Night*, and finally, *We Wish You A Merry Christmas*.

With the *tintinnabulation* complete, traditional hymns were sung, and then the ceremony of lighting the candles to signify Christ as the light of the world. The Reverend Murray reminded them of the reason to celebrate the birth of Jesus Christ.

"And now let us pray." He spoke with a full voice and bowed head. "Our Lord we humbly beseech thee..."

Bob and Aileen had moved from the center pew and left the family to take their places beside the organ.

As prayer finished, the lights went out, so only candles flickered in hands and at the altar. Contrasting lights and shadows warmed and enriched the stained maple woodwork. Then Bob and Aileen joined in a duet of *Silent Night*. After a pause they finished with, *Away in the Manger*.

There was a stillness as Reverend Murray bowed his head to lead the congregation in prayer, then the choir offered it's own contribution of *Hallelujah Chorus*.

Outside again there was much congratulating and shaking of hands and sisterly and brotherly hugging. Mary was glad to have Bob at her side again. He had introduced her to so many people, and she couldn't remember any of their names.

༄༅༅༅༅

After weeks of Yuletide preparation, then sadly, the day had passed so quickly, and all wondered where it went. Just one day later they were contemplating the everyday commitment to school and work that lay ahead.

On Sunday, the family visited the Waterbury Center Methodist Church where Bob again introduced Mary to Reverend Murray. She had been impressed and immediately understood why her husband thought so highly of him, and in some way her woman's intuition told her why he hoped to pattern his own life after the man. She felt proud of him then.

Just two days later, Bob and Mary with Aileen, George and Bill had decided on a drive to Camel's Hump Mountain for some hiking and camping. They knew of an old single room cabin with a fireplace in the center. After gathering wood, they had built a fire, and all had slept in circle with their feet to the hearth. On the way up the car's tires had gotten caught in some ruts and Bob decided to leave it there with plans to dislodge it the next day.

At night they took turns reciting poetry and telling stories and together they sang songs, staying up most of the night in an attempt to keep warm.

Finally rolled up in blankets and sleepers they dozed off by early morning, only to be awakened later by someone stirring about to start the fire again.

Their last day at the farm seemed the happiest. A time when new friends have become old friends. It was Sunday and they went to church again and Aileen sang *In The Garden*, and *Whispering Hope* as a solo. Mary began to feel accepted as a part of the family. She felt closest to Aileen, perhaps because she was the nearest to her own age, and also because she both appreciated, and envied her singing voice.

That evening was the last time the men joined together for the chores. Family pictures were brought out and the girls studied them together. There was one of the five boys, Bob with a cast on his arm. "How did it happen," Mary asked; Leslie went on to explain: "It had been the first year after their father had died, and Bob and the boys were lowering an old ensilage cutter from a bridge in the hay barn. The rope broke and Bob and machine were both thrown over the side to the ground below. Bob had been knocked unconscious, and Bill looked at him, saying, 'he's as dead as a doornail.'" Bill winced at the memory. "Bob had been shaken up, but fortunately a broken arm was his only injury."

"He insisted on working the rest of the summer, though he had only one arm," said Mother Marshall from her rocking chair, a lump of knitting in her lap so far untouched.

Next came a picture of Bob and Bill in funny looking swim suits. They were standing together, and the letters across their chest, read LIFE GUARD. Aileen said: "oh that was the summer they were life guards down at the lake, 1927—no 28, I think."

Mary asked about their singing. Aileen said that Bob always liked music, and Leslie told of the time he got the other boys to help move an old organ in to the cow-barn so he could play to the cows while the others did the milking. He claimed the cows liked it and it made for better milking. The others argued he did it just to get them to do all the milking. Aileen had said, his singing had really started with his first year at Montpelier, after high school he stayed to work the farm for two years while Bill and Leslie went off to college. He was short of credits for college, so that's when he went to Montpelier Seminary for a year before going to Wesleyan.

"Yes, a funny thing had happened," Aileen said. "That's when the senior's were hazing the freshman, and three of them tried to throw Bob into a fountain, but he didn't let them, instead, he threw all three of them in and just walked away, dusting his hands as if it was nothing." Mary looked up to Bob, her eyes beaming and filled with admiration.

There were some old sepia colored pictures of great-grandparents with stern and scowling faces. Mother Marshall explained: "in those days you were required to hold a straight face for portrait taking. I remember when I was a child, and the portrait taker became furious because every time he got ready, I smiled, and he refused to take a portrait when a body was smiling. Still to this day many think it is only proper that they must pose a serious face for a portrait."

With a soft smiling face, she sat rocking and knitting, without lifting her eyes she said, "who will recite the first poem?"

As if on cue Allen jumped to his feet first and he recited his version of *Our Cousin Jack* and *The King Is Sick*. Then he and John joined to recite alternate lines of *Our Cousin Jack*.

When they finished Mary prompted Bill to recite his version of *The Lady of Shalott*.

Ten

Robert Marshall placed the photographs in his lap and shifted in his wheelchair in one quick animated motion like a bird sensing sounds. He looked at Odelia, then past her, seeing her, yet not seeing at all because it was space and time he was locked into. She had entered the room quietly to sit on the couch opposite and facing him, waiting and not impatient.

"You know me too well, Odelia," he said at last. "I know you can read my most inner thoughts like spoken words... And yes I do remember that time in Cincinnati, the day and night after we got married, like it was yesterday now. Like I know the sounds and queerness of this old house, every mouse and cockroach, and every thing in that time before the dark age of my present existence... Little things come back to me now, the times of our youth when we thought we were invincible and our faith protected us from all wrongs—we were blind to the choices then—rationality governed and dictated choice, and we went stumbling blindly along the path of least resistance as though we had all the answers. We responded to whims like petals in a breeze, and it is we who were the petals.

"At first I tried to make sense of it, but there was no logic, nor was there sanity. I've been too involved with the years and managing to get by to think of the past—it was another time and I was all too willing to forget, less I should fall deeper into the well of self-pity and depression. Even simple body functions had to be learned all over again. The sound of my own voice betrayed me, and it was a long time before I came to understand the uncertainty of that voice. I tried to set the two apart—different lives, split in two by a period of darkness—the one put away under lock and key. Now all is returned, and reality is a fearful and desperate thing. I'm not sure I can handle reconciling the two into one.

"Odelia, if you were to ask me now how many years the dark period lasted I couldn't say, two, six, maybe ten years. It was a gradual awakening into the healing process, and most of all, acceptance. Legs taken for granted, once useful for walking and running, and so many other things, now became a burden like worthless pendulous dead weights, and all the while the ghost-like pain as a wicked reminder. Yes, acceptance of a body leaden with ineptness and failings, until that other body no longer existed in my memory. It was a necessary evil in order to get on with the business of living. There was no such thing as something for nothing or wealth without effort. That was before, but now, hard work and effort and dedication didn't even pay off. During that black time I hated everybody, and blamed God—yes even God for forsaking me, and I trusted no one—despised even those who tried to help me, because I was dependant on their help. Before that dark period I was in charge, or at least I thought I made my own decisions, and charted my own destiny. I served God because I had decided it was serving God that served my purpose, and being a minister was a good thing to do. It would bring prestige and approval to my mother and family—recognition to my good father's name and memory. I was in turn struck down with my affliction in the prime of my youth, and that meant I was a failure. How do you fight back against a bug, an invisible germ? Then I met another man who was to become president, and he too had been struck down years before me in the same way, and he overcame his affliction to show the way. It was a long time, this time of brooding and despair in which I despised and blamed everyone—filled myself with self pity and self recriminations. . . This other man was a wealthy man and he purchased Warm Springs and formed a foundation so others less fortunate like myself could afford to go there to aid their healing process. When I arrived he had just become president and that time may have signaled the turning point without my even knowing it, to restoring my faith and motivation towards survival. During that time and the following forty some odd years I began to detach myself from that other time of anticipation and energetic youth. Over the years those letters from him became a constant reminder and support. God had set a mighty task for this man, so much greater than my own, and he found a way with the energy to succeed and to lead us in our direst time of need. Who am I to pine and waste away when God gave me strength by way of conditioning before, so that I might endure these trying years for a purpose—perhaps as no more that a simple example to others. Do you suppose the president gained something too—rose above adversity by having someone like myself to guide and motivate. His letters certainly bear that out. Back in those early days we, the *polios* were all inspired merely by his and Eleanor's presence. The *polios* had become an affectionate term among all of us. We all, in time spoke it and used the term openly. Some even learned to show amusement with our own ineptness. When she asked me to sing it restored my confidence in my own voice. Each of us in turn gave something to the other, even if my contribution was the far lesser of the two.

"I'll tell you something else, Odelia, a confession if you will— I haven't been this honest with anyone—myself included in all these forty some odd years—perhaps in my whole life. God must be chuckling up there now—a big belly laugh, as if he planned it this way, and knew the answers all along—when the pieces would come together. I'll bet he didn't count on it taking me this long though. Yes sir; a big belly laugh. . ."

Odelia came to her feet, as though sensing the time had come again for his sojourn into the past. "You passed through the stage the Lord set forth—you know the Holy Scriptures, and His word— Emotions is the hardest, I think. You learned when a thing is wrong you got to fix it; if you are criticized you put it aside and don't take it personal— I never hear you say 'why me?' You get on with life as best you can. That what counts most. The Lord works His mystique in mysterious ways, Robert. Could be more pieces got to fall in place yet."

Even as she spoke his mind was drifting back again. He had left telling Joe about Mary being pregnant to Edith. Edith wanted it that way. After that Joe hadn't spoken to him for days; then, if he had any reservations he seemed to have forgotten them. But Joe never invited him to play basketball again. Ross was a different story though. He stared with piercing eyes but said nothing. It was the only time Bob had been able to read the other man's thoughts; *preachers are no different than other people*;

then he turned on his heels and walked away.

He picked up the photo again; his window into the past. "Those were good times, Odelia—Christmas at the farm, and the journey back to Delaware. An automobile is a fine thing, but so is walking, even if you have to stuff cardboard in the soles of your shoes to plug up the holes, like a walk in the woods at winter time, with the sound and luxury of snow crunching beneath your feet, or along a city street looking for work, even when you are hungry and have no idea where the next meal is coming from, and you got this baby coming into the world. . ."

In the early hours of Monday morning they departed. Bob planned to drive all day and night if needed to arrive in Ann Arbor the next day. It had warmed a bit by mid-morning and once more they were rolling down the highway, telling stories and chanting as they had done before, with the Hundred Pipers as the favorite.

Back In Delaware, Bob and Mary soon settled into their familiar routine. Once again he poured himself into his studies with a renewed vigor.

On days when weather permitted, they traveled to adjacent towns to perform on radio and at school auditoriums. Once, they made three appearances in the same week.

It was late March, and with spring promising new things, Bob's interest in studies began to fade. He had mentioned that he was a doer and not a studier anyway, and maybe they should think about moving to an apartment of their own, Mary had agreed to accept whatever he decided. After all, she was happy with the life inside her and just to be with him, and she was growing plumper by the day.

On their return from an appearance in Columbus one day, Bob said after driving quietly for a long time: " I think it's time we moved. Edith, er Mom I mean; well she's been wonderful with us, and I hope it doesn't hurt her feelings. She could certainly do better by renting the room out."

Mary sat quietly, listening and waiting. She had sensed the surging tides of change in him, especially at night—the tossing about in bed—the aura of uncertainty—the sleepless nights standing by the window.

"I've written a letter," he continued, "to apply for a position with the Chautauqua lecture circuit. . . if I'm accepted, I can earn twenty dollars each time I speak, and another twenty if I sing. If I get to do both in one day, I could make forty dollars. We would have to travel though, and . . . "

"What about college? You can't just give it up. I mean just like that? You're so close to getting your degree?"

"I'd come back later, after the baby comes." He patted her belly, then caressed her thigh next to his own, "and we'd have some money saved by then. I need to pay Ross the rest of what I owe him for the Chevy. . . "

"No you don't, he won't ask for it."

"Yes I do," he jerked, sounding harsher than he had intended. "I couldn't continue like this, accepting charity from your Mom."

"You're not accepting charity. Beside she wants to help."

"Well, it won't be long now, for you, and it wouldn't be proper for you to accompany me. Pregnant and all, you know. Just not proper. Also there's the matter of privacy, we could be in an apartment of our own, and who knows what next." He smiled easily, as if getting it out in the open lifted a weight from his shoulders. He reached over to squeeze her hand affectionately. "Besides, it is time to move on."

"And no more donuts in the morning," Mary said, remembering the first morning sickness, though she really hadn't been sick since. Still there were many mornings in which she had stuck her head out the window for fresh air, or even dressed quickly and went outside for a walk.

"So. . . it's all settled," he said, resolvedly, with a slight nod. "We'll look for a place in Columbus, and then we'll tell Edith the news." He glanced in the rear-view mirror, then out both sides and made a u-turn at the cross-road.

They headed back to Columbus.

The apartment they settled on was a two room affair with a semi-private bath on the second floor. In one corner there was a small alcove to serve as a kitchen. The rent was six dollars a week and there was just enough money to keep going, yet they were immensely happy. It seemed like an adventure.

Mary stayed at the apartment and sometimes took short walks while Bob went door to door trying to sell Wearever Cookware.

On one occasion Bob arranged a demonstration in which Mary was to cook a whole meal in a waterless cooker for a group of eight women.

She had been terrified, always it had been Edith who cooked at home, and always it had been she who helped; Edith was in command.

Now the prospect of having to demonstrate by herself was terrifying. Bob repeatedly encouraged her, saying, "You can do it—I'll help." The demonstration had been a complete success. The women were congenial and all had complimented her on her plumpness, "a healthy sign," they agreed.

On another occasion, they were to demonstrate a new type of sandwich toaster by making toasted cheese sandwiches. There was not enough money for cheese, so they decided to make applesauce sandwiches from some homemade applesauce given them by her Grandmother Norris. Once again they had been lucky and the ladies accepted them without reservation. It was a time like that—when a body felt good to help another.

Meanwhile Bob wrote more letters in hopes of gaining acceptance by the Chautauqua lecture circuit, certain it was his best chance for a real break.

The fourth week in Columbus came and their performances at W A I U had been cut to once a week. Bob decided this would be their last.

Standing by the second floor window, Mary waited as she often did each day when he was due. When he left that morning, she had asked him about supper. He had been vague and told her not to plan anything.

From her window she watched the Chevrolet park directly below. As he closed the door they exchanged the ritual of blown kisses. She could tell he was happy by the way he moved and hurried to the stairway. She waited eagerly as he bounded upward, two, three steps at a time. He gathered her in his arms.

"Guess what?" he said, anxiously, a wry smile flashing over his face... he waited.

"Well... what?" she insisted, "come on tell me, why so smug?"

"We're going to Chicago."

"When?" Her voice filled with ambivalence at first.

"Tomorrow, tomorrow morning. I spoke with a Mr. Bailey, and he told me I would have a very good chance to get on the Chautauqua if I went to Chicago. He gave me a letter of recommendation and told me to see a Miss Abigail Rellquist. She's the circuit manger... so... we leave tomorrow. What do you think?"

"Why not? I've never been to Chicago," she glowed.

"Of course it still may take a little while, and I may have to look for another job in the meantime, perhaps a radio station there. Radio is the coming thing, singing and talking on the radio. Anyway, I'm not very good at this selling business."

"I'd better start packing," she said, throwing her arms about him again. "I know you'll make it, I just know it."

"Wait," he said, his eyes teasing her. "Tonight we go out on the town."

"Where?"

"To our favorite Italian restaurant," he said, "that's where. Spa-gett, or maybe ravioli and maybe a leetle ah-vino."

On the way they toyed with some words to an obscure Italian tune.

The apartment in Chicago was very much like the one in Columbus, two small rooms with an alcove kitchen, except this one included their own bathroom. Like the one in Columbus, it was on the second floor but, had French doors that opened onto a wrought iron balcony.

Again, they had been fortunate to find the apartment district and it had not been difficult with so many 'For Rent' signs. They settled in a second floor apartment they looked at. Being tired, they bathed quickly and then piled into bed, sleeping long and soundly. Even the initiation ritual had to wait till morning.

Waking eager and energetic, Bob hurried to the French doors, apparently blown open by the winds in the night. Snow had blown in and lay piled at his feet.

"Mary, come here. I want you to see something?"

She drew tighter into the covers, but he insisted. Eventually she tip-toed, shivering, to his side.

"Well. . . I'll be. . . " she stammered, "and look-k, our k-car, it's c-covered with s-snow."

"Who'd believe it, snow in the springtime. . . but in Chicago, anything is possible."

She drew her arms tightly about her and shivered to brace against the cold.

Scooping her in up, he rushed to the bed.

"It's time to christen another bed," he said, as they wrestled to get beneath the warm covers, head and all.

"What about the doors, people, they might hear," she giggled.

"Let them."

Two weeks passed since Bob's first meeting with Miss Rellquist. She could promise nothing, saying only that she would let him know as soon as she could.

Meanwhile, he looked for other work, only to learn there was so little to be found. He contacted people at two radio stations, offering to sing and talk, and had been rejected even when he offered to perform free at first. He applied for selling jobs, with little success.

After paying the rent with the last of their money, he walked everywhere to save on what gas was left.

It was a depressed Mary who awaited his return this day. She watched from the balcony as he turned the corner below and threw a kiss, and wondered about the load of books in his arms.

She hurried to the steps and eagerly helped him with the heavy load, pleading anxiously, "what are all these for? where did you get them?"

"I have to study, for work" he said proudly. Then added, "I stopped at the library to pick up these; to work on my lecture."

She started to jump but thought better of it. "Tell me all about it. What happened?"

"Well. . . this morning when I started out, first I stopped at the hardware store again, and still they weren't hiring anyone, then that little restaurant. . . and still nothing, then a couple of filling stations. Downtown, I tried more restaurants and stores, and still nothing, and by then I was ready to come home. . . but

I decided to stop and see Abigail, er, I mean Miss Rellquist and that's it. I start day after tomorrow, Thursday, and I'll make twenty dollars."

"Oh. . . so it's Abigail now, is it?" she said, her stare penetrating, her voice playfully menacing.

"Say, do you have anything to eat? I'm starved."

She eyed him cynically. "I used the last money to buy a soup bone and some vegetables. And two potatoes for mashing, and some French bread. Oh yes, two lemons for lemonade and we're broke. I figured the soup could last a couple days. Here sit down. It's almost ready. Tell me the rest about the books and all."

"Boy does this smell good," he said, sniffing at the pot while reaching to break off a piece of bread. He dipped it into the simmer, holding it there to soak up the juice.

"Careful," she warned, "it's *hot.*" It was a warning she had cautioned him with many times.

He blew on it, and sat down to taste it, carefully. "Don't want a burnt mouth for my first lecture in Chicago," he mused.

"What is it going to be about? she asked, mashing the already boiled potatoes and thinning with a little milk.

"Well. . . after discussing it with. . . ah, *Miss* Rellquist," he shot her a teasing glance, "she agreed that Bible History would be a fitting subject, and birds, or maybe the history of birds in the Bible, and later maybe. . . " He took a bite of bread, chewed, gaged because he ate too fast, and muttered something.

"I could help," she said, indicating the books. "I could look up things to help, and if you need any typing."

Immediately after eating, Bob went to a small table near the French doors and dug into the books while Mary cleaned up.

It was getting late and she watched him bent over seriously locked in the rigors of research, often scribbling after accumulating a tid-bit of information. She picked one of the books and leafed through it, hoping to discover something that would be of interest and a contribution.

It was past bed-time, and she flung her arms around him from behind, and teased, then coaxed, begged even; "come to bed."

"You go ahead. . . I'll be along later."

In the later hours he relented to her pleading and rubbing his eyes, he stretched and staggered to her side, explaining: "after the Thursday appearance I'm due to lecture again on Sunday, and this time I may be given a chance to sing. It's too far to walk—clear across town—to the outskirts, so I'll have to drive there. I am supposed to join some other lecturers at a tent that afternoon, and I won't be home until late in the evening."

"It doesn't matter," she argued. The issue had been one of mounting importance between them—her plumpness and the proper perspective in public. "I've gone with you before to the radio stations, and to auditoriums, and sometimes we've returned late."

"But... but there's you... and the baby now, and well, it's just not fitting."

Again she pleaded. "This is your first big break—you may need me, for a cue or something. I don't want to miss it. And I promise not to interfere. I'll stay in the back..." Then came that look; the eyes of a doe, or was it a puppy dog look?

"Okay— okay," he relented; "but just this once... agreed?"

After attending morning service at a local Methodist Church they were driving to the lecture location.

Sitting quiet, Mary was mindful of his rapid mental activity. She even felt he was unaware of her presence by his side.

"Want to tell me about the lecture?" she said, even though she had heard him practice it many times as he paced the floor back in the apartment. At times he had paused to seek her opinion, only to ignore it.

She recalled one occasion while he was sitting at the little table, she had pulled up a chair to his side, and leaned low to the table, and watched. She had tried to catch his eye. He had brushed aside her teasing advances and continued seriously reading and then jotting down notes. "What are you writing about this time?" she persisted, in an effort to interrupt and draw his eyes to hers; waiting for a response.

"Birds," he muttered, undaunted.

"Are you going to tell about the Preacher Bird?"

Finally, he paused, leaving his stillness behind, he gazed into her eyes, and said, "no... I don't think so. That will be our little secret."

The next evening when he returned to their apartment Bob explained that they would be in Chicago one more week, and then they would move to Milwaukee for the next series of lectures.

When he introduced her to Miss Rellquist, Mary had guessed the other woman's age to be thirty-ish. She was plainly attractive, tall and business-like. Her hair was light brown, like her own, yet pulled into a chignon. She wore an air of discreet and conservative reserve; not at all prudish as Mary had expected.

It was early May when Bob returned from his lecture to tell Mary it was time to move on to Milwaukee. He said, they would be there for a couple of months, and then maybe move on to Buffalo, Cleveland and finally Cincinnati.

Upon arrival, he took Mary to a maternity clinic at the nearby suburb of Wauwatoosa. The doctor confirmed that the baby was due in early July.

As they drove back to their upstairs apartment, Mary was saying: "Somehow, the apartments all seemed the same no matter where we go, and I sure wish the baby was ready now," she spoke wistfully. "Another six weeks like this," she patted her plump, rounded middle. "I don't know how I'll make it. . ."

"Oh you'll make it just fine." He tried to sound reassuring.

"Okay, that's easy for you to say. . . you don't have to waddle around like a duck, and bump into things, and can't sit, and can't sleep and— I can't even find my feet to put on shoes that fit too tight."

"So, that's why you go bare-footed?"

Mary did just fine, waddling like a duck and bumping into things and scolding *it* to hurry up.

Late June was the beginning of a hot and humid period. Bob prepared for a lecture due in three days. Speaking had become difficult lately, and rubbing his neck, he discovered soreness and swelling. Mary remembered he had mentioned he hadn't felt good for a couple days and maybe it was a cold or sore throat, and that it would go away in a day or two.

She tested his face and neck while he sat awaiting the verdict.

"Maybe it's the mumps. . . sure looks like it. Hmm. . . swollen on both sides too. You better lie down in bed," she ordered in a motherly tone of voice. It was that maternal instinct exerting itself.

"Oh it's nothing. . . it'll go away in a while, just a little rest."

"You better stay down just in case. . . while I go downstairs and ring for the doctor."

She hurried away in her waddling fashion, and returned shortly. "He'll be here as soon as he can, probably an hour or so. And he said for you to *stay down* until then."

The doctor was a small man in a dark, worn suit and his hair, all that was left was gray around the edges with a balding spot in the center. He wore a platonic manner like a shroud, placed his black leather bag on the floor at bedside and opened it, felt his patient's throat and considered it—then said: " say ahhh," as he pressed a flat stick on his tongue.

"Hmm," he muttered, feeling below one ear, "does this hurt?"

"Uhh," Bob winced a little in obvious pain.

"Does this side hurt too?"

He winced again.

"Well, you got em all right," he tried to sound nonchalant. "Here, take one of these now, and another at bedtime. Gargle three times daily with salt water, or more if you feel a need to. Drink lots of water and most important of all, stay in bed. In a week, you should be fine."

"But doctor, I have to give a lecture," he struggled through pain for the words, "in three days," he gulped; that was his own answer.

"The lecture will just have to wait, and call me if you have any trouble." His words ended with finality, as he scribbled his fee on a note-pad and handed it to Mary.

At the door she paid him the four dollars.

Two days passed and Bob was up, claiming to feel better, and once more studying his material, when he started feeling pain in his abdomen. The pain worsened and he finally consented to lie down.

The doctor arrived in an hour, same dark, worn suit, same black bag and after lowering Bob's pajama bottom, he confirmed the mumps had gone down. After a stern scolding he handed Mary a small jar of salve and instructed her to apply it two to three times a day to the genitals. He then scolded Bob, "you, young man must stay in bed for at least another week."

Bob did not argue this time. He didn't feel much like a young man either.

At the door, Mary asked if Bob would be all right.

"Well, when this happens, it can mean sterility. And you, young woman?" he indicated plumpness, "when are you do?"

"In July, maybe ten or twelve days yet."

"He should be up and about by then, barring any more complications. I'll stop by and check again in a few days ."

"Your bill?" she asked.

He dismissed it with a wave of his hand and said to her: "take care of yourselves."

A short time later Miss Rellquist stopped by to see Bob. When Mary explained that he had the mumps, she sincerely wished them well, and said to have Bob contact her when he was better.

Four days later when he could wait no longer he climbed out of bed. It felt good to be up and about. June had passed into July with nary a blink, and the baby was due in four days.

The tough reality was: they were broke. Broke, if you can consider total liquid assets of $2.32 worth much. And the rent was due. He had agonized about it many times especially during his illness; if it came to this, and what to do? He had even made tentative arrangements through the church. For her remaining days Mary was put in a home for unwed mothers supported by the United Christian Brotherhood, and then transferred to the local hospital for birthing. By time for her release he expected to have finances under control again, and the apartment secured for her return. Meanwhile he would sleep in the Chevy and walk to save gas. At least he could remain close that way. When he told her about the idea she said nothing; only packed her things and went to wait in the car.

The whole affair didn't take long once the signals started. Some women are blessed in such things, excruciating pain turned to joy after the final labors are done. It was a boy, born on the ninth of July in the early morning hours. Bob, after a long and worried night saw it for the first time from behind glass as the nurse held it up; red faced and squealing, in blue; so fragile and mystifying. Mary was beautiful, more so than he had ever remembered her before.

Four days later Mary was to be released. Bob picked up Edith at the train station and together they went to the hospital where both held the baby for the first time. It cooed for Edith, but when Bob tried to handle it he became awkward, fussed and squirmed and was given back to Edith.

On the way to the apartment, they discussed names. The birth certificate read, "infant Marshall."

"I think we should name him, Robert Taylor. . . Robert for his daddy. . . and. . . "

"Why Taylor?"

"Well, because. . . there have been presidents and writers and poets named Taylor, and besides that, your mother said it was a family name, and it was good enough for a president. We'll call him Bobby, how's that?" she said decidedly.

He was a fussy baby, and often cried when held by his bewildered father.

When Edith walked to the corner store to purchase some sandwich material they found themselves alone. Bob had been distant and quiet the past four days since their return from the hospital. Mary knew something was bothering him.

"It's not going to work," he said, laboriously. "The baby and us traveling. I mean the lecture tour and . . . maybe he would be better off with someone else. The Chautauqua is not doing well I've known that for some time. Many have closed down for lack of funds—and with radio becoming so popular this one may not last another year.

"Abigail thinks the future lies in radio, and I should concentrate on that and singing. In California a singer named Bing Crosby is becoming the rage—and there is another named Ruby Valee. If I could try to get on with one of the big bands like Fred Waring, or Wayne King—but I would have to travel a lot and. . . and change my style. It would take time."

She stood stunned and speechless as he went on—the words interrupted by frequent pauses became more difficult, until at last he stood in mute silence staring at the street below.

Then he said, as if choking for a moment, "Put him up for adoption. He would be better off that way. Or, Bill is married now and ordained with a steady position—I've talked with him, and he and his wife would take it. . . "

"No," she said emphatically, and turned to stare at the baby sleeping on the bed, guarded between two pillows. He went to the bed opposite her, and waited there. She turned away and went to the window, like a storm in the early stages of mounting fury; without another word.

When Edith returned to the icy atmosphere of the apartment, Mary told her they would be leaving for Delaware immediately. She was going home.

On the way home Edith asked Bob to stop in Indianapolis for the night so she could visit a cousin. She stalled for time and hoped a reconciliation. . . that never came.

The baby fussed and cried most of the trip, and upon arrival in Delaware, Bob and Mary parted without words, like two opposing forces in deadlock.

Bob drove to the station and met with Ross, where he left the car, saying he was sure it could be sold for the balance he owed. He told Ross that Mary would explain.

Then he walked to the edge of town and there on Route 23, he raised a thumb hoping to catch a ride back to Milwaukee.

Eleven

For a few years the two grandmothers exchanged letters and from this correspondence plus various other sources Robert Taylor Marshall later pieced together from his own recollection some of the events that transpired in each of his parent's lives. Both grandparents favored a reconciliation and both failed to comprehend the silent stubbornness in the young lives of two people they loved.

For Mary the days passed in a cloud of gloom and she remained sad and depressed most of the time. Often Edith tried to console her, saying he'll come back, or you'll hear from him, and he really does love you. . . have faith. Little Bobby, as he came to be called had settled down and adjusted to his new environment with little difficulty.

Joe paid particular attention to his toy nephew. If only he could handle a football and basketball. The old house buzzed with new life. Lullabies became the common tunes often being played at the old piano. Mary checked the mail each day, hoping for that special letter.

She visited Ross almost daily, as she had before, but for that too she had lost some of the old enthusiasm. By the end of July Bobby had become a happy baby who slept a lot. Mary started taking him out, carrying him when and wherever she walked.

After helping her mother with the housework, Mary would often go for a walk while Bobby napped. But this day she had a different plan. "Mother, I think when Bobby wakes up I'll take him over to see Ardith and her. . . " she stopped mid-word, hand to her mouth, recalling that she had not seen or heard of her two best friends since leaving for Columbus. "My God, how could I, forget. . . Ardith's baby, what was it? A boy or a girl, or maybe twins." she said, her voice full of excitement once again with the prospects of sharing baby talk with her old friend. She knew Ardith hadn't married. The boy's parents had removed him from college and sent him away, yet her parents had accepted her and looked forward to her coming baby.

Edith stood quiet, a room away in the kitchen; "you mustn't go there," she said, her voice pained.

"Why not?"

"You just mustn't go, child."

"Why not, Mother?" Mary insisted.

Edith hesitated.

"Something has happened, hasn't it, something—" Terrible thoughts flashed through her mind, unable to separate them, she envisioned the worst.

"You just can't go, that's all, honey," Edith's voice struggled again for words.

"I'll go anyway, I'll find out for myself."

Edith despaired, moved wearily to be close. "No, wait child, sit down, it's so tragic, only the Lord knows why. His ways may seem mysterious to us at times, for this He requires our good faith... It happened while you were in Milwaukee, and I was going to tell you then, but couldn't... I didn't know how." She stalled, wondering why it was she who had to be the one who must hurt her child so.

"Moth-ther... what is it?"

"Here, sit down child," she said, once again patting the couch while wiping her damp hands nervously on her apron.

Her glance settled for a spell on Bobby sleeping peacefully in his crib nearby.

"She's gone... to heaven."

"Gone... you can't mean—dead!" She groaned painfully; her hands to her face, as tears poured like opening flood-gates, and both wept together. "No, no, no, she can't—my best friend—we were like sisters. I should have been here—"

The mother hugged her daughter, and rocked back and forth, trying desperately to absorb the grief.

"How did it happen?" Mary groaned.

"During the birth... the baby too. It was a girl, but both are in heaven now," Edith held her close, rocking her gently wiping the tears with her apron, then with a hankie drawn from her bosom, again and again.

"How could he... desert her like that, and his family, how could they just do that to her. Where was she? When? I knew she went to live in the country with an aunt because her family wanted her to."

Edith paused and they sat quiet for a time.

"You know the Lord works in mysterious ways... only He knows."

"They're the ones who deserted her... Christians, ha..." the tears stopped, her face became sad and drawn, but she had spit her words with a decided bitterness.

With the passing of weeks Mary's sadness began to subside. For days she had settled into a sudden pit of despair, and then when the spirit could sink no lower she began to rise above the pain. But the girlish youthfulness had gone in the process—as surely as day folds into darkness of night, and the new reality appears. To aid in the healing process she returned to some of the old ways. After helping her mother in the morning with housework, she would take Bobby to visit Ross and her brother Joe at work. With the demise of the CD&M Interurban, Ross had opened a filling station south of town on route 23 on property he had purchased from the bankrupt CD&M. He was involved in building cabins for rent and Joe would ride his bicycle there to work with his dad.

Still, there came no word or letters from Bob, and she had almost given up hope of ever seeing him again. One day after bathing and changing Bobby where he lay happy on his pad with squirming and jerking limbs; his face ever smiling joyfully in a baby way. She tickled his chin and made mocking infant sounds and he responded with coos and giggles of his own.

Suddenly, there came a knock at the door.

"Mary... is somebody at the door?" Edith called from the kitchen.

"Yes... I'll get it Mom," she answered, giving one more cooch-e-cooch-e-coo...

At the door she said: "yes, who is it?"... then came the answer; "BOB!" she stared in quiet surprise as their eyes mingled, while all the doubt gave way to a trembling anxiety... "What... are you doing here?"

She threw the door open, and for an instant almost flung her arms around his neck, then catching herself in that reserved composure she hesitated.

"Who is it Mary?" came Edith's voice from the kitchen.

"Hello Mary—" he said.

Both stood quiet in the foyer, facing one another, but saying nothing.

"Who is it?" Edith called again.

"It's Bob, Mother," she called back in a voice small.

"Robert!" Edith choked, rushing through the parlor. "Well Robert, gracious sakes alive, what a surprise, so good to see you." Her arms moved to encircle him with a matronly hug. For Edith there was no time for reserve—only long overdue affection. Then drawing back, she said: "let me look at you, you're so fine and gentlemanly in that dark suit and tie and all, but my lands you're a little peaked. What on earth happened to you, it's been so long." Then, without reservation she hugged him again. "That's it, you're starved. You haven't been eating well... come." To Edith the key to health and well being meant eating well, and in circumstances requiring drastic measures; an occasional hot toddy.

"No thanks, really. . . I'm not hungry at all. I just stopped by. . ."

It was not without design that she coaxed him by the arm into the parlor where they paused to look at wide-eyed little Bobby, cooing and stretching to play with his own toes.

"Nonsense, I'll fix something and I won't take no for an answer either. You two just visit for a spell, and I'll call when it's ready. Then you can tell us all about yourself." When she spoke, her last words trailed off musically as she paddled back to her kitchen.

"Look," Mary said softly, "he's happy to see you. Come. . . he won't bite." She coaxed him closer to the crib-side, "see, he looks just like you—" To the father, any resemblance escaped him—he looked like a baby, any baby.

He moved warily. "He is kinda cute isn't he?" he inched his hand near, offering a finger for the little fellow to hold onto.

Arms and legs jerked erratically while one hand clutched his finger with a tight grip. The mouth gave a wry twisted smile as if it were trying to say something, gurgling bubbles and garble.

So many thoughts raced through Bob's mind, she's so beautiful he thought, and wanted to touch her and hold her again, and this infant of his own making. . . it too. He could smell it's baby smell, baby powder and oil, sweet and fresh, the scents of life brand new with innocence. "Look," he said. "He's trying to suck my finger."

"Babies do that—put everything in their mouths."

"No milk in that, little fellow. . ."

"He has your eyes see. . . and nose. Do you want to hold him? We call him Bobby. But you know that." Her words came soft while her eyes watched him curiously.

He didn't answer, but watched it longingly. He remembered having held it before, in Milwaukee, and each time it had cried and fussed and left him feeling helpless and frustrated.

She picked it up, offering it to him gently. "See, like this," she said. "With one hand right here for his bottom, and the other here for his head. His little neck isn't quite strong enough yet." She watched with anticipation, hoping and praying the two would accept and want each other.

Tiny feet kicked spasmodically, arms swung, reaching everywhere as if to grasp at something—anything, moving with tiny sensitive fingers desperately trying to articulate while it's head lurched. At first the eyes smiled grandly and again the pure tiny lips twisted and pursed in uncertain meaning.

He contemplated it momentarily; this thing she saw in his own likeness. Little eyes opened wide—staring at the man's face, wary. . . and then a pucker and a frown formed. Innocence faded as the face twisted fearfully while arching it's back, and it started to cry.

He wanted to say to it, "I won't hurt you."

Edith returned. "Come Robert, I've fixed a little something for you. The others have already had supper and left."

"But I'm really not hungry."

"Oh come now, Lordy, a man needs some good food, something to stick to the ribs, and Lord knows you can use some rest. Come, tell us about yourself," she insisted.

Mary joined them swaying Bobby in her arms.

Bob ate and explained they had lectured in the Milwaukee area for two weeks, then to Akron, then to Buffalo, and finally back to Cincinnati for the last two weeks. Now he was on his way back to Milwaukee, and decided to stop. He went on to explain that in his spare time, he was doing research on natural history for material he used in his lectures, and that he was uncovering some amazing statistics. In particular, things like the number of bones and muscles in the human body, and even things like the number of muscles in an elephant trunk. Pausing to chew a mouthful, he continued, unwittingly stirring his mashed potatoes and gravy into a paste. "The lectures on birds of the Bible have been well accepted. . . and after assembling some statistics on how many species were mentioned in the Bible and then how many times each was mentioned. . . Perhaps someday I'll put it all together in a study or manuscript and who knows, maybe get it published. . . there I go again, carried away and talking too much."

Even Bobby seemed quietly caught up in the sound of his father's words.

"Well then," said Edith, when he had eaten his fill; "I'll just tidy up a bit, and then I'll be off to Jess and Izetta's—leave you two to be alone for a spell. We're playing at the square dance tonight. I'll be in a little late most likely, maybe even ten o'clock."

Mary was playing *Fur Elise* on the piano while he leaned back in the big leather chair and listened. After that she eased into *Moonlight Sonata* while Bobby rested peacefully. Then she changed to a soft sounding lullaby as his mind struggled with forces inside. He studied the babies subtle movements across from him. . . and he remembered the past. . . the times they were together, he rested and dreamed. . . a kaleidoscope of dreams struggling with outside forces—all doing battle for the influence over his mind.

It was dark and quiet when his eyes opened sometime later. He heard her light footsteps and felt her hand's presences tugging at his.

"Come," she said.

"Where?"

"Our room is still there."

She undressed him at bedside with moonbeams striking in through the open window and a gentle breeze stirred the curtains. Nearby, the baby lay sleeping soundly in his bassinet. Together they tip-toed over to stare at his innocent peacefulness, then back to the bed. He tried to tell her he must leave in the morning. . . even as they drew close with flesh caressing flesh until nothing else seemed as important for awhile.

Both were sound asleep when Edith and Joe came in.

In the early morning hour just before sunrise, she lay close when he awoke, and together they remained quiet for a while. She spoke first. "You don't have to go; you could go back to college, or anything. I could get a job and work to help while you study."

Turning to her, he said: "I want you to come with me."

"And Bobby?" she indicated the bassinet.

"You could leave him with Edith. . . or your aunt, just until we get settled. . . then."

"*No*. The three of us belong together. . . we can make it, even here with a place of our own, or where ever you want, I'll go anyplace you want and I'll work to help."

He eased himself from the bed and started to dress.

"Don't go," she pleaded.

"I must. . . I have a commitment."

"A commitment. . . what about me, and. . . Bobby. I guess we don't count," she snapped, jumped out of bed and moved to confront him. "Is that it? We don't count. Just those damn lectures. . . and your Bible." She was almost hysterical then, biting back the tears; I won't cry.

He dressed and started through the door.

"If you leave this time. . . don't come back. Do you hear? Don't ever come back. . . never."

Hurrying to the window, she watched as he turned the corner below to walk out of sight, carrying the one bag he had come with.

Twelve

*A*rthur Brown made a right turn and wheeled his taxicab onto Ponce de Leon Avenue from Spring Street. He was saying: "Arthur Haley went back to Africa, you know the guy who wrote *Roots*, to visit the home of his ancestors, in Gambia—the people there was all black, and he was brown—what did he expect? Wonder what my ancestors looked like? I read that in Life Magazine. Good movie series too.

"Now they pardoned those Vietnam draft dodgers, and our Justice Department is investigating Korean officials for trying to buy off our congress reps—"

I spotted a building number 222, odd numbers on the right and even on the left. Mentally he tried to calculate the blocks to go to 1723—

As for the events after Bob last saw Mom I had to put together the answers from a combination of sources. Most of it from what she told me over the years, when I asked. A little from Frances Milton, my stepfather and Grandmother Edith when I visited her in that summer of my teens. I got a little from my brother too—he by way of our grandpa Ross.

When I got older Ross, didn't seem to care much for me—I didn't fish, hunt or play cards that he knew of—but he and my brother Bill, who was still in high school at the time, became real chums—they could sit by the Olentangy River and fish for hours—often not saying much even then; "yup," or "nope," or "I reckon so." Catching a fish though, now that was something to get excited about.

That first summer I went to Delaware for a visit, Grandpa Ross was pretty friendly to me, until one day standing in front of his old rumble seater he covered the hood ornament and coaxed me to spell 'Chevrolet'—I couldn't get it—I don't know why—but from that day on he concluded I was a dummy and not worth much of his time. Maybe he didn't hold much use for preachers either.

Anyway, in those last years he and Edith had gotten back together and on Saturday night he would drive her into town to her Spiritualist meetings on his way to card games. That summer I was full of questions and often when alone with Grandma Edith Swaren she would tell me how it was and what happened after my father left Mary that last time:

When Edith came in the room to find Mary sitting on the bed crying, and Bobby crying in his bassinet, then sympathy tears flooded her face also. She rocked both of them desperately.

"He never cared for us. He never loved us—just like it was with Ardith they're all the same. . . *preachers, ha,* some religion, the Bible, it means nothing. . . nothing." Abruptly the tears halted, replaced by a new and angry determination.

"Child, here now, you mustn't punish yourself."

"No. . . nothing counts but themselves. They don't care about anybody else."

Bobby started crying louder and Edith sobbed for their pain as Mary suddenly rushed to scoop him up and hold him close. "Now, now," she said, trying to calm him while she swayed and paced the floor, rocking him closely. "Now, now. . . don't cry, he's gone, didn't want us anyway."

"Here child, let me take Bobby for a little. . ."

"NO!. . . no, he's not Bobby anymore. His name is Taylor now. . . *not* Bobby."

Later that same afternoon, Edith returned from the garden to find Mary sitting on the parlor floor by the piano stool. Bobby played with his toes innocently unaware of his mother grief as she sat tearing music sheets into shredded pieces; music that she had proudly collected over the many past years, tearing and throwing them at the floor with a vengeance wrought of mounting anguish.

Edith stood speechless.

Bobby played and giggled.

"Mary... what are you doing?"

She only stared at the pieces of torn music sheets strewn about the floor, and ripped another. "I'll never play again!" With that as her final declaration her voice had found a new level of harshness.

Robert Marshall still sat in his wheelchair by the desk at 1723 Ponce de Leon. He fingered the aged envelope that had never been mailed—and in his mind he returned to that time he had last seen Mary in her room, and his son sleeping in his bassinet.

He had walked to the station and paced nervously, waiting for the early morning bus to Marion, there he took a direct train to Milwaukee.

It was late evening when he arrived at the hotel where he was to meet with other lecturers in the morning. He had walked from the train station and checked into his room, and hadn't eaten all day.

Lying on his bed, tired, and weary, he agonized and struggled with himself, his mind tormented with confusing visions and signals that stabbed at his conscience. Always, he had known what he must do, and always he had a strong conviction in his decisions. But now, he didn't know and he wished, prayed for sleep, escape.

But he could not sleep, and he struggled and pleaded with his God for help. "Yes... I have made a commitment to serve thee God... and I want to serve thee, but Mary and the baby, do I not have an obligation to them." Alone in his room he said the words aloud and in the dark empty chamber they hung still in the air like evoking aura of suspense and uncertainty. . . "Why is there this strain between the two?" Then there came a time of lucidity—all things seemed rational.

He lay there on his back looking up to the ceiling motionless for a while till he felt at ease with a new calm, then he jumped up and to himself, he said aloud, "I know what I must do." There was a small table and a chair with a light. He pulled the chain to turn it on. From a drawer he drew a piece of plain white paper and envelope. Lifting the pen and opening the ink bottle he dipped it and started to write:

August 19, 1931
Dearest Mary,
    I've been a fool and I realize now that what I love most is you and our son. After tomorrow I have two more lecture commitments, and then I shall return to you.

    We can rent a place of our own and I'll continue with college, perhaps change my major to teaching. Music and physical education, or history, yes history. I have always found history one of my favorites. I may not take a full schedule at first and thereby allow more time to work at a job. I'll find something and we'll get by. Perhaps carpentry. I always liked making things, and fixing things. It may take longer to earn a degree, but it'll be better for us, all three of us. I'll count the minutes till we're together again.

All my love,
Your Bob

After reading it back once he folded it neatly and placed it in the plain white envelope.

As if someone else was there in the room he found himself, saying "I'll address it and mail it first thing in the morning," then undressing, he turned off the light and crawled back into bed.

Atlanta, September 1977

*M*rs. Odelia Bright was a rather large-boned well built woman in her late forties. She wore her long black hair with traces of gray gathered in the back neatly. She went about her usual daily business humming tunefully much of the time.

When she tapped him lightly on the shoulder as he sat still holding the aged photo and envelope his thoughts returned from the past.

She said, "Robert. . . a taxicab just pulled into the driveway. It must be the one you're expecting, with your son."

"Oh. . . yes, of course," he answered, placing the pictures neatly on the table before him. "My crutches Odelia, please. I surely don't want to greet my son in this confounded wheeling thing."

Maneuvering to a corner nearby, he reached for them as Mrs. Bright hurried to hand them over. He struggled to stand and balance himself. "Amazing isn't it. . . after all these years;" he paused, managing to position himself on them. "Wonder what he's like, what he looks like. I suspect he wonders the same about me." Moving into the hallway, he chuckled, "He says he lives in California. . . and here he is, right in Atlanta. . . just imagine Odelia. . . my own son, here."

"It most certainly is Robert," she agreed. "The Lord works in mysterious ways."

He paused at the ornate door with glass sections in the upper half, pulled the curtain aside and peeked through.

When Arthur Brown turned into a tree lined gravel driveway to stop before an old two story red brick structure, evidence of some past glory seemed almost certain. I don't know what I expected; it was neat and looked well kept, not at all what I might have expected. For some strange reason something Mom had said once struck me as ironic: "we never missed a meal, but there were many times we didn't know where the next one was coming from."

I wondered how a man burdened with so many years in a wheelchair could struggle to survive. Mom told me how tall and athletic he had been, inches taller than myself. And that he always stood straight with a certain personal pride that had become his trademark back then.

The taxicab stopped in front of steps which led to a small front porch with the ornate door. The door opened and there stood a thinly built man with gray hair, straight and tall as he could manage. A large well built woman dressed in white like a nurse stood at his side.

I stepped out as Arthur Brown placed my only bag at my feet. "Can you return for me here at eight thirty?" I said to him, "better make it eight for a return trip to the airport."

"You better call in cause I might be busy with another fare or on the other side of town. If I'm nearby and hear your call I'll come if you could ask for me, I'd like to come—hear how you and your dad got on—you take care now, hear?"

I paid the fare and added a generous tip and thanked him, promising to call.

For a long time it seemed, I stood there, struggling to control the welling inside, and to force back any emotions that might betray me. Then I climbed the steps one at a time and set my bag down.

"You must be Robert. . . "

"Yes of course."

We both seemed speechless and then reached to shake hands. The man on crutches balanced skillfully and reached to grasp my hand, then clasping his other hand on top we held there for what seemed like an eternity. There was a certain manliness in his grip—the hands of an old man. There was eagerness with a measure of anticipation there too.

"Come in, come on in," he offered graciously. "Come on in." He moved backwards. "So it's Taylor is it, your mother. . . she liked that name. Oh let me introduce you," he said. "This is Mrs. Bright, my housekeeper. . . and a very good friend. She comes to see me, and I couldn't get by without her. Three days a week she's supposed to, but she stops by more often to check on me. Likes to keep me on the straight and narrow. Don't you suppose?"

"I'm pleased to meet you." She smiled a broad smile. "This sure is a happy day. Your father has hoped someday to find you he tells me now, but he never said a word till this day."

"You say he looked too?" then looking back to my father, I waited for the answer.

"Oh yes, many times. Just a minute." He shifted about as if

to make himself as comfortable as practical. "So much to talk about. . . let's see forty five, forty six years. How time flies." While he glanced about, Mrs. Bright had brought what he was looking for. "You sit down and get comfortable while I change into this confounded contraption. Spend most of my life in this contemptible chair on wheels. You just make yourself comfortable. How about some ice cold lemonade. Do you like lemonade?"

"Yes sir I do."

"Odelia, would you please?"

"Most certainly," she said, hurrying away to where the kitchen must be.

I studied the room curiously from where I sat on a firm provincial style couch with dark wood trim aged well into comfort. In front a stylish coffee table waited as though arranged for company and standing next to the wall where I had just entered stood an antique looking bookcase with glass doors. Placed inside neatly were some framed photos and select porcelain figurines. Near the opposite wall and next to a brick fireplace was a brown overstuffed leather chair and footstool. Through an archway of retractable double doors I could see into the adjoining room. At the far end of the room was a neatly made bed and in the opposite corner was a table. When I first entered the room I immediately noticed three television sets side by side on a table. In the other corner stood an age darkened desk with some letters and photos apparently recently set there. I couldn't tell what they were but did recognize a worn leather covered Bible with several red ribbon markers hanging out. I wondered if it was the King James version, because Mom had told me that he said it was the most *lyrical* of all Bibles.

"Now young, man," the older man said, having made his final adjustments. "You must tell me about yourself. For years I've looked for you too—in phone books. Always I looked for Robert Taylor Marshall, but nothing, not even a clue. When ever I've traveled, oh yes I travel." His response seemed more an answer to my expression of surprise. "Oh yes I travel, even in this condition," he tapped the armrest of his wheelchair. "A few years back with my sister Aileen, your aunt by the way, we covered nine different states and saw the Grand Canyon. One of the Lord's great wonders. My brother, Bill once remarked when we visited Niagara Falls, actually it was more like a declaration;

anyway he said, 'that here more than any other place on earth you can see the hand of God at work.' I don't think Bill ever got to see the Grand Canyon—" His face revealed thoughts reminiscent of that past experience. "But enough from me now, I want to hear about you."

"Yes, I did the same thing." He inclined his head a little and tightened his eyes—waiting on me. He did a neat job of breaking the ice, I'll have to give him that.

"You'll have to forgive me, but I think I'm still in shock," I said. Secretly, I scolded myself for not having come better prepared, and wondered if perhaps he really never expected this meeting to happen. "Anyway, from time to time I travel, and I too often looked in phone books, I've been right here at Atlanta airport several times, and this time. . ." I opened my hands expressively in a gesture. "Well here we are. Oh what does the S stand for?"

"Sidney, for my grandfather," he said.

"I wasn't sure and Mom had never said for certain if it was Stanley or Steven or Spencer. I suppose I should have considered that too."

He smiled, his face all at once filled with the wisdom of age.

"Anyway, I didn't know until I was about fourteen. That's when she told me. . . about you and that my real name was Marshall."

"She told you about me?" he asked, with a hint of curiosity.

We sat there quiet, each wondering what to say next, like measuring each other. I decided to speak candidly.

"She said that you had a wonderful singing voice, and that you were a theology student at Ohio Wesleyan when you and she met, and you lectured and wanted to be a preacher. . . and that you just weren't ready for children." The last seemed to carry a sting to it I had not intended, like paying off an old debt.

"That was kind of her," the older man said with a nod. It did sting though; quick and prickly, then he hid it.

Breaking their silence, Mrs. Bright entered the room to place a glass of lemonade in front of each of them, the ice cube tinkled as she sat them down. "Would you like some sugar cookies or something to eat?" she asked.

"No thanks. I've eaten too much already, and with all that sitting. . . but thank you very much just the same. Then I changed my mind. "Is that sugar cookies I smell baking? Grandma Edith used to make sugar cookies. I remember how she used to always smell like things baking; sugar cookies most of all—I can see her now in my mind's eye, in her kitchen, wiping her hands on her apron, busy, and pleased with what she was doing..."

"I remember her that way too, especially since you called—truly one of the Lord's chosen ladies—a kindly person to so many—" he paused momentarily. "Odelia, Mrs. Bright has worked long and hard to duplicate them—including the toasted edges, so they're just right, without being burnt."

"It's the baking soda and flour, and not too much sugar, I think—"

"I think you're right, and cinnamon—perhaps a pinch of this and that; her own secret ingredients. She did everything in pinches and by instinctive measures. Nothing was written down—"

" But it always came out the same and perfect. That was her all right. If that's the case then how could I refuse. I'll try some—they're best with cool milk though—"

"Or cocoa—cocoa in the wintertime—milk or lemonade in the heat of summer."

Mrs. Bright beamed with pride. "Your father is an exceptional man," she said. "Why he sings a gospel right from his wheelchair and he preaches a powerful sermon—but his best work is in Sunday school—with young folks—"

"Now Odelia, lets not fill this young man with false notions—you go and get us some of those sugar cookies—and some cold milk."

"Lemonade is fine—even with sugar cookies. I've tried them with lemonade too. Peculiar isn't it; sugar cookies with lemonade, but it works."

"It sure does," he agreed.

I smiled back, anxious at the thought.

"Tell me about yourself, are you married, any children, and what kind of work do you do?"

"Yes I am married, a building contractor... in Northern California, small time, up in the mountains, I have three or I should say *you* have three *grandsons*." He would be pleased to hear this—and the pride suddenly flashed across his face and I knew I was right.

"*Three grandsons!*" he said, almost leaping from the wheelchair. "Lord God," he declared inclining his head a little. "Can you imagine that? Did you hear that Odelia?" He called to the kitchen, and repeated it, "three grandsons," then wiping his eyes he said, "tell me about them. Do you have pictures?"

"Well no I don't. I guess I didn't come very well prepared. I didn't know this would happen. . . the eldest, is from a first marriage. I've lost track of him, from time to time, but I think the last I heard he was in Houston. The next one started in college, just this last year. How ironic, you know, oh I guess you couldn't though. . . I have never understood religion." This last statement sounded like a confession I wished undone. "I don't know why. I have read my share of the Bible though, but anyway a friend stopped me one day and congratulated me—you can imagine my surprise when he explained that my son had chosen the ministry and was going to college to study for it. It was his senior year in high school and he had considered law enforcement, the Coast Guard Academy and also architecture. . . so it came as a complete surprise to learn that he wanted to be a preacher. Of course, his mother and I were the last to find out. Seems he was going to keep it a secret and surprise us, don't you think?

"The youngest, as far as I know plans for a career in Radiology or Inhalation Therapy, but it wouldn't surprise me if he ends up in construction—he likes making things. Both do, and both are very independent, with minds of their own. Later, the older one confessed that to be a preacher was not his goal, but he wanted to work with young people, or in athletics."

"That's very interesting. I'd like very much to meet them, and the rest of your family. You know I often wonder about Edith, your grandmother, a wonderful woman, did you get to know her well? And Joseph, your uncle, and Ross. . . and Mary too. Did you know that your grandmother and my mother corresponded for a while, but then I was in Warm Springs, and lost contact. Edith and Ross were divorced. Did they ever get back together?"

"Yes, for several years in fact. They lived in Stratford until she died and then Ross passed on some three years after that. . . 1952 or 53, I think."

"A pity, wonderful people. And Joe, how is he?"

"Uncle Joe was killed, about 1947 I believe. . . very tragic."

"Oh Lord no. . . we used to play basketball together, before these." He slapped his legs as a reminder of the days before. "Lord knows I liked Joe and thought of him often. . . how did it happen?"

"It was from a football injury he got in his senior year in high school. He had a trick knee from the injury. He was married did you know that?"

"No I didn't."

"Well, he had four children, three girls and a boy. Jon was the boy's name. Anyway, he worked on the railroad and it was a rainy night; he was doing something on the ladder between the cars; there was a bent step and his trick knee from his football days gave way. They figured he fell between the cars while the train was moving."

We sat there, quiet and saddened, neither able to speak next as though sharing a moment in silence.

Finally he found words to gently end the stillness. "And Mary, you see I never heard much about her, after that day. . . when we parted. Did she tell you much about that time? I always wondered about her. . . "

"For some years she didn't, but yes, later she did. When she thought it was time I knew, I suppose. I didn't want to press her. . . but some years back when we were talking alone, and I guess she must have felt like talking. That's when she told me. Said she was very bitter afterwards, for some time, and then with a smile she had said, 'time heals all.' She also said that for a long time she refused to attend church, and that her mother had even tried to force her, but she didn't explain why."

I had touched a raw nerve and it showed for an instant, so I watched for a clue, uncertain if I should continue. The older man's eyes gave me the answer I needed. . . I tried to think ahead choosing my words with better care this time:

As the scene unfolded in my head I started putting together the pieces from what I had learned of that time when my mother learned about the tragedy of my father. It happened on a mid-October Sunday morning, Grandma Edith told me that much. The events that followed had been etched in the recesses of her memory as eternal as life itself. The day was an especially nice one. Mom, Mary, was busy helping her mother with the clean-up after breakfast. Church had become a sore subject between them, yet Edith had persisted.

"What a beautiful day the Lord has given us for worship."

Mary said nothing, but continued wiping a pan.

"It's been so long now Honey. . . come to church with me, bring the baby, " Edith pleaded.

"Mother, we've talked about this before, and you know how I feel. I've made up my mind," Mary's words came with cold determination.

"But child, you need to. . . to rid yourself of sadness, and the bitterness inside."

"I'm okay. Really, and I don't want to go to church, ever. They're all hypocrites anyway."

"Surely you don't believe that child. You're just hurt. . . and Lord knows Bob would write or contract you *if. . .* " she hesitated, then a small *if,* "if he could."

"Oh, all he wants to do is run around giving his precious lectures and having a good time. . . he doesn't care one little iota about us," her voice was uncharacteristically petulant for the recent days. "Why should I care?"

"But. . . he needs. . . your prayers and compassion."

"He doesn't need, or *want* anything from. . . prayers, for what? Mother! Is something wrong?" Mary studied the saddened face of her mother for long moments, and she wondered. These last weeks, and how often she had mentioned forgiveness and compassion and the need for prayers for others. And that Bob would come back to her if he could.

"Mother! something has happened, and you know it, why won't you tell me?"

"Lord knows child. . . only the Lord understands our trials and sufferings. . . only he knows. . . "

"Mother, what is it? Tell me."

"There's a letter. . . from Bob's mother. It came two weeks ago. . . he's. . . he's paralyzed, only God knows how I wish I didn't have to tell you this."

A pan hit the floor, yet she hadn't heard it, for she too stood poised momentarily in the clutches of her own rapidly mounting dilemma.

Edith moved to her side and guided her so both sat down at the kitchen table.

Wiping her eyes, she pleaded, "how did it happen? The letter. Let me see it."

"You don't need to. . . ."

"But I want to read it, please, I'm okay, really I am," she said, her voice became calm as she straightened with a certain forced dignity.

Leaving the kitchen, Edith soon returned with the envelope and handed it to her.

Mary removed a single page, unfolded it and studied the writing on both sides. She hesitated. . . then read quietly to herself, her lips moving intensely with each word.

Nov. 19, 1931
Dear Friend,

I grieve deeply as I write this letter to tell you of the very sad news. It was on the 20th of August in his hotel room in Milwaukee when a friend of Bob's (who was also on the lecture tour), found him. He was delirious and could not move his legs. He was taken to the hospital and was later diagnosed as having a severe case of poliomyelitis. It really wasn't diagnosed until later, by then it was to late for proper treatment.

About the only organs in his body left functioning properly were his heart and lungs, and for a while he wasn't expected to live. Doctors had almost given up hope, but finally he did improve. They said probably because of his good physical condition.

A high school friend of Bob's, named Leander Basset who was living in Milwaukee discovered his predicament and visited him regularly. He handled Bob's affairs and I'm sure his loyalty and generosity proved a great source of strength for Bob.

After months in the hospital he came home where we worked on his legs daily, but unfortunately they did not respond.

Yesterday he was taken to Warm Springs, Georgia and we all hope and pray for his recovery. However, the doctors give little chance he will ever walk again.

He insisted that I not trouble you with this, but I felt you should know, and that you would wish to remember him in your prayers.

Sincerely,
Florence Marshall

After reading the letter, Mary sat reflecting on the sudden impact, her brow set in a somber frown. "I have to go to him," she cried, placing the letter tentatively on the table and rushing off to her room.

Edith hurried behind her.

In a sudden rush, Mary threw a suitcase on her bed and proceeded to stuff it with clothing.

"But Mary, what will you do?"

"I don't know, but I have to go. He needs me. I'll get a job, somehow, and a place to stay nearby," she rattled on while stuffing the suitcase in a frenzy.

"But child, there are no jobs... Lord knows I hate to say this, but these are bad times, especially in the big cities. People are starving, and there are no jobs. You know how it is, even here... and you'd be a stranger down there, with no training, and no one to go to. Lord knows we're not rich... and your father would surely help you... and I'd do what I could."

She continued with her frantic stuffing, then stood poised as a feeling of complete hopelessness crept over her. She said nothing, then started tossing shoes and other items out and about in a fit of despair.

Edith went on sympathetically, "and you have a child to care for... Robert is getting the best treatment possible, and it would be a long time..." Edith sat down wearily on the bedside.

Suddenly, Mary stopped. Holding a shoe in each hand, she slapped them into her case of chaos, sobbing again and sagged as if suddenly weighed down by the gravity of her situation. Edith pushed the suitcase aside and pulled Mary to her as the tears poured together.

"Nothing's changed, really. He didn't want us before." She straightened to wipe her eyes. "Why should he want us now?"

I paused momentarily, looking to the man in the wheelchair. There was a pained expression on his face, and he wiped it away. "Please continue," he said.

This story unfolding in my head was not a pretty one and I wondered if he could handle it; but then he has handled tougher ones already I concluded:

It was after Christmas, in January or maybe February, Mary found a job with the Smith Liquidation Company, doing typing and inventory work. That's when she learned to take direct dictation on the typewriter.

The manager, an older man with a family liked her and on Mother's Day gave her a bouquet of yellow roses. The job lasted almost a year, until the company moved to another town. She said she could have kept the job but decide against moving.

Eventually she started to shed her bitterness, and attended square dances again at Mingo Park where her aunt and uncle played. She loved to dance. Her Uncle Jess was the caller, and he played the harmonica. Another uncle played the fiddle, and another old fellow played spoons and scrub-board. I remember, cause she said they were a real show to watch.

At times she would leave me with her grandparents, and sometimes they would come to watch and mind me while she danced.

It was in June in 1932, at one of the square dances, that she met this guy Covet, Brice Covett. She had been sad much too long and his friendly, cheerful manner pleased her. A friend she had known in high school was married to his brother-in-law, or something like that. Anyway, he apparently seemed to be a sort of cheerful character. He had been drinking and she danced with him. Later, they went outside together.

"Here have a drink of this," he said, pulling a bottle from his pocket, "just what you need."

"No, I don't drink whiskey," she said.

"Well don't mind if I do." He tipped it up for a long swig, grinned, wiped and said: "Best shine ever come out of Virginia."

Mary watched. She was aware that Ross took a drink in the morning and one before bedtime, for medicinal purposes Edith had explained. But that's all, and he never got drunk.

"Come on you have one, it'll do you good, come on, don't be a stick in-the-mud," he pressed. But he apparently had a certain charm about him, like being used to getting his way, and Mary needed cheering up.

"No thanks, I don't want any. . ."

"Here you gotta," grabbing her arm, he pushed the bottle to her mouth.

"I said *no!*" twisting free, she started back to the dance alone.

"Wait, I didn't mean to... look I'm sorry—only kiddin. Just tryin to cheer you up, you know, so we can have a little fun. Ain't no harm in that, now is there?"

He had stopped, and was standing in front of her. He smiled and put the bottle in his hip pocket then held his hands up in a placating gesture. "Look... I'm sorry, it won't happen again, promise." He smiled convincingly.

"Well... okay."

"Wanna danse, let's danse. Come on, they're forming for another square right now. We can get in if we hurry," he took her hand and they hurried inside; "*Swing your partner...*" the caller sang out. She laughed as his jovial manner raised her spirits.

A week passed and another Friday came at the dance. They met again and when he asked her to go to a show in Columbus, she consented.

Brice Covett always drank, yet she found him fun to be with. So their meetings and dates continued. Always he encouraged her to drink with him, but always she refused, and when he became amorous, she put him off, though each time he became more aggressive. He spoke of marriage and she stalled.

Summer passed, then fall. Christmas was near.

I remember Mom said they couldn't keep me from climbing the Christmas tree. She said I would get into all the presents and climb the tree, so they had been forced to put the tree and packages in my playpen... sure wish I knew what had been so fascinating about that tree. Well Uncle Joe had made a hobbyhorse in woodshop for me for a Christmas present.

I paused in a effort to collect my thoughts, watching his eyes for a clue, wondering if he played poker, then returned to where I had left off.

It was mid-March and she found work at the local five-and-dime store on Sandusky Street. Covett had still been pressuring her to marry him.

Ross came to the store and asked her to have lunch with him one day. They went to a little sandwich shop nearby.

"Do you know Brice Covett," she asked.

"Yep."

"He wants me to marry him."

Ross said: "worked with him once, some years back. He's no good Mary. Stay away from him." Grandpa Ross was a man of few words. She knew that. She should have listened.

She started to explain, but realizing her father's opposition, she decided to change the subject.

Two days later on a Friday, at closing time, Covett picked her up and they went out to eat and then to a show. He had been drinking and was in one of his mellow pleasing moods.

After the show, they sat in his car in front of her house and talked.

"You know that old store job ain't no good for you. An you got that kid. Why don't you marry me? I got a good business and you sure could help. . . typing bills and doing other things an all. I could provide for you and the kid. And you know how much I love you." He pulled her close for a kiss.

She wondered what Ross had meant. Still, Covett seemed so sincere. . . and he had told her many times how much he loved her. The thought of working at something useful again, and taking care of her own home, and a father for her baby all seemed so appealing. "Okay," she consented, "I'll marry you. When do you want to do it?"

"How about tomorrow, we can drive down to Newport, get hitched and back in the same day, then you can move in right away," he said, satisfied. He reached for his bottle and pulled a long swig.

They were married and she typed his bills and cooked his meals, straightened his house and delivered his lunch daily to wherever he worked. She even drove delivery trucks on occasions. She got pregnant right away.

With the passing of six weeks Mary had been happy, and spring was near. Brice had been unconcerned when she had given him the news. He drank as usual, and soon undertones of sarcasm surfaced as she was treated to a different side of his personality. There were times when he drank too much and became belligerent and mean, seemingly for no reason. There were also times when he had gone wild in a tantrum, and thrown things and had punched the walls or anything in his way. On two occasions he had blamed her for something menial and threatened to hit her. That time she was able to fend him off. Always, the next day he had apologized and sworn it would not happen again. Yet more and more periods frequently surfaced in which he became increasingly sullen and threatening.

Covett came home late from work one night and he had been drinking heavily. He muttered unpleasantly and started to sit down to the kitchen table.

"This damn food's cold—garbage anyhow," he grunted.

"It was ready hours ago, and I couldn't keep it warm forever," she said flatly.

Stopping at the opposite end of the table, he studied the typewriter and the papers nearby, then stared at her with contempt. "You got them bills done like I told you this morning?" he glowered.

"Some of them, most of them," she answered cautiously.

"I thought I told you to get them all done. What you been doin all day, just sittin around, thinking about that goddamn preacher guy, is that it... huh? Is that his kid in your belly—huh, instead of mine?" With a swipe of his violent hand he knocked papers, plate and food across the room. Then lifting the typewriter, he hurled it. Barely missing her head it smashed against the wall. "I'll show you, you worthless bitch."

From the nearby room, Taylor came at his leg. "You leave my Mommy alone."

"Why you little brat... I'll..."

"Don't you dare touch him. You leave him alone."

Grabbing Taylor by the arm, he shoved him into a closet and closed the door, locking him into blackness. When she grabbed at the door his hand caught her across the face with a glancing blow that sent her reeling backwards. She picked up the typewriter, raised it above her head and rushed past him to throw it crashing down the cellar stairs.

"There," she said, "do your own damn bills."

"Why you bitch, I'll show you a thing or two."

As he grabbed her by the arm and spun her around, her knee caught him full in the groin. Loosening his grip, he staggered back for an instant... only to come back with a fist that barely missed her face. Again he grabbed one arm while her free hand scratched his face and desperately pulled at his hair. They struggled until finally he punched her full on the face with his fist, and then another, and another. She lay slumped on the couch where he left her, until she heard cries from the closet.

The Roadhouse was a private club on a secluded road east of town and a usual haunt of working men. This night was no different. The local sheriff was an honorary member but never put any time in there. It had been a hot and humid day and finally the night air offered a small measure of relief.

At the bar on the left stood five or six regulars, while still others lined up on stools chatting and laughing at old worn out stories. In the center of the floor stood a pool table with a colored Tiffany glass shade suspended low over it's center. Two player's plied their skills at a game of eight-ball, one against the other. Another stood nearby with a glass of beer in one hand and cue-stick in the other, waiting his turn patiently.

A few feet away and to the right was a green felt covered table with a single lighted shade and pull-chain lamp suspended low from the ceiling. Five players sat, cards in hand. Sometimes there were others to fill the other tables behind, but not this night. The back room otherwise looked dark and foreboding. Dealers choice was the rule. Some liked draw-poker and others preferred stud.

Jake Buttercroft sat across the table to the rear, and John Miller to his right with Huey Littlejohn to his left. Ross sat opposite them with his side to the pool table. Then there was Milt Pepper. With sober faces, they studied the cards fanned in their hands. Jake had dealt.

"Take three," said Huey, tossing three away.

Ross discarded two and thumped two fingers.

Milt took two also, and John Miller discarded one.

"Dealer takes three," Jake said with a gravelly voice, after scratching his bushy mane of red hair.

A familiar figure entered and took a place at the bar next to Ben Crump.

"Shine," growled Covett.

"What in tarnation happened to you?. . . Looks like you run into a wildcat, Covett," exclaimed Ben.

He downed the whiskey in a single gulp, "Showed her a thing or two. . . by God you better believe it, bet she'd listen next time I tell her to do a thing."

"Looks like she got in a few licks herself," Ben taunted.

"Well maybe that's a fact, but let me tell you something, I knocked a shit right outa that wench. . . showed her a thing or two... whuped her sumpin fierce... hey, another shine. Double..."

"A body ought to go up there and smack him right across the mouth, by thunder. Got a notion to do it myself," Jake fretted.

"Nobody'd hold it against you Ross, him being a younger man and all, if you just let it pass."

"They say he can get kinda mean and wild," added Milt Pepper.

"Oh, everybody knows he's just got a big mouth, likes to shoot it off, that's all," said Huey. "Pay him no mind—"

At the bar Covett went on. "Whuped that wench sumthing fierce... and I'd do it again, teach her who's boss, by God." bragged Covett in a louder voice, taking notice of Ross for the first time.

"Shhh," whispered Ben Crump, "Ross is over there, and he'd hear..."

"Screw Ross, never liked him anyhow, and I'd just as soon stomp a tird right outa him too," he growled, turning to the card table, so all were sure to hear.

The words of his card playing companions meant nothing as they fell on deaf ears. Ross had already decided what he must do. Closing the fanned cards, he laid them face down on the table and came to his feet.

A loud crack chilled the room as a body hit the floor with a heavy thud. A man stood over the moaning, wretching figure at his feet. The man stood there silent for a time, tensed and waiting, still holding the remains of a broken cue-stick he had taken from the hands of a waiting player standing nearby.

Ben Crump was first to break the silence.

"Nobody would blame you none, Ross... he had it coming sure's Hades has hell-fire."

Without looking down at the writhing body clutching the pained face Ross flung the splintered cue-stick down, stepped over the body and left.

The road shone ahead like an endless darkened pathway in the headlights, except for a quarter moon hanging like a sickle ready to swing. He should have no trouble finding the old single story farm house from what Mary had told him in their recent visits. Ross knew every road and structure anyway. He hadn't approved of her marriage to Covett, yet said nothing when she told him about it. Later on he had regretted holding his peace.

Inside, the lights were on, and the front door was open. At the sagging screen door he paused. There was no sound. Opening the door, he stepped in, looked around the front room and down the hall to the kitchen to survey the mess and evidence of a struggle. Then he followed another sound to a doorway and stopped.

Mary had an open suitcase on the bed, and some boxes, all over-stuffed with their belongings.

She turned to him, "Oh Pops," she cried.

Holding her close, he patted her back, comforting her as best he could.

"I should have listened. . . " whimper, "I should have known," she said, wiping her eyes.

He touched her bruised and swollen face tenderly, and asked, "what now, Honey?" For the moment, seeing her face that way he was inclined to go back and finish the job by knocking the *rest* of Covett's teeth out.

"Go somewhere. . . anywhere away from here, I don't know, anywhere. Oh Pops, what a mess I've made of my life, of everything. . . "

"Now there, it's not that bad, tomorrow, and time heals all. Time heals all, daughter. At Stratford, I've just finished another cabin. It's not a mansion but you can stay there for a spell anyhow."

After that Joe was working at the station one day and told Mary that her room was still available. He told her Edith said she and the baby were both still welcome anytime.

Time passed slowly for Mary, and if she had been bitter before, she was doubly so now.

Mary gave birth on December 28, 1933 to Ruth Mae Covett a beautiful baby girl with gorgeous red hair, and though Mary named her, her continued bitterness left no room in her heart for joy.

A new boarder named Frances Milton drove Edith to the hospital for visits. On the day Mary was to be released Milton offered to picked her up and brought her home. Edith was busy baking pies at the time.

When the car pulled up, Edith rushed eagerly to meet her

with Taylor stumbling close at her heels.
Without a word, Mary went past her and directly upstairs.
Bewildered, Edith asked Milton, "Where is the baby?"
"She wouldn't take it. . . it's at the hospital," he said, lamely.
"You mean she just left it—? Oh my Lord." Edith's own words came back at her in shock. She lumbered up the steps to discover Mary rocking solemnly, arms folded in protest. Hurrying back downstairs, she asked Milton to take her to the hospital.
Taylor was playing innocently and Mary still sitting there rocking when Edith returned to stand in front of her cuddling the new baby.
"This is your child, a beautiful child," she scolded, "and you should thank the good Lord you are both healthy." That is all she said. That was all she needed to say. Placing the baby in Mary's lap, Edith waited. Soon the mother's fingers inched to touch the sleeping infant and it's own tiny fingers. Taylor stood by inquisitive and touched it also.
Scooping it into her arms, she rocked. Holding it close to her bosom, she tearfully repeated, "I'll never let you go, never, and I'll never let anybody take you away from me."
"Come Taylor," Edith said, taking his hand, "let's go downstairs and you can help grandma make some sugar cookies—a big one like a Teddy-bear."

"Well that's about it I guess. Milton was very patient with her and they were married some time later. Then we moved to Columbus where he was doing well in business for some years. He was one of the depression era casualties and lost everything. He was always trying to climb back up the ladder of success. I remember in Columbus—I was a little kid then, we lived in a big house with servants and a gardener—a whole city block with lots of rooms—he wound up as a clerk in a hardware store after that. Mom had two more children in Columbus, a girl and another boy. Then about 1937, I think it was when his business failed, we all moved to New Orleans where she gave birth to another boy."
"New Orleans. . . imagine all those years, and you were that close." He shook his head thoughtfully, as though sorting the

pieces of a puzzle; "and Mary, she was okay then?

"Oh yes, except during the war, about 1940 or 41— I think it happened one night while she was doing Air Raid Warden duty, somehow she injured her right ankle and infection got into the bone, she spent the better part of two years in the hospital."

"How is she now?" he asked, his voice deeply concerned, "I mean. . . she's still alive, and well, is she?"

"Oh yes, yes of course. She lived with us for several years, but has her own apartment now. She stays busy with clubs and lady-friends since Milton died about five years ago."

The older man waited, his eyes and mind busy and inquisitive; "do you play the piano?" he asked.

"No. I love music, but for some reason the talent for making it seems to have escaped me. I can drive the hell out of a backhoe, but I can't get any work done with one."

"Strange isn't it? Your Mother always wanted us to dance together—she did the Charleston once for me—and I was so clumsy—she danced the Kinkajoo and Lindy Hop. After we moved to Columbus to be on our own, it was."

"She always says the thing she misses most is not being able to dance—her condition—the doctors were barely able to save her foot—but it left her. . . "

"Crippled. . . how ironic. Both of us, after all these years. She always wanted us to dance together—and we never did."

For a moment he hesitated, then: "You don't happen to have a picture of your mother with you. . .?"

"Sorry. . ."

He nodded as if dismissing it but I could tell he wanted to see what she looked like.

"I can see her now," he said. For an instant he drifted. I think in his mind's eye he could see her then, the girl of another life-time.

"She hasn't changed much over the recent years," I said. "A little grayer perhaps, and maybe a few wrinkles. . ." If you don't notice that she has a limp, I thought.

We sat with eyes locked for a time, each not sure what to say next—then he, as if searching for a way to keep the conversation going, said; "do you sing?"

"Only in the shower, or sometimes when I'm driving alone on the highway. Guess I never learned that either. I remember, Grandmother Swaren used to tell me I should sing. 'You know your father had such a beautiful voice,' she would say, 'and you sound just like him'. . . but unfortunately no, I never learned."

"Your grandmother was an extraordinary woman, she played a beautiful piano. She could hear a piece of music once or twice and play it, and she could change the tempo, improvise. She could read music, but apparently didn't feel a need to." His eyes closed blissfully for a brief interval, as if to hear the music once again.

"It was when I visited them that one summer when I was fourteen. That's when Mom told me my name was really Marshall. But yes, I remember her well, she always smelled sweet and floury, like sugar cookies, and pies, and cakes. At times, yes I think maybe I can hear someone playing the piano, way off in the distance. It has always been a mystery to me, until now."

"Yep, sure enough, that was her all right, same woman. And your mother could play too. Yes, she could play beautifully, but they were different. . . different styles. Did she ever tell you we performed together on radio?"

"Yes, she mentioned it a few times. . . and something about a canary. . . and something else too. . . about a preacher bird, and then she smiled. I sensed there was something of a personal secret there—so I didn't press her. But she smiled when she mentioned it, so I knew it must have triggered a pleasant memory."

"A preacher bird huh—those were happy days; yes indeed," he said, and his own smile betrayed a reminiscent quality about the incident too.

Mrs. Bright filled the glasses with lemonade and placed more cookies in front of us. "Your father is a very extraordinary man, did you know that? Over the years he has managed some ingenious things, mechanical things, like hooking up controls and such."

"Odelia, he's not interested in those things."

"Sure I am. Please go on Mrs. Bright."

"He connected some controls to his Buick so he could drive it. And he could put his wheelchair in the trunk, and then with his arms, he could work his way around to get in all by himself. And then he made some levers and pulleys so he could get himself in and out of the bathtub, and some more cables and pulleys so he could go down to the basement and tend the furnace without help. Yes sir, quite a clever man, I'd say."

"Oh she just likes to brag on me, really nothing though," he shot her an accusatory glance.

She returned his glance and continued, "he loves to travel too. Took a trip with his sister Aileen a few years back, nine states it was they visited, and the Grand Canyon. Drove his Buick too, why you ought to see the way he has got it all hooked up."

"So you really like to travel?" I said.

"Oh yes. . . even with these," he slapped his knees. "I manage, but the old Buick's not so dependable anymore. Then I only go with someone else. I don't dare go alone." As he spoke, his words came soft and easy as though the key to common interest was at hand.

"Even though he's retired he keeps busy you know." She smiled a big gracious smile with white teeth that sparkled like pearls, all the more evident against her smoothly chocolate complexion. She had moved to sit on the edge of the big leather chair. "He teaches Bible classes, and he's a lay-minister in our church, preaches a powerful message too, and spends lots of time researching and writing, birds, history, the likes. You know what I tell him, I tell him he should write a story about himself, his life, his memoirs. . . "

"Now Odelia, there's nothing in my life worth writing about."

"He always says that, but, I think he's got a lot he could write about, but he always says, *'nothing in his life worth writing about.'* Maybe he should call it that; *Memoirs of a Man Who Has Nothing To Write About.* Then again, maybe he *could* tell a lot." She pushed herself to her feet, walked a few steps through the archway into the next room, stopped at a desk, and returned with a framed picture. "I bet you didn't know that your father knew the president," she said, polishing the ornate metal frame and glass shinny with her apron before handing it to me.

Sure enough, it was the president sitting in a wheelchair, and there beside him, another man in a second wheelchair. "This you?" I asked, holding the picture up in his direction to make a comparison.

He nodded.

I also recognized the lady standing between them as the president's wife.

"That was when he was still Governor of New York state and he was in Warm Springs. They were quite close, and used to sit together by the poolside with their legs in the water, and talk, and they told lots of stories." She glanced at my father, but without seeking his approval to continue, "and he would sing. Miss Eleanor always like to have your father sing, she loved his voice."

Without thinking I glanced up at the clock on the mantle and then to a window. I suddenly realized it was getting dark outside.

"They corresponded for many years and even when he became president—he would call sometimes to talk and pass the time with your father."

"Oh, my God. . . oops pardon the expression, the time is five minutes to eight. Where did it go? My flight is at nine thirty six. I think I better call a taxi. May I please use your telephone?"

"Certainly. . . there in the next room. Uh, Odelia, would you please?"

She was already headed for the phone. "Any special one?" she asked.

"No, anyone will do," I replied. "Wait—call the one I came in—if you will please, and ask for Arthur Brown."

When I looked back to him his expression showed the sadness he felt—and then I felt it too. "Where did the time go, and it is getting dark outside. . . seems like I just got here. . . and now it's time to go," I said, looking for excuses.

"Yes it seems such a shame, after so many years, we have so much to talk of yet. Of course, this is just the beginning."

"Mrs. Bright is a wonderful woman. . . I suppose you're glad to have her. . ."

"Yes, I certainly am—known her for many years, even before retiring. She insisted on helping me with the house. Very active in our church. So much energy and generosity. She has a family of her own and still finds time to do for others. . . I have come to depend on her so—don't know what I'd do without her helping hand."

"I love her Southern accent, so gracious and delightful. . . I bet she tells a good story."

"That she does. Teaches children's Sunday School classes. And they love her."

She returned, "One's on the way, ten minutes they said."

I stood and stretched. "What a pleasure this has been," I said, as I thought of the fleeting minutes just past. When we had met it had seemed strained at first, yet now I hated the thought of leaving. I felt I knew something of this other man, and had shared his warmth in a manly hand-shake, and now looked forward to a time together when we could get to know each other better.

"I wish you didn't have to leave," he said. "There's room here. It's humble, and if you could find some way? Where is it you're going? Dolphin Island? Did you say you'll be there three days?"

"Yes. . . This is the last flight of the day, and my brother will be on his way to the Mobile Airport by now. I called once to tell him of the change."

Mrs. Bright was saying: "one time four boys tipped your father over in his chair and poked fun at him. Three run away but he talked one into helping him back in his chair and that boy is a regular church member now. Studying for the ministry too. Another time when he was working late at the lumber yard one night a robber came in and your father talked him out of what he come to do. . ."

"Now Odelia. . ."

"Oh my, the taxi is here, Lord that was quick," said Mrs. Bright.

I watched as he maneuvered to the hallway and struggled to pull himself up on his crutches. I wanted to help, but didn't know how, and reasoned he has been doing it for years. "You needn't get up," I said, feebly, but there he was, showing a certain pride in a little thing like standing—a small thing to some, yet it meant so much to him.

Together we made it to the door. Arthur Brown came to the steps and I handed him the bag. My dad stood there in the doorway with Odelia beside him. As I reached out my hand, he balanced skillfully and held it strongly in his own while clasping on top with his other hand for a long time. I felt a surging gift of energy and I wondered if this was really what it was like to be a preacher man—one without pretense—just energy and a spiritual vitality to pass on in a simple hand-shake.

Finally, without words I turned and started down the steps. Hesitating, I turned to see them still standing there... "You say you like to travel... where would you like to go?"

It took him only a few seconds to come up with the answer; "Oh, the farm in Vermont, brother John still has the family farm, and I haven't been there in years. Soon the fall colors will be out, very easy on the eyes... and there's Claire and Harry Ellwood, very dear old friends in Niagara Falls; haven't seem them in too many years either." His words seemed reminiscent again, then in a voice that seemed to drift far away to another time, he added: "that's where I'd go."

"In three days. I could be back here in three days, and rent a car at the airport. Could you go then?"

"Why—why yes, I suppose I could," he looked to Mrs. Bright.

"Yes sir, he sure can," she said.

"But your work, what about your work, and your family?" he said, his words and face became anxious.

"Now is as good a time as any. I have some free time, and I'll call home and explain."

The older man nodded with a smile.

"Then three days it is... I'll make the arrangements."

"Maybe we could stop in Delaware, I haven't been there since that day..."

"Then it's Delaware too, along the way."

"Do you know the song, *We A Hundred Pipers?*"

"No, I've never heard of it."

"I'll teach you; lot's of fun, while driving along on the road."

I waved, pleased with my sudden ingenuity, and opening the cab door I turned once again to wave for the last time, "Anyplace else you'd like to go?"

"Well yes, those Redwoods in California. I always wanted to see those big trees... say you live in the mountains? Near those big trees do you?" he called out.

"Yes I do, very close; we could go there also." As I settled in the cab I closed the door, still watching them..

The taxi started to move and I leaned out the window, "Maybe you can tell me more about your time with the President," I called back.

"I'd like that," his voice returned. Then: "if I were a betting man I would bet you can see the Lord's hands at work among those giant trees."

As the taxi pulled away I watched the tall gray haired man standing erect and proud on his crutches. I didn't have to wonder why I could see only the man and not the supports and I felt a mounting eagerness to return and resume a time together when we could get to know each other better. I watched until he was out of sight.

When they had disappeared, he returned to his wheelchair. "Imagine that Odelia, three grandsons, three," he said, slipping into himself once again.

Sitting before his desk once more, he held the photos of a baby and a young woman in his hands, then placing them down gently he lifted a packet of old letters and separated one, a plain white envelope yellowed with age, and opened it. He removed and unfolded a single sheet, pausing there to study it as his lips silently mouthed the words. . .

August 19,1931

Dearest Mary,

THE END

BOOKS AVAILABLE FROM PRETANI:

Fiction: by *Robert Clifton Wallace*
Ka-Batin-Guy: A light-hearted novel of suspense and rein-carnation at the Big Water Basin, hc, ISBN 0 963-4992-1-1, 336pp, $12.00

Mons Graupius: An historical novel about the first recorded events in Caledonian history and the events leading to Hadrian's wall, A.D. 83, hc, ISBN 0 963-4992-1-1, 600pp, $15.00 (first of a four book series)

The Preacher Bird: Atlanta, 1977; a series of flashbacks in the depression years of 1930-31; to Delaware, Ohio. Inspirational true story about a man in a wheelchair; builds steadily to a powerful and gripping conclusion, hc, 224pp, ISBN 0 963-4992-2-X, $12.00

Non-Fiction:
William Wallace, The Guardian of Scotland, by James Fergusson, revised edition, 152pp, pb, ISBN 0-963-4992-3-8, (other bio's due for future release), $8.00

Poetry:
Batiste Lives: A collection of witty and humorous Acadian poems by Daniel T. Trombley and Seth Clement Towle, 104pp, pb, ISBN 0-963-4992-4-6, $7.00.

All books listed above may be purchased from your local booksellers, or may be ordered directly from the publisher. To order please indicate selection and send check or m/o to: **Pretani,** 268 Sayre St., Lakeport, CA 95453, (707 263-0514)

S&H, plus sales tax (Calif.), is included. Novels signed if requested.

Prices and availability subject to change.